Grant couldn't tend a baby. Period.

His cell phone chose that moment to buzz at him. Clumsily, he dug around with his left hand, just managing to extricate the thing before it was too late.

He answered without looking at the caller ID, because he didn't have time. Just his luck. It was Ginny.

He glanced at Crimson. Maybe something in his face alerted her to the problem. Or maybe she had just put two and two together from hearing his end of the conversation.

She raised her eyebrows and tapped her index finger against her collarbone. "Me," she mouthed. She held her elbows out, cupped one hand behind the other and mimicked rocking a baby. "Me."

He nodded. *Yes. Oh, hell yes.* He didn't have to think twice.

"I've already got the help I need," he said into the phone, though he kept his gaze on Crimson, who was smiling her approval. She was extraordinarily beautiful. Was that the painkillers talking?

Maybe it was just that, at the moment, she looked like his guardian angel.

Dear Reader,

I'm a talker. I don't know if it's my DNA or my upbringing, but I've always needed a special someone to confide in. When I'm upset or anxious, nothing calms me like a long heart-to-heart with a friend.

Sometimes exposing your honest, inner truths is frightening. Often, our first instinct is that the pain is too great, and no one can possibly help. But I've always felt there's a high price to pay for locking your emotions inside.

Hundreds of years ago, a pretty smart guy agreed with me. In *Macbeth*, Shakespeare wrote a beautiful line in which a grieving man is told he should "give sorrow words," because if he doesn't, his heart may break.

In *The Rancher's Dream*, both Grant and Crimson have broken hearts. It's time for them to heal and move on, but they can't. They're too afraid to open up and be vulnerable again.

Love is said to heal all wounds...but what if you're afraid of love itself? Though deep feelings are growing between them, caring has brought them so much pain already. Can they find the courage to take that risk again?

I hope you enjoy watching Grant and Crimson find the words to open their hearts. And may you always find an understanding ear when you are ready to open yours.

Warmly,

Kathleen O'Brien

PS—I love to hear from readers!
Please come see me at kathleenobrien.com,
or stop by facebook.com/kathleenobrienauthor.

KATHLEEN O'BRIEN

———

The Rancher's Dream

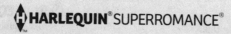

Recycling programs
for this product may
not exist in your area.

ISBN-13: 978-0-373-60908-6

The Rancher's Dream

Copyright © 2015 by Kathleen O'Brien

Printed in U.S.A.

Kathleen O'Brien was a feature writer and TV critic before marrying a fellow journalist. Motherhood, which followed soon after, was so marvelous she turned to writing novels, which meant she could work at home. Though she's a lifelong city gal, she has a special place in her heart for tiny towns like Silverdell, where you may not enjoy a lot of privacy...but you never really face your troubles alone, either.

Books by Kathleen O'Brien

HARLEQUIN SUPERROMANCE

The Sisters of Bell River Ranch

Wild for the Sheriff
Betting on the Cowboy
The Secrets of Bell River
Reclaiming the Cowboy

The Heroes of Heyday

The Saint
The Sinner
The Stranger

The Homecoming Baby
Christmas in Hawthorn Bay
Everything but the Baby
Texas Baby
Texas Wedding
For the Love of Family
Texas Trouble
That Christmas Feeling
"We Need A Little Christmas"
For Their Baby
The Cost of Silence
The Vineyard of Hopes and Dreams

Visit the Author Profile page
at Harlequin.com for more titles.

To Manning, Irene and Mike, who stand by me during my descents into the deadline pit and always keep a firm grip on the safety rope. You guys are, to put it mildly, the best.

And to Colorado, for its wildflower springs, its majestic winters and its endless inspiration as I wrote these six Bell River books.

CHAPTER ONE

I'VE GOT TO get out of Silverdell.

The sentence kept running through Crimson Slayton's head, clogging up her brain waves. She ought to be thinking of something clever to say to keep this foolish girl from getting an incredibly dumb tattoo.

But she couldn't think of a thing. All she could think was...

I've got to get out of Silverdell...before I start to care about this kid, too.

She frowned, annoyed with herself, and repressed the urge to pick up one of her own homemade lavender Earl Grey tea cookies, which she kept on hand for her clients. The cookies were great for calming nerves.

Why should she need calming down? Why should she be in any danger of feeling emotional about this lovesick girl across the table from her in the tattoo parlor?

It was ridiculous. Becky Hampton was nothing to Crimson. The two had met twenty minutes ago...and if Crimson did her job, she'd say goodbye to Becky in another twenty minutes, and that would be the end of that.

Stay out of it. When Crimson's sister, Clover, died, and Crimson left her hometown of Omaha, Nebraska, those four words had been her new sworn life motto.

Stay out of *everything.* No ties. No roots. No attachments to things or people she could lose. She'd be a gypsy, a loner. Get in, get out and nobody gets hurt.

For the first few weeks after Clover's funeral, she'd done just that. Three towns in three weeks.

But then she'd hit Silverdell, Colorado, and, though she told herself every month that she'd probably leave soon, somehow she never did.

She'd been here thirteen months, more or less.

Clearly that was much too long. Somewhere, over that time, she'd started to feel things. Instead of staying free, cordial but unattached, like a bird on a wire, she'd started getting involved. Making friends.

First Mitch and Belle, and all the Bell River family. And Marianne Donovan, who owned the café and shared Crimson's love of cooking.

Those weren't the most dangerous attachments, though. The real threat had snuck up on her. First she'd met Grant Campbell, a nice rancher who had helped her figure out how to mortar bricks when they were paired up to build a playground for the Silverdell Outreach charity she'd gotten involved with.

Then she'd met Grant's friend and temporary roommate, Kevin Ellison.

And finally, the biggest danger of all, Kevin's precious, motherless baby, Molly.

At the thought of the warm little bundle of sweetness, her heart squeezed.

Oh, yeah. I've got to get out of Silverdell.

But first she had to handle Becky. The pretty blonde had been leafing through Crimson's sample book for nearly twenty minutes now, exclaiming like a little kid every time she passed a pretty flower or a colorful fairy.

"I just don't know! They're all so cute!"

Crimson managed not to groan. *Think, think.* The girl was obviously nervous, ripe for being talked out of this. She'd come in alone, hovering in the doorway without entering, grabbing the shoulder strap of her purse as if it was a lifeline, and twisting her legs so nervously it looked as if she badly needed to go to the bathroom.

When Crimson had approached her, she'd confessed shyly that she wanted to have her boyfriend's name, Roderick, tattooed on her left buttock, along with "something pretty." But she had to wait for Rory to come "give the okay" to the design.

Her body…but his decision? That had been Crimson's first red flag. If Roderick was that bossy, he probably wouldn't be Becky's boyfriend for long.

Crimson collected Becky's ID, always the first step.

Believe it or not, the girl—woman—was going on twenty-two. Amazing. Crimson was only twenty-six, but she would have guessed she was at least ten years older than Becky.

Still, you could count rotations of the earth around the sun, or you could count life experience. By the latter calculation, this poor kid didn't seem old enough to drink root beer.

"If you call him Rory, how about getting that tattooed, instead of Roderick?" Crimson raised her brows. "It's shorter. Cheaper. Less painful."

And easier to remove or cover up when Becky and Rory split.

"No. He wants the tattoo to be his real name." Frowning, Becky shifted her sandaled feet nervously on the scuffed black floor and nibbled on her index fingernail. "Why? Does it hurt a lot?"

"It's uncomfortable," Crimson said carefully.

Out of the corner of her eye, she saw Pete look up from his station, where he was inking a skull and crossbones on the one clear piece of real estate still left on the forearm of their favorite regular customer, Butchie the bronc rider.

Pete, a sixty-five-year-old former pro wrestler, owned the tattoo parlor, and he'd already warned

Crimson he'd have to let her go if she didn't stop talking customers out of getting work done.

"Some people say it's very painful," Crimson said. To heck with Pete's glare. She'd signed on here as a tech and, at his urging, had learned to ink tattoos over the past few months. She'd become pretty good at it, if she did say so herself. She'd brought in a lot of work. She didn't turn away the Butchies of the world, who genuinely wanted and loved their tats. Just the people who would end up regretting the decision within six weeks.

Sometimes six minutes.

The way Crimson saw it, she was saving Pete a load of bad publicity from unhappy customers. If he couldn't see that...

"Tell you the truth, Becky," she added firmly, "I've seen grown men cry." When Pete growled, she just gave him a bright smile. It was true, so live with it.

Biting her lower lip, Becky flipped a few more pages, though her fingers had become clumsy. They were both silent a few minutes. Crimson considered offering Becky one of the cookies, but decided against it. She didn't want her to calm down. She wanted her to leave. Without a tattoo.

But when the girl encountered another rainbow-colored fairy, her mouth relaxed, and her blue eyes lit up.

"Oh, that's adorable!"

Crimson sighed.

Becky held up the plastic-covered picture. "Do you think that would look good above the name Roderick?"

"No." Crimson stared at the foolish fairy blandly. "Not really. It's too girly. You wouldn't want to threaten Roderick's virility."

Becky nodded, the sarcasm clearly lost on her. Crimson's throat tightened as she looked at the sweet, trusting face. Darn it. The poor thing was in love. Capital *L*, Love. And with an insensitive guy who kept his sheltered girlfriend waiting in a tattoo parlor, getting more scared by the minute. A control freak who wanted his name on her rear end like a brand. His full name.

So maybe a sadist, too. Roderick was twice as long as Rory…

Impulsively, Crimson reached out her hand and caught the slim fingers. "Becky, look, maybe you ought to consider this a little longer."

She thought fast. What was the secret tunnel into Becky's psyche? Everyone had one. Even Crimson's twin sister, Clover, had had one.

Unfortunately for Clover, Crimson had known exactly what it was and how to exploit it. If she hadn't, Clover might be alive today.

But she wouldn't let herself think about that right now. Back to Becky.

What was Becky's secret tunnel? She'd just demonstrated she wouldn't flinch from the prospect of pain. Crimson tapped her fingers on the table, eyeing the girl thoughtfully. Vanity, maybe?

Might work. The girl's skin was almost flawless, and her one scar, a small, starry patch of white in the center of her forehead, was mostly buried under several layers of thick foundation. She obviously hated that scar.

"You look like someone who takes good care of your body." Crimson smiled. "You eat healthy. Work out, right?"

Becky nodded. "Oh, yeah."

"So…think how hard you work to keep your skin so pretty. You don't let it burn in the sun, and you don't let it break out or get dry or freckle. You don't want scars or cellulite…"

Becky was frowning again. The thoughtful furrow on her brow creased around the tiny white scar, giving Crimson hope.

"So are you sure you want to mark it up with permanent ink?" Crimson turned to the back of the portfolio, where she kept her secret pictures, the ones designed to scare the bejeezus out of innocents like Becky. "See this? This is what's left when you have the tattoo removed. I mean, it's not awful, but it's certainly not as pristine as your skin is now."

She let that sink in a minute before lowering her voice. "I always feel terrible when women come in to get their tattoos removed because they've finally found the right guy, the guy they want to marry and spend the rest of their lives with, and they don't want the constant reminder about Rory…" She waved her hand to make the statement more vague. "Or whoever."

She was taking a chance here. She was banking on having read this Rory character correctly—and she was counting on Becky being smart. Her instincts told her Becky knew, if only subconsciously, that she'd never walk down the aisle with Rory, and didn't really want to, anyhow.

For a minute, as Becky remained poker-faced, Crimson thought she'd miscalculated. But then Becky closed the portfolio slowly.

"Yeah, maybe I'd better think about it some more." She scraped back her chair and stood. "I'm sorry. I feel bad I took so much time, and then didn't even—"

"Don't feel bad." Crimson stood, too. "I think you're making the right decision." Impulsively, driven by some unnamed instinct, she grabbed one of her business cards and held it out. "And listen, if you ever…if you ever need anything…"

The girl looked confused. Well, of course she was confused. Crimson wasn't sure why she had said that, either. Except…her gut told her Rory was not a good guy.

Becky took the card, glanced down at the odd name, Crimson Slash—the name Crimson had adopted when she took the Needles 'N Pins job.

Crimson's cell number was on it, too. This was the card she gave only to her regular, trusted clients.

Becky didn't react, simply shoving it into her jeans pocket. She cast a doubtful glance toward the door, as if she were afraid her boyfriend might saunter in now and force her to get the tattoo after all. "If Rory comes..."

Crimson smiled. "If Rory comes, I'll explain you got called away."

"Yeah." Becky nodded. "Yeah, that's good." She started to offer to shake hands, but clearly decided that didn't make sense and settled for a wave and a smile as she hurried out the door.

Relieved, Crimson sank back onto her chair.

"Not so fast, Doctor Freud."

She looked up. It was Pete, all six foot four inches of him, standing in the spot where Becky had just been. His gloved hands were fisted on his hips, which accentuated the fact that he'd rushed over in the middle of Butchie's tattoo.

"Pete, please don't give me a hard time about this."

She wasn't in the mood. She'd have quit this job ten times during the past few weeks if she could just decide where to go next. If she could just get up the courage to leave Silverdell. "She would have regretted it before she got home, and then there would have been hell to pay."

"Hell I can handle. But employees who chase off the customers...that I can't afford." To her surprise, Pete's brown eyes seemed to hold an undercurrent of sadness. "Clear out your locker, Red. You're fired."

ACTUALLY, IT WAS perfect timing. She'd been planning to meet Grant Campbell for lunch at Donovan's Dream, at noon, anyhow. Grant had given Kevin a lift into town for a meeting, which meant he'd probably be bringing Molly, Kevin's baby. That was all the consolation Crimson could ask for. At six months, Molly was a dream, warm and loving and absolutely adorable.

And if Crimson was leaving Silverdell soon, she was glad of every minute she could get with the baby.

It didn't take her long to pack up.

She always traveled light and didn't have much to clear out. The plate of cookies, her tea mug, her purse and a couple of spare black T-shirts she kept in case she spilled something…that's all she'd ever moved into the shop, even after a year.

She dumped her portfolio in Pete's trash can, where it hit bottom with a thud. A swoosh of relief moved through her as she realized she wouldn't ever need it again. However much she loved Pete, she wasn't a tattoo artist. This job had only been an attempt to leave behind the old Crimson, the "real" Crimson, who would have been happier in a restaurant or a kitchen, or waiting tables, or anything that involved food.

At the last minute, Pete came out to the car and hugged her awkwardly. His droopy brown eyes made him look like a basset hound with indigestion, and she patted his shoulder as if he were the one who'd been fired, not her.

"Damn it, Red," he said thickly, "if you'd just behave yourself—"

"But I won't. You know that."

He shoved his hands into his pockets. Glancing at the sky, which was as lumpy and gray as a pad of old steel wool, he sighed. "Look, it's going to rain. Why don't you come on back inside? We can talk it over."

She shook her head, smiling. He was so softhearted, poor guy, and he'd been good to give her a job sterilizing his equipment when she didn't have a single reference, or a single day's experience. She didn't want him to agonize over this.

"It's okay, Pete," she said. "It's time. Past time. I needed a nudge."

He squinted as a few fat drops of rain splatted against his cheeks. "Maybe. Hell, at least don't be a stranger. Come see me sometime. If you ever decide to get that tattoo we've been talking about, it's on the house."

The tattoo had been a running gag. She was the only person who had ever worked for him who didn't have a single spot of ink on her skin. Probably that should have tipped him off that her heart wasn't in it.

She laughed, and he hugged her again, clearly relieved there would be no hard feelings. He didn't seem to be in any hurry to let go. The rain fell harder, but she didn't mind. Her hair was in that awkward, growing-out phase, anyhow, and never looked exactly great.

"Hey, what are you doing, hugging my girl on the public streets?"

Crimson and Pete broke apart at the sound of the deep, male voice. Grant Campbell stood there, with little Molly in his arms, the baby carrier and diaper bag dangling from the crook of his elbow.

He looked as gorgeous as ever—maybe more so, because, *wow*, there really was something about a man holding a baby…

He winked at Crimson, the thick black fringe of lashes dropping briefly over the gold-flecked brown eyes. His lopsided smile gave her a rush of warmth, as if he'd leaned over and kissed her… though naturally he hadn't.

He was just kidding about the girlfriend thing. For a brief second, Crimson wondered why. Why hadn't she ever let herself fall for this amazing specimen of male magnificence? Why was she dating his single-dad friend Kevin instead?

But then she remembered. First of all, Grant was a very satisfactory friend, and it was much easier to find dates than friends. Secondly, it was almost impossible to catch Grant between girlfriends, anyhow. He was like a thousand-dollar bill…if any woman was dumb enough to let him slip through her fingers, he wouldn't hit the ground before another woman grabbed him up.

"Red's not your girl, Campbell." Pete sounded cranky. "And she's not mine anymore, either. She just got fired, so you better be buying lunch, big shot."

Grant glanced at Crimson, raising his eyebrows.

"Yeah, he's serious," she said. "I'm unemployed. But don't worry. I'm buying lunch. I feel like celebrating."

With a final, teasing smile at Pete, she took custody of the diaper bag and nudged Grant into motion. They needed to hustle before they got drenched.

Marianne's restaurant, Donovan's Dream, was a couple of blocks down, on the chichi end of Elk Avenue, the main downtown street of Silverdell. As the rain intensified, they started to run. By the time they ducked into the café, sweeping in on the familiar notes of "Danny Boy," which played whenever the door opened or shut, Molly was red-faced and crying.

Immediately Grant handed her to Crimson. Crimson took over without complaint—this pattern had been established a couple of months ago, when Kevin and Molly had first come to stay with him. Grant was fine with Molly most of the time. He changed diapers like a champ, and he could play peekaboo for hours. He was even unfazed by spit-up milk and slobber.

But if Molly started to cry...that was different.

Then he just withdrew, somehow. Emotionally, a door slammed shut, and he was no comfort at all to the poor little thing.

"Red! Thank goodness you're here!" Marianne Donovan came rushing to their table, her hair stuck to her damp forehead and a spatula in her hand. "Come quick. The meringue is weeping. It's a mess."

It wasn't unusual for Marianne to consult with Crimson about her menu. At a potluck dinner a few months ago, a small get-together hosted by the Silverdell Outreach group, Marianne had discovered that Crimson wasn't your average store-bought cookies kind of gal.

Crimson never advertised her history with cooking—and she certainly never mentioned she'd been to cooking school, or that she'd been *this close* to opening her own restaurant when her world fell apart. But it was hard to completely squelch your most primal interests, and gradually the two women had bonded over their mutual love of herbs and spices, pots and pans.

So. She considered the problem. Weeping meringue.

She ought to take a look. But...

Crimson glanced at Grant, who was already studying the menu. She jiggled Molly a few times, making soft noises and wiping the chilly rain-drops from the baby's fine hair. Molly seemed to be settling down, but she wasn't calm enough yet to leave her with Grant.

"It's probably just the humidity," Crimson assured Marianne. She wouldn't even have at-tempted meringue with such a bad storm com-ing, especially in an older building that wasn't exactly airtight. Donovan's Dream had been ren-ovated enough to look delightful, but not enough to eliminate all the old windows and doors, which always let the outside in. Marianne had explained that she'd left those features partly to maintain the original feel—and partly to keep from going broke.

"Can you just lower the oven and cook a little longer? Or you could start over and add a little cornstarch."

"Okay. I'll try starting over, unless you'd like to…"

Crimson shook her head, looking down at the baby.

Marianne sighed. "Fine. I'll do it. But I'm not a dessert chef. I make a fabulous Irish stew, but…" She held out her hand, spatula and all. "Quit that other job, darn it, and come work for me. Please. I clearly need you more than Pete does."

Grant glanced up from the menu, his half smile back in place. "Funny you should mention that—" he began.

"Hush." Crimson stopped the sentence in its tracks. She sat, and then she began arranging Molly in her baby seat. "Go fix your meringue, Mari. And when you get a minute I'll take some of that stew."

"Me, too." Grant tossed his menu onto the table. "Gloomy days like this call for hot stew."

Soon they were alone again, and Molly cooed contentedly. He leaned back in his chair and yawned, eyeing Crimson curiously. "Why don't you take the job, Red? Unless you're secretly loaded, you could use a new source of income."

Crimson felt herself flushing. Secretly loaded? He was just kidding, of course. He couldn't possibly know...

Her thoughts shot immediately to the life insurance check she always carried in her purse. It was hers, fair and square, made out to her, but she couldn't have felt any guiltier if she'd acquired it at gunpoint.

"Oh, well." She shrugged. "Sometimes, when you start doing the work you love for a paycheck, it ruins your pleasure."

He frowned. "Baloney."

He was right. It was nonsense. She would have adored working as a pastry chef—if she'd been able to do it with Clover. The two of them had dreamed of opening their own restaurant since they were toddlers making mud pies in the backyard. Even back then, Crimson had been the "sweet" cook. She'd decorated her mud pies with violets and rose petals and sprinkled her mother's white beads of vermiculite over them for "sugar."

But now that Clover was dead, Crimson had no desire to pursue the dream alone.

She had no *right* to.

"Come on—you know that's absurd," he went on, watching her as if he were trying to figure something out. "I still love the ranch. I might even love it more, actually, now that it's a reality instead of a dream. Why on earth would getting paid to cook spoil your fun?"

"Never mind," she said, bending over Molly with her napkin, though the baby was fine and didn't need tending. "Maybe it wouldn't. It's just—don't listen to everything Marianne says. She's exaggerating. I'm nothing special in the kitchen."

She began cooing to the baby, hoping to prevent Grant from pursuing the subject. And he got the message, of course. He was one of those rare men who could read nonverbal cues.

He dropped the topic. And he was kind enough not to discuss her getting fired, either. When the stew was served, they talked about his horses. He was in the early stages of building an Arabian breeding program, and one of his young fillies was turning out to be special. A three-year-old copper-colored beauty, her name was Cawdor's Golden Dawn, though Grant called her Dawn.

It was kind of cute, how crazy he was about this horse. Even Crimson could see how beautiful Dawn was, and how elegant, but the bond between her and Grant was adorable. Grant obviously thought she'd hung the moon, and the feeling appeared to be mutual.

And of course Crimson wanted to hear about the foaling schedule. His main mare had delivered a promising little colt in April, which had been exciting for everyone at the ranch.

"So have you decided what to name the new colt?" Crimson knew he'd been trying to come up with the perfect name for days. She and Kevin had offered about a hundred suggestions, but nothing had hit the spot.

"Not yet. Kevin's most recent suggestion is Kevimol, which he said was a brilliant combination of his name and Molly's. But I think it sounds like a periodontal disease."

He smiled, popping the last piece of bread into his mouth with gusto. He worked hard, and he could eat all day without putting an ounce of fat onto that lean, muscular frame, lucky devil. "Besides, what kind of egotist thinks I'm going to name my horse for him? Talk to Kevin about that, would you?"

Crimson laughed, but something about Grant's easy assumption that she was the one who could make Kevin see reason left her uncomfortable.

She'd known Kevin almost two months now,

ever since he'd shown up at Campbell Ranch, his four-month-old motherless baby in tow, asking Grant, his old college buddy, if he could crash there temporarily. Because Crimson and Grant were friends, Crimson had of course met Kevin, too.

They'd begun to date maybe a month ago— if *dating* was even the right word for this oddly platonic relationship they seemed to have forged.

She, at least, knew full well that the friendship would never be more than that. She'd known it almost from the start. She was half in love with Kevin's baby, but she'd never be in love with Kevin himself.

She'd always assumed Kevin understood that. After all, he'd clearly just embarked on single parenthood. Though he never seemed to want to discuss the details of Molly's mother, she deduced that the two had never married, and somehow he'd ended up with custody.

A daunting prospect, and a situation in which you wouldn't want to take any new risks with lovers lightly. Crimson had assumed he couldn't possibly be ready to start something serious.

Lately, though, she'd seen a look on his face… heard a tone in his voice…

She wondered whether Grant had seen and heard those things, too.

Well, bottom line, it was time to break it off before Kevin got the wrong idea. And if she was moving away from Silverdell, which she *obviously* should, that would be the easiest out, wouldn't it?

She bent over the baby again, first taking care to tuck her gold necklace into her shirt. Molly had recently become fascinated with anything shiny, and consequently Crimson had stopped wearing most jewelry. Except the necklace, a small shamrock. That, she never removed.

"Where is Kevin, anyhow?" She glanced briefly at Grant and then returned her attention to Molly, who was starting to get fussy again. "Molly needs feeding. You dropped him at the law firm, right? I thought the meeting was supposed to be over by now."

"Guess it ran late." Grant leaned back in his chair and stretched. His impatience was palpable, which Crimson understood. Horse breeding was a demanding job, and he couldn't afford to cool his heels in town all day just because his houseguest's car was on the fritz and the man had hitched a ride into town.

"I certainly hope this law firm is paying him enough to buy a house, and a new car...and hire a nanny." Grant raised one eyebrow. "I know you and I would both like to see the man move into a place of his own."

Again, that tone—as if Crimson must be dying for some privacy with Kevin, so they could take their relationship to the next level.

If Grant only knew! The fact that Kevin lived

in Grant's spare bedroom was probably his most attractive quality. She lived in a tiny efficiency apartment with paper-thin walls and never, ever brought anyone home. So if Kevin didn't have privacy, either...well, that settled the whole "will we or won't we" debate before it could even get started.

She smiled neutrally. "I take it the charm of having a boarder is fading?"

"The charm of having a boarder is nonexistent." Grant scooped up the check, waving off her protest. "It's killing my love life. Correction—it's already killed my love life. Ginny broke up with me last night, after about three hours of listening to Molly cry."

Crimson wouldn't have thought the woman was that foolish. She frowned. "Molly cried all night? Why? What was wrong?"

"Beats me. My guess is Molly's an undercover operative with the morality police. Her assignment, and she's definitely chosen to accept it, is to ensure I never have sex again."

Crimson shook her head. "Seriously. Was she sick?"

"*Seriously*. She's the president of the Abstinence Vigilantes."

"Grant."

He grinned. "She's probably just teething. As I recall, this is about when the first ones start coming in. I told Kevin to buy one of those nasty plastic rings you can put in the freezer, but he hasn't done it yet. Apparently, he's the *vice* president of the abstinence club."

As he recalled?

For a minute, she couldn't move past that comment. What did he mean? Grant didn't have children...

Or did he? Crimson hesitated, her curiosity warring with her vow to always, always stay out of it. Still, it was strange. If Grant had children, he'd certainly never mentioned it before. In her experience, people who had kids couldn't *stop* talking about them—how good they were, how bad they were, how underfoot they were or how much they missed them.

Her mind sifted through the possible scenarios. She had the impression he was divorced—though she couldn't pinpoint what made her think so. Perhaps she just couldn't believe a man like him could have reached his thirties without getting scooped up by some lucky lady. But he'd never hinted anything about children.

Maybe he had siblings, and those siblings had kids. Or maybe he was divorced, and he'd lost custody for some reason. Or maybe, like Kevin's runaway ex, he'd left his family behind to pursue his dream of a horse ranch in Colorado.

Or maybe...

She shook herself irritably. Maybe it was none of her business. She knew all too well that when a person imposed total silence on a subject, those wishes should be respected.

For instance…heaven help anyone who brought up Clover's death with *her*.

Molly had begun to strain at the strap that held her in the baby seat. As she squirmed, she grew red-faced, and the whimpering escalated into full-blown crying.

"Sweetheart." Crimson stroked the baby's cheek. "Poor little thing."

Grant glanced at his watch. "Maybe I should go see what's keeping Kevin. I've got to get back to the ranch. With all this rain, I'm worried about the stable roof. Any chance you could…"

She was already unfastening Molly's strap. She lifted the warm, damp baby out and folded her up against her shoulder.

"Of course," she said, patting Molly's back. She was well aware he hadn't been asking if she'd pick up Kevin. "How about if I take your truck because you've got the car seat, and you take my car? I'll stop by the pharmacy and grab a teething ring and then meet you back at the ranch. If I get there first, I'll feed her, change her and put her down for a nap."

"Perfect." He nodded. "Mine's right out front, so you won't have to get wet." He frowned, glancing at the front windows. "You drive carefully, though, okay?"

"I will. The truck's four-wheel drive will be safer in this weather, anyhow."

And wow, what weather, even for late May! The rain had grown steadily more intense while they were in the café. She'd heard about these wet Silverdell springs. The gully-washers were mostly short-lived and profoundly welcomed by the ranchers, who appreciated the free irrigation—as long as none of their own gullies got washed out.

Plus, the storms apparently were a boon for the wildflowers. She'd been hearing for weeks about how, if the drought continued, the annual wildflower festival might have to be canceled. Apparently, that would be a historic failure for Silverdell, and everyone had been eying the skies glumly, calculating the chances of rain.

"I'll be careful," she promised again, holding out her key ring. "You do the same, even if Kevin keeps you waiting and you're ticked off." She held his gaze sternly, daring him to deny he could get impatient behind the wheel, especially when he wanted to get home to check on the horses. "Deal?"

He smiled. "Deal."

From her perch on Crimson's shoulder, Molly wailed, suddenly at the end of her rope. Standing quickly, Grant leaned over and planted a firm kiss on Crimson's cheek.

"Thanks, Red," he said. "You're the best. Be good to Auntie Red, kiddo."

He patted Molly's head perfunctorily as he moved away. He had paid and disappeared to the notes of "Danny Boy" before Crimson could even get the baby reinstalled in her carrier. Molly definitely wasn't happy to be strapped in again, but she had found her fingers and begun to suck on them.

Crimson watched as Grant's silhouette dashed past the front windows, his head ducked against the rain. He appeared in one window, then another, then the third, and then he finally disappeared.

"Interesting, isn't it, sweetheart?" She bent low to rub Molly's pink button nose with her own. "I'm pretty sure our friend Mr. Campbell is allergic to crying babies. What I can't quite figure out..."

She glanced back at the windows, but no one else was walking past, not in this weather. All she could see was a thick sheet of silver rain that sparkled as it caught the reflected brilliance of streetlights that had blinked on, fooled into believing it was night.

"What I can't quite figure out is why."

CHAPTER TWO

AFTER SHE LEFT the tattoo parlor, Becky drove around Silverdell for a long time.

Even when the storm broke, she didn't stop driving. She cruised down Elk Avenue, around the square and over to Callahan Circle, which Dellians always just called Mansion Street. She didn't stop when she got to the blue French château with the mansard roof, even though she'd called that particular mansion home for twenty-one years.

She didn't even look at it. Didn't make any difference whether her dad was home or not—she wasn't going to stop. She just kept driving. North, and then west onto Cimarron Street. After that, she went back into town to start the figure eight all over again.

Truth was, she really, really didn't want to go back to Rory's apartment. He was going to be mad about the tattoo…or the lack of a tattoo. And when he was mad, it was awful.

It was actually more awful than it ought to be, considering he didn't scream or yell or break things. She almost wished he would. At least that kind of anger made sense.

Her dad was a yeller. He blew up like the storm

that was turning Silverdell black as an eclipse right now, flooding the streets and shaking the traffic lights as if it wanted to yank them from their wires. But, like this storm, his anger blew over. Things might be damp and uncomfortable for a while, but the sun always came out again eventually.

Rory was different. He didn't ever let loose. He got snake-eyed and sarcastic, but behind those curled lips and cold eyes, you could tell the same storm was raging. It just didn't have an outlet, so it never blew itself out. It kept building, and it spit out in little scalding spurts, like when you over-heated grease in a pan. It shot out in small, oddly painful insults, in little unexpected cruelties.

As her car sped through a pool of water so deep it sprayed out like a white fan from her tires, she realized she was going too fast. She had a head-ache from peering through the rain, and she'd been gripping her steering wheel so tightly her hands hurt.

Consciously flexing her fingers, she took several deliberate deep breaths. She should go home. So what if Rory was mad? She lifted her chin. She wasn't afraid of him. That wasn't why she didn't want to go back. She wasn't afraid of anybody.

It was just that, when Rory was mean, she didn't like him very much. And when you loved somebody, it hurt to discover you didn't like them. It hurt a lot.

Still…the later she showed up, the madder he'd be. And besides, where else did she have to go?

Half-consciously, she slid her hand into her jacket pocket, where she'd put the card that nice woman at the tattoo parlor had given her. But she almost had to laugh at how naive that was. Crimson Slash couldn't be her real name. But anyone who chose a name like that for herself wasn't likely to be Mother Teresa.

Which proved that, however nice she seemed, Crimson Slash hadn't been serious when she said Becky should call her if she needed help.

If Becky were stupid enough to take the offer seriously, the woman probably wouldn't even remember who the heck Becky Hampton was.

Suddenly, a traffic light swam at her out of the turbulent black ocean of the sky. The light was red. Her heart jumped, hot and huge, and tried to explode in her throat.

She stood on her brakes…belatedly hearing her father's voice warning her never, never to stop too fast in the rain.

With a sickening awareness that her tires were only barely connected to the tarmac, Becky felt her car fishtail, as if it were hinged in the middle—and not under her control at all.

Oh, God, oh, God, oh, God…

She'd barely had time to register fear when, like a miracle, her tires gripped the road again, and the car shuddered to a stop.

Her eyes darted to the rearview mirror, and she prayed she wouldn't see headlights barreling toward her like white bullets. *One second...two seconds...*

Nothing. She raked her hands through her hair and made a strange, gulping sound. She was going to be okay.

For several seconds, she sat there, thanking God and trying to stop her hands from shaking.

When the light turned green, she didn't want to take her foot off the brake, but she had to. She'd be a sitting duck if she waited there, immobile and invisible, for some unsuspecting car to smash into. She probably was almost as dumb as her father always said she was...but she wasn't that dumb.

Somehow she reached Cimarron Street. Apartment Alley was this one's nickname, because one anonymous building after another was lined up there, shoulder-to-shoulder and face-to-face. Instead of circling through, this time she turned onto Coyote Lane, where Rory lived.

Where she lived, too, she reminded herself. This was home now—not Mansion Street. And that was okay. Compared to splatting herself all over a rain-drenched road, Rory and Coyote Lane had started to look pretty good.

MOLLY FELL ASLEEP on the way back to Grant's ranch, probably lulled by the rain pounding against the truck's roof and the rhythmic swishing of the windshield wipers.

Crimson, who needed to concentrate on maneuvering the flooding streets, was relieved. If she'd had a choice, she would have pulled over and waited out the storm, but Molly was hungry and uncomfortable, and Kevin hadn't packed enough bottles to see her through such a long afternoon.

She drove no more than ten miles an hour the whole way, aware of her priceless cargo and the treacherous nature of slippery roads. Luckily, Grant's truck rode high on its big tires, and its bright red paint would be fairly easy for other drivers to spot, even in this monochromatic, underwater gray world.

Once Crimson crawled out of Silverdell and onto the winding rural road that led to the ranches west of town, the traffic thinned out nicely, and the wild rain eased to a simple downpour. Way up ahead, just above the horizon, she could even glimpse a sliver of blue sky.

It felt symbolic, somehow. She might be caught in a storm, but there was light up ahead. Hope still existed. All she had to do was get there. For some inexplicable reason, for the first time since Clover died, Crimson believed she might make it.

As she neared the last real intersection with a traffic light before everything turned to rolling acres of pasture, she began to hum under her breath, choosing a sweet old lullaby her mother used to sing. It had been Clover's favorite.

Sleep my child, and peace attend thee,
all through the night.
Guardian angels God will send thee,
all through the night.

Suddenly, out of nowhere, the air was filled with a horrible shrieking sound…as if an eagle was dying. Some part of her mind understood it was a car horn, a desperate, endless, metallic warning. And then a crash so abrupt it was more like a bomb. Just a loud, terrifying, glassy explosion, followed by ominous silence.

Ahead of her, the rain filled with smoke, or dust, or… She smelled burning rubber. She touched her brakes, somehow forcing herself not to panic and slam them. The truck slowed down and then stopped just as she drew close enough to see what lay in the road in front of her.

Oh, dear God.

That mangled mass of silver wreckage…that was her car.

Molly was crying now. Crimson dimly heard it, but she was fumbling with her cell phone, dialing 911, and she didn't have time to do more than murmur a numb, "It's okay, baby" before she had to talk to the operator.

As she stammered out the details, she was automatically easing the truck onto the right of way. She tucked it safely behind a tree, so no one could accidentally clip it going past, and then she opened the door and went streaking out into the rain.

Another car was in the road, too. A bigger one. Black. Expensive. A man stood by it, his cell phone in his hand.

"I didn't see them," he said to her, in the mono-tone voice of someone in shock. "I didn't see them."

She didn't answer, didn't even look at him. She ran to her car, drenched and shaking and numb with cold.

"Grant!" She rushed to the driver's side, the side that had been T-boned by the big black Mercedes. The door was crumpled like an old tissue.

"Grant!" She banged on the window, willing the man slumped over the air bag to raise his head and tell her everything was all right. But it wasn't all right. It couldn't be, not with the door like that, and the man so limp, his dark brown hair falling forward, obscuring his face…

His dark brown hair…

It wasn't Grant. It was Kevin. Kevin had been driving. She glanced at the passenger seat, not breathing. It was empty. It was empty.

Her heart began to beat quickly. "Grant?"

"Yes. I'm here. I'm all right."

He appeared suddenly on the other side of the car, as if he'd rolled out, and then dragged him-self to a standing position. His shirt was muddy, clinging to his shoulders, and he held one arm strangely, clutching the elbow with the other hand and propping it across his chest. Above that, his hard-boned face was pale, his golden-brown hair drenched, water streaming down his cheeks.

"Are you all right?" The bulk of the car was between them, and she couldn't think how to fix that. She couldn't think at all. "Are you hurt?"

"No. But Kevin's unconscious. I've called 911, but—"

"I called 911, too," the man from the Mercedes said. "Are you okay?"

Grant ignored him. He kept his eyes trained on Crimson, as if she were the touchstone that kept him focused, kept him from sinking back into the mud. "Where is Molly?"

"In the truck. She's fine. We're fine. Is Kevin—" Her teeth chattered, as if it were deepest winter, and she couldn't form words. Not that word. It was not a word you spoke aloud. It couldn't be true, anyhow. It couldn't be true.

She put her hand against the window, as if she could touch Kevin through the glass. But Kevin wasn't aware of her. His face was turned sideways, pointing toward the passenger seat, and she couldn't tell how badly hurt he was.

"Oh, God," she said. "Kevin…"

"He's breathing. It's okay. He's breathing." Grant started to take a step, as if to come around the back of the car. As if he wanted to comfort her. But something was wrong with one of his legs, and he stumbled, falling against the hood with his bad arm.

He groaned, clearly in agony.

"Grant." A pain shot through her own chest, as if she could feel what he felt. His contorted face was so tortured she could hardly bear to look at it. His arm must be badly broken.

"He'll live, Crimson," he said thickly. "I promise."

And with a low moan, he slumped to the ground and out of sight.

Every part of her body felt cold and numb and strangely distant, as if she weren't really here. As if she might, please God, be dreaming.

Dimly, she heard Molly wailing from the truck. In front of her, Kevin was still slumped over the wheel, motionless. Unconscious, unresponsive, unaware.

And Grant... She couldn't see him at all, and somehow that was the worst, as if she were an astronaut free-floating in space, her lifeline snipped in two.

The emptiness of infinite space roared in her ears, and she wondered if she'd gone deaf.

But then, finally, she heard the noise she'd been waiting for, the one sound her ears, her heart, her entire soul had been listening, straining, praying for.

The sound of the ambulance, screaming toward them through the rain.

CHAPTER THREE

IT WAS ALMOST midnight before Grant was able to go home.

Actually, he was secretly shocked that he'd been able to talk the doctors into discharging him at all. Given how scrambled his brain was right now, he wouldn't have thought he could talk a bear into sleeping in the woods.

But luckily Harry Middleton was the doctor on duty, and Harry had bought Grant's first foal, Tender Night, out of Charisma Creek. So a few corners could be cut. Besides, once they set Grant's arm and did a CT scan on his brain, they didn't have anything left to hold him for.

"Observation" wasn't a good enough reason to keep a man in the hospital, not when he had a ranch to run single-handedly.

He looked down at the cast that covered his right forearm from palm to elbow. Single-handedly, indeed. He might have smiled at his inadvertent pun, except his head hurt like a demon, and his bruised ribs were killing him.

And who could feel like smiling about anything while Kevin lay up there on the third floor, unconscious? Sure, Grant's right ankle was sprained and his arm broken, but that was nothing compared to the crushing Kevin had suffered. He'd never regained consciousness after the accident, and no one seemed sure when—or if—he might wake.

Condition serious but stable, they called it. Whatever that meant. Grant shook off the memory of Kevin's bandaged form. He didn't have time to dwell on worst-case scenarios. He had to stay focused. Not only were there chores to do, horses to look after and accounts to settle…but he also had a baby to take care of.

With one hand.

Earlier, while he'd been waiting for his CT scan, Crimson had sent word that Marianne Donovan would babysit Molly for the evening. He'd been surprised at first, because Crimson normally never missed a chance to be with the baby. But he realized how dumb that was. Of course Crimson would want to stay at the hospital as long as she could, even though they wouldn't let her in Kevin's room.

She would want to be as close to him as she could get.

If Grant had ever been fool enough to wonder about Crimson's feelings—to wonder whether maybe Molly was more the attraction than Kevin himself—he knew better now. The look on her face when she first saw Kevin slumped over the steering wheel had said it all. She had been pale with terror, mute with grief.

God, the quiet hospital hallway seemed end-less. The polished floor reflected the overhead lights in hazy circles, as if someone had spilled milk at intervals—and the line of circles seemed to stretch on forever.

He'd lied to Harry and the nurses about how much his ankle hurt, hoping they wouldn't insist on a wheelchair. Limping as little as he could, he followed the path of watery lights to the waiting room on the second floor.

Crimson had sent word she'd be there, and she was.

To his surprise, though, she was deep in con-versation with another female, a teenager, he'd guess, and a bottle blonde. The two huddled to-gether in adjoining chairs by the far wall, talking in low tones even though they were the only two people in the room.

They both looked up as Grant entered. Only then did he see that the blonde had a black eye, a swollen upper lip and a bandage across the bridge of her nose.

"Grant!" Crimson rose jerkily. "Is there news?"

He shook his head. "Nothing since I sent the note around nine."

She nodded. "Thanks for that. No one would tell me anything."

He'd figured as much. A couple of weeks ago, when Kevin had learned that his new law firm would be sending him overseas periodically, he'd filled out forms naming Grant his official health-care surrogate and the emergency guardian for Molly.

It was a sudden outburst of practicality, which, frankly, had been a shocker. In their college days, Kevin had been the least sensible person Grant knew.

Of course, he hadn't seen Kevin in years, so maybe he'd grown out of that long ago. Working with the law could make you overly cautious. And fatherhood changed even the craziest frat boys.

Grant knew that, too.

So now Grant got all the medical updates. Crimson, who had no official standing, couldn't force the doctors to admit Kevin existed, much less that he lay in one of these rooms, unconscious.

"They may move him to Montrose in a day or two," Grant said, uncertain whether he'd included that in his note. The painkillers they'd given him were powerful, and a lot of tonight was a blur. "They don't have neurosurgeons here in Silverdell. The brain scan looks normal, and he does respond to light and stimulus…"

He let the sentence drift off. He'd included the details to provide hope, but even he wasn't sure what they meant. Clearly the doctors weren't sure, either. All they were certain of was that Kevin wasn't brain-dead, and therefore he would prob-ably require a higher level of care.

Crimson nodded silently. She didn't look shocked,

so he assumed his note had covered the basics well enough. But she did look grave. She must hate the idea of Kevin being moved—it would be harder to get to Montrose, which was about an hour away from Silverdell.

On the other hand, she would want him to get the best care possible. Poor Crimson. Her emotions clearly were a heavy weight to carry. Her hazel eyes, normally lit with both intelligence and mischief, were dulled with grief and fear.

Without ever meeting Grant's gaze, the mystery girl standing next to Crimson fidgeted with her purse strap. She tentatively touched Crimson's arm.

"I probably should go. Rory's waiting for me downstairs, and he has to work in the morning."

Crimson frowned, but even the frown was blunted. When she didn't agree with something, she ordinarily zapped you hard. Now, though, her voice was softly troubled. "Becky, Rory isn't—"

"It's okay!" The girl smiled so brightly it looked out of place here, in the dim, hushed chill of a hospital waiting room at midnight. "He'll watch out for me. After I fell, he practically carried me to the hospital. Honestly. I stumble on one wet staircase, and suddenly he thinks I can't walk without tripping over my own feet."

Crimson shut her eyes and took a deep breath. She swayed slightly. Grant wondered whether she might collapse right there. He'd never seen her look so dead-dog tired.

She opened her eyes. "You still have my card?"

The girl nodded, never letting the smile drop. "Sure do! Thanks. Pretty crazy, huh, both of us showing up here tonight?" She transferred the high-wattage beam to Grant. "Good to meet you," she said, though she hadn't. "Glad you're okay!"

Wiggling her fingers in a goodbye better suited to friends parting at the dance club, she left.

Grant went over to where Crimson stood. She'd let her shoulder drop against the wall as if she needed the support. Beside her, through the window, he saw flashes of silver, which made the ugly metallic rooftop air handlers look almost pretty.

"It's still raining." He was surprised, though he wasn't sure why. Silverdell springs could be wet as hell. But he felt as if he'd been inside this hospital for days, instead of hours.

"It's okay. I drive pretty well in the rain."

Right. He'd have to leave the driving to her, wouldn't he? He wasn't even sure his sprained right ankle would be capable of making the transition from gas to brake—and the last thing they needed was another accident.

He almost asked her where her car was parked—but he remembered in the nick of time. She didn't have a car anymore. They'd towed it to the junk lot down by Mark's garage on the south side of town, waiting to be crushed, no doubt.

And suddenly, like a tsunami, all the practical details of this mess rushed into his head. None of it had seemed to matter earlier, when he'd been focused on Kevin's condition and on persuading the doctors to let him go home.

But it mattered now. Thanks to that fool tourist, who had been texting when he should have been watching the road, Crimson was in a fix— and so was he.

What was he going to do with Molly? He couldn't tend to a baby with only one good hand.

He couldn't tend to a baby. Period.

"Hell." He frowned, getting a sudden glimpse of the long list of things he wasn't going to be able to do one-handed. It stretched from the profoundly important, like grooming, feeding and training his horses, to the ridiculously trivial, like buttoning his jeans and squeezing toothpaste onto his own toothbrush. "I'm screwed, aren't I?"

His cell phone chose that moment to buzz at him. Clumsily, he dug around in his pocket with his left hand, barely managing to extricate the thing before it was too late.

He answered without looking at the caller ID, because he didn't have time. Just his luck. It was Ginny.

And apparently, she'd heard about the accident. "Honey, are you okay?"

"I'm okay." He wondered why they were back to *honey*. He'd been so relieved when she broke up with him. Surely she wasn't going to try to patch things up now.

Crimson was staring at him, her face set as if she feared it might be bad news, so he smiled a little and shook his head to set her mind at ease. "My arm's broken," he explained into the phone, "and I'm on some serious painkillers, but I'm alive."

He winced when he heard himself say that. *I'm alive, but Kevin…*

"Are you still at the hospital? Let me come get you. You shouldn't be alone tonight."

Instinctively, he began to protest. "No, really. I'm fine. I know you decided we should take a break, and just because I've had an accident, you shouldn't—"

"I want to! You know I wouldn't leave you in the lurch!"

"Listen, Ginny." He was suddenly so tired he wasn't sure how much longer he could string words together. "I'm fine. I don't need any help."

"What about the baby? If your arm is broken, you'll need someone to help with the baby, surely. Diapers? Feeding?"

She was right, of course. He would desperately need help with all that. But he'd learn to change diapers with his toes before he'd put Molly in the Ginny's care. The breakup over late-night wailing was only the last in a long line of small indications that Ginny wasn't fond of babies.

He glanced at Crimson. Maybe something in

his face alerted her to the problem. Or maybe she had just put two and two together from his end of the conversation.

She raised her eyebrows and tapped her index finger against her collarbone. "Me," she mouthed. She held her elbows out, cupped one hand behind the other and mimicked rocking a baby. "Me."

He nodded. *Yes. Oh, hell, yes.* He didn't have to think twice. Even his muddy brain could see how perfect that solution was. Crimson was capable, kind and newly unemployed. She loved Molly, and the baby had clearly bonded with her.

"I've already got the help I need," he said into the phone, though he kept his gaze on Crimson, who was smiling her approval. She was extraordinarily beautiful, he thought suddenly, and then pulled back from the thought. Was that the painkillers talking? He didn't concern himself with the beauty of women who belonged to other men.

Maybe it was just that, at the moment, she looked like his guardian angel. He hadn't even realized how daunted he'd felt at the prospect of handling things alone until he didn't have to. She was the perfect candidate.

Honestly, he couldn't think of anyone else he could stand to have living at the ranch right now.

"What do you mean, you've already got help?" Ginny sounded suspicious. "You've been in the hospital all afternoon. What did you do, hire a nurse straight out of the ER?"

"Better than a nurse," he said. "Crimson's offered to move in till Kevin wakes up."

"I'VE GOTTA TELL YOU, pumpkin, you're cute, but you're exhausting."

Crimson dropped a kiss on Molly's head as she spoke, as if to offset any implied criticism. But it was true. She was dog-tired. And she'd only been a substitute mother for about—she glanced at the alarm clock on the nightstand by Kevin's bed—about three hours now.

Three hours out of...how many? How many days, weeks, months, even, would it be before Kevin was well enough to come back to his infant daughter?

If he ever was.

She shivered, even though this bedroom, one of the few completely renovated rooms in Grant's comfortable ranch house, was cozy warm. She could see a peaceful spring dawn rising over the greening mountains through the window.

About half an hour ago, the rain had finally stopped—and Molly had woken up. Maybe the sudden silence was the problem. Maybe the deep drumming of water against the roof had provided a lullaby of white noise. Or, heck, maybe waking at 5:00 a.m. was normal for Molly. Crimson had never been intimate enough with Kevin to learn such things.

She'd never spent the night in this bedroom. Not until tonight.

She looked at the baby, who looked back, wide-eyed and curious.

What had she gotten herself into? Was it really just yesterday she'd been saying she needed to get the heck out of Silverdell? She should have listened to her gut. She should have gone straight to her car and…

As if Molly sensed Crimson's distress, she frowned. She puckered up and inhaled, clearly prepared to wail.

"Shhh…no, no, we have to let Uncle Grant sleep." Crimson patted the baby's back, wondering what on earth to try next.

Clean diaper? Well, she wasn't an idiot. She'd taken care of that first. She'd also offered a bottle of formula. Kevin had cleverly turned this guest bedroom into a self-contained baby-tending unit, with a small refrigerator on the dresser, and an electric bottle warmer conveniently situated on the end table.

After Molly had eaten, Crimson had patted her back until she burped. Serenading her softly, she'd walked her around the room.

And around. And around.

She'd been pacing a cramped circle through this small space for half an hour now. From the crib, down around the foot of the bed, over to the window, past the armoire and back to the bed.

Every time, the minute Molly saw the crib, she started to fret, so Crimson would start the loop all over again.

But still Molly rode her shoulder with her head erect, her body tense, her feet kicking slightly. She was 100 percent wide-awake.

"Hush now, pumpkin. Hush."

But Molly was clearly not in the mood to be hushed. Jiggling the baby with one arm, Crimson snatched up her long bathrobe with the other and made her way out the door, worming her arm into the sleeve awkwardly.

She still had only one arm in by the time she hit the staircase, and the robe dangled from her shoulder. Gingerly, she made her way down the beautiful Australian cypress treads, being careful not to trip on the untied belt, which dragged beside her like a snake.

The staircase seemed to fascinate Molly, who instantly went silent. She gripped the neck of Crimson's nightshirt in one fist to steady herself and used her other hand to push upright so she could gaze at the big house with her liquid blue eyes.

She smacked her lips, and then she made a noise that sounded a lot like a kitten purring. Crimson had to chuckle. It was undoubtedly an expression of approval, as if saying that Crimson had been a little slow on the uptake, but she'd finally gotten it right.

"I hear you, girlfriend," Crimson said, kissing the warm, silky head again as they made it to the bottom of the stairs. "A lady's gotta have space. A lady's gotta have a little excitement."

"I'm not sure I can offer excitement this early in the morning," Grant said, appearing suddenly from the shadows of the dining room, where it led into the kitchen. "Frankly, it took me half an hour to manage coffee. Want some?"

"Grant!" Crimson frowned. "What on earth are you doing awake?"

He couldn't have slept more than two hours. If that. They'd decided not to leave Molly with Marianne, who had the restaurant to handle and needed rest. But by the time they'd picked up the baby, and stopped by Crimson's apartment to grab a toothbrush and a change of clothes, and driven back to Grant's place, it had been nearly 3:00 a.m.

"Did Molly wake you? I tried to keep her quiet, but—"

"No. I haven't even been upstairs." He turned and led the way into the kitchen, talking as he walked. "Too much to do."

She watched him move away. He was limping more than he had last night. Shifting Molly to her other shoulder, she followed him into the kitchen.

"Tell me what needs to be done, and I'll take care of it. You need to get off that foot, and you need sleep. You look awful."

He turned, raising one eyebrow and giving her a small smile. "Gee. Thanks."

She refused to smile back. He'd been born gorgeous, and he knew it, but she wasn't kidding. He looked done in. His thick, brown hair fell onto his forehead in unkempt waves. Dark blue shadows sat like bruises below his heavy-lidded eyes. His skin, which ordinarily glowed, bronzed by the hours outside, looked oddly sallow. His full lips seemed to have thinned from pain.

"You look terrible," she repeated.

"Oh, well." Tilting his head, he let his gaze quickly scan her from head to toe. He brought his coffee mug up for a quick sip to hide his smile. "Obviously we can't all be as splendid first thing in the morning as you are."

Aw, crud. Belatedly, she remembered she hadn't even run her fingers through her hair when she got up with the baby. Last year, she'd cut her hair in edgy, red-tipped spikes, and growing that stupid style out was an ordeal. If she didn't slick it down, it stuck out all over like a sick peacock in molting season.

And then there was the sexless gray bathrobe, which still hung over one shoulder, half on, half off, and dragged on the ground behind her.

"Yeah, well, I didn't expect to find anyone down here," she said brusquely. It annoyed her to realize she was embarrassed. What did she care how bad she looked? If he'd wanted eye candy,

he should have stuck with Ginny, whose magic mascara probably never gave her raccoon eyes if she forgot to take it off.

She felt around behind her, blindly rooting for the other side of the robe so she could at least cover herself up. It was probably obvious she wasn't wearing anything underneath this ugly cotton nightshirt.

With a small chuckle, Grant set down his coffee cup. Reaching his good hand around to help her, he lifted the terry cloth and guided the opening of the sleeve toward her fingers. When that was on, he tugged the robe up over her shoulders and tucked the edge under the other side, while she held Molly out of the way.

He grabbed the short end of the fuzzy belt and slid it through its loopholes to pull it even.

"You'll have to tie it, I'm afraid." He smiled. "I'm already discovering how many things I can't do with one hand. Making a bow is one of them."

"Thanks," she said awkwardly. He was still holding the edge of the sash, and Crimson's skin prickled with an odd awareness. When he'd brushed her breast, she'd felt it like a burn. She needed to remember not to come down half-dressed ever again. Clearly it made her way too sensitized and silly.

As if he understood, he dropped the sash and instead put his palm over the crown of the baby's head and softly stroked the carroty hair.

"Hey, cutie," he said. "You look sleepy, too. How about a nap, so Auntie Red can get a little more shut-eye?"

Molly seemed to love the touch of his big, gentle hand, and she clearly recognized the name "Auntie Red." Kevin had given it to her when they first started dating.

The baby sank against Crimson's shoulder with a contented chirp. She nuzzled her collarbone for a second or two, and then she shut her eyes and went instantly limp with sleep.

Grant smiled, and their gazes met over the baby's head. Crimson shook her head slightly, a mute acknowledgment of the irony. She'd tried for an hour to accomplish what he'd been able to do with one touch.

"It's a guy thing," he whispered, but his eyes were teasing.

She ought to take Molly upstairs right now, ease her into the crib and grab a little more sleep. And yet she felt oddly fixed in place.

After the hell of yesterday, there was something so intensely intimate and good about this moment. The kitchen was fresh and pink with dawn light. The coffee gave the rain-freshened air a homey flavor. The warm infant in her arms smelled like baby powder, soap and everything simple and sweet.

"Thank you, Crimson," Grant said, his voice quietly solemn. He rarely used her real name, which he knew she didn't like. But it sounded oddly feminine and lovely now. "Thank you for being here. For being willing to help."

Crimson started to protest automatically—it was nothing, she was glad to do it, she adored Molly, she'd do anything for Grant...

But as she gazed into his eyes, she felt a strange shift, as if she'd momentarily lost her balance. When she centered herself again, she felt different. The whole room felt different.

He blinked and frowned slightly, as if the same tremor had just run through him, too. His beautiful brown eyes, flecked with gold, were just as shadowed and tired as ever, but they suddenly held a new gleam. When he gazed down at her, it was as if he could see beyond the surface, beneath the skin, down to something very private. Something no one else could see.

She'd do anything for Grant...

Heat shot to her cheeks as a jolt of electricity moved through her midsection. Confused and deeply embarrassed, she fought the feeling. This was ridiculous. She must be imagining it. She and Grant...they weren't like this. They weren't lovers. They hadn't ever even considered it. They didn't even flirt.

They were just friends.

And yet, she didn't seem to be able to pull her gaze from his, and she was tingling all over...

"It's nothing," she said, desperately clutching at the pat phrases. "Really. I'm glad to help. It's nothing."

She backed off a clumsy step or two, ignoring the way her robe slid open again, exposing her bare legs and the outline of her breast. If he dropped his gaze, he would see what these invisible shivers had done to her...

But he didn't look down. The minute she began to move, he turned away.

"Better get some sleep while you can," he said briskly. "I'm trying to line up more help. I'll let you know what I can get."

And then, as if the electricity that arced between them had never happened, as if she had imagined it, he turned back to the counter where the coffee was brewing. He was pouring himself another cup when his cell phone rang.

"Get some sleep, Red," he said again. He smiled casually at her over his shoulder as he answered his phone. "Olson...thank God. Did you catch up with Barley? I'm going to be useless for weeks. Can he be here by ten?"

THESE DAYS, WHEN the alarm on Rory's cell phone went off at 6:00 a.m., Becky pretended to sleep through it. She used to get up with him, eager to be supportive and "wifely." But she'd quickly learned he wasn't a morning person. He didn't eat breakfast, hated to make small talk before

the coffee kicked in and was always running late, anyway.

Besides, their apartment was too small, and no matter how careful she was, she always seemed to be standing right where he needed to be. If she asked him questions like "When do you think you'll be home?" he'd get that cold, contemptuous look. He'd sigh and repeat very slowly, "What did I tell you the *last* ten times you asked?"

I don't know when I'll be home, Becky. Remember? It depended on how many cars there were to fix, and how hard the problems were to diagnose, how long the supplier took to deliver the parts, how obnoxious the customers acted or how lazy the other mechanics were when it came time to clean up the bays.

Of course she remembered all that. She was just making conversation. It felt weird to watch him shave and gargle, drag on his underwear, guzzle milk from the carton and pee with the bathroom door open…all without saying a word.

It hadn't always been like this. When she'd first moved in, he'd usually been horny in the mornings. When his alarm went off, he'd hit the snooze button, and then he'd reach over and shove her nightgown up around her waist with a quick jerk that was supposed to be a joke. She slept on her side, so he'd angle her hips and take her in a spoon position, sometimes before she was even fully awake.

He'd always be finished long before the alarm went off again.

Funny. She could remember when she'd found that kind of primitive dominance weirdly thrilling. It had seemed manly. Simple, earthy and real. Maybe it wasn't technically satisfying, in that she never…well, it never made her…

But it had turned her on, even so. It made her feel female and desirable. It had made her feel alive, as she had never felt alive in the mansion on Callahan Circle.

But Rory hadn't touched her in the morning for weeks. They still had sex, of course, but mostly at night, after he got home from work. He'd shower first, naturally. He hated the stink of the shop. All through dinner, he'd bitch about the customers and the other mechanics, and Joe, the owner. He'd keep up a running monologue as he wolfed the food down, even when she'd made something really complicated and special for him as a treat.

And when he was finished eating and complaining, he'd want to have sex. Lately, she'd stopped even thinking of it as "making love." It was just sex. Just a way to let off steam, like eating or complaining.

She knew what this change in him meant. It meant he was terribly, terribly unhappy. He hated his job. He hated his poverty, this apartment, the fact that her father had disowned her for moving in with a blue-collar loser like him.

What she didn't know was what to do about it. She didn't know how to make him happy again.

She listened to him moving around the small apartment now, mentally following the routine, gauging how long till he would be gone. She had to pee, too, but she didn't want to risk tying up the bathroom at the very moment he needed it.

He was in a superbad mood today, she could tell. His steps were heavy on the uncarpeted floors, and he made a big to-do of trying to find a clean spoon for his coffee in the silverware drawer. She wondered whether, at least subconsciously, he wanted to wake her, specifically so they could have a fight.

He resented that she only had a part-time job at Fanny Bronson's bookshop and didn't have to get up as early as he did. He was always telling her she needed to look harder for something full-time, or at least another part-time gig.

He was running late. She could tell by how rushed his movements were. Too rushed. Suddenly she heard his coffee mug hit the kitchen floor. The ceramic splintered on the wood like a china bomb.

He cussed loudly, using the F word, which he once had kept off-limits, around her, anyhow.

"I don't have time for this shit," she heard him say. She did not hear the sound of the broom closet opening, or the swish of bristles across the floor or the clink of broken pieces collecting in the dustpan.

She merely heard the cabinet open, the trickle of coffee filling a new mug, and then Rory slamming the pot back on the stove with undisguised hostility. As if she, not he, had broken the first mug.

Becky wondered whether she could get away with feigning sleep any longer—even the dead couldn't sleep through all this—but she didn't have the courage to open her eyes.

She heard him stomp to the bedroom door. He stood there a minute, and she knew he was staring at her. She tried to breathe regularly, but her lungs felt like iron. And she wasn't sure what her real-sleep breathing sounded like. Was it fast? Slow? Noisy? Did she snore? She ought to record herself sometime, she thought numbly, so she could imitate it more accurately.

After what seemed an eternity, he cursed again, smacked the door frame with the palm of his hand and left the apartment. Even then, she didn't get up. She waited until she heard his truck rumble to life in the parking lot outside their window. When he turned the corner onto Cimarron Street, and its sputtering sound died away, she finally pushed back the covers and stood.

Her legs were oddly unsteady, and her stomach felt loose and unpleasant, as if she'd swallowed a gallon of dirty water. She put her hand over her navel, hoping to might stop the sudden surge of nausea.

Was she coming down with stomach flu?

She hoped not. Fanny was a good boss, but she didn't offer sick leave to her part-timers, and Becky needed the money. She'd sold a gold chain last week to cover her half of the rent, and she didn't have much more of her good jewelry with her at the apartment.

She'd left most of it back at the Callahan House on purpose. To make a statement. To show her father she didn't give a damn about his money. She didn't need it. Where she was going, the currency was love.

Her father had laughed. "Let's see how much he loves you when you're not decked out in diamonds and gold."

How sad, how indescribably sad, to discover her father was right, after all. It wasn't that Rory didn't love her unless she had money—it was just that nothing could bloom in an atmosphere of this much stress and financial worry. Not even love. Nothing could go right at home when a man spent all day at a job he hated, with people who didn't value him.

After she used the bathroom, her stomach felt a little more settled, so she cleaned up the broken mug, made the bed and took a shower. She still felt light-headed, but not actually ill, so she decided not to call in until she tried having some breakfast.

But when she sat down at the kitchen table and ate her first spoonful of cereal, she suddenly doubled over with nausea. She rose blindly, knowing she would never make it to the bathroom. She turned toward the sink.

And vomited.

She stood there many minutes afterward, shaking strangely, her elbows pressing against the cold stainless steel. She stared into the sink. She'd had nothing in her, really, so nothing much had come up except greenish bile that had slipped right down the silver drain.

At the thought, her stomach turned again. Helplessly, she retched, desperately trying to gather her long hair and keep it from falling into her face. Again, nothing came up except a thin, sickly stream of water.

So it couldn't be anything she'd eaten. What was it? Was it nerves? Was it Rory?

Bowing her head, she made a small sobbing sound. She felt confused and weak, as if she wanted to curl up on the floor and cry for her mommy. But she hadn't had a mother since she was eight years old. And she hadn't had much of one, even before that.

"Jesus, what the hell is this?" Rory's voice was suddenly right behind her. "Don't you have to be at work in half an hour?"

She let her hair drop from numb fingers. She whirled around to face him, too shocked to take

offense at his tone. What was he doing home? He should be at the garage, shouldn't he?

"I...I'm not feeling that great," she stammered. "I was thinking I might call in sick."

"Oh, yeah?" His handsome face looked menacing, suffused with dark, angry blood. He strode to the sink and caught her by the arm. His fingers were so tight she swore she felt them reach her bone.

"Well, you better think again. You're going in no matter how you feel. We need that money. Especially now."

She swallowed. Her mouth felt sour and unclean. "Why especially now?"

"Because only one of us can sit around in our pj's eating bonbons, princess, and it's my turn now. That bastard Joe Mooney just fired me."

CHAPTER FOUR

"You know about this horse, I guess."

Dusty Barley, the crusty old trainer who had answered Campbell Ranch's call for help the other day, shot a quick glance at Grant, who was watching the halter training from just outside the paddock fence.

"Know what?" Grant was definitely interested in Barley's opinion. Cawdor's Gilded Dawn was the horse he hoped to sell to his deep-pocket buyer Monday night. Grant thought the three-year-old filly was fabulous, but if she had a defect he needed to know about it now.

"Ah, well, yep, of course you know." Barley always talked softly, as if he were thinking aloud, which maybe he was. He also sounded as if he had a mouth full of gravel, probably the result of his crowded and crisscrossed teeth. "But I still gotta say it. This one's gonna be special, Campbell."

Grant held back a sigh, watching as the copper filly flicked her beautifully elevated tail. As Barley prompted her to step to the right, her muscular hips caught the sunlight, gleaming as if she truly were made of gold.

Barley was right, of course. Barley was always

right. That's why Grant couldn't afford him at Campbell Ranch, not full-time. It had been a small miracle he'd been able to get him on such short notice Wednesday—and hold on to him for three whole days now.

"So…I'm just saying." Barley kept his voice steady as he moved around the young filly, careful not to spook her. "You sure you don't want to keep this one?"

"I never said that." Grant leaned on the post, taking the weight off his bad foot. The grass was soft, but right now it felt harder than concrete. "I just said I've got a buyer coming from California to look at her."

"Yep." Phlegmatic as ever, the older man put the crop close to the young filly's nose. She didn't flinch. "Good girl. Good girl. Still. This one's got star quality. Look at that neck."

Grant didn't answer. Truth was, he was 100 percent sure he did want to keep her. But he was 99.9 percent sure he couldn't afford to.

She would have been perfect, though. If he was going to maintain a breeding program, and not just a boarding and training stable, he needed a foundation mare. Up to now, Charisma Creek had been his dam, but she was reaching the end of her breeding years.

If Campbell Ranch was going to make a name for itself, Grant needed a champion maker, a con-

sistent producer with a good bloodline. And he
needed her soon.

Dawn could be that mare.

Though she was very young, she already had
the most extraordinary elegance—a high, airy
motion and impeccable conformation. She had a
swan-like neck, a flat topline, a perfectly dished
head. Her eyes were soulful and intelligent.

Plus, as Barley pointed out, she had that inde-
finable something that made a star. Everyone fell
in love with her. The best Arabians were as pretty
in the face as cartoon horses, as powerful in car-
riage as thunderbolts and as graceful in motion
as water. Dawn was all of that...and then some.

Barley finished the lesson, led Dawn to the car-
rots and then let her loose to romp a bit in the outdoor paddock.

Grant followed the filly with his gaze. She
covered so much ground when she ran—and yet
she still had amazing elevation. He wished he'd
brought a video camera. It was a beautiful morning, the sun sparkling like an enormous gold
sequin overhead, and the grass studded with a
thousand wildflowers that seemed to have sprung
up all at once.

Amid all that picture-postcard color, Dawn
looked like a dancing sunbeam.

"Thanks," Grant said as Barley sauntered over
toward him at the fence. "You really brought her
along today. If you can stay, the boarders need

turnout, too. And I'd love to hear what you think about the horse in stall five. His owner wants to sell, but I'm not so sure. I'd planned to ride him a bit this week, but..."

Damn his useless arm. It was going to cost him a fortune to hire out all this work. And he hated feeling cooped up. Pinned down. Irrelevant. He loved the horses, and he loved this land. He wanted to be doing something active, something that mattered.

Instead, for the past three days, he'd been clumsily typing with one finger and making endless phone calls. And watching while other people did the real work.

"I can stay." Barley shrugged, as if it was no big deal. "Olson said you needed help, and that cast there says he wasn't kidding. I'm yours as long as you need me."

Grant was relieved—and a little flattered. Everyone knew Barley operated more on gut instinct than on schedules. No one else could get away with being so elusive, but Barley could.

At first glance, he didn't look particularly impressive. A scrawny older guy, probably not even ninety pounds dripping wet, with a big black mustache and curly black hair that fell to his shoulders. He walked bowlegged and dressed scruffy.

But he knew horses, and he could work miracles.

That meant he didn't have to commit to anyone

long-term, and he rarely did. He was like rain—you couldn't summon it, and you couldn't keep it from floating away to the next guy's acres, but you were grateful for every drop that fell your way.

"Actually," Grant corrected ruefully, "you're only mine as long as I can afford you. Which, if I don't sell Dawn Monday night, isn't very long."

"Monday night, huh?" Barley made a thoughtful sound between his teeth. Soberly, he bent over and plucked a snowdrop from a cluster of wildflowers growing beside the post. He threaded its stem into the top buttonhole of his vest. Then he tipped back his hat and watched Dawn cantering in the sunlight.

"That's a damned shame, Campbell. Truly."

"Yes," Grant said with feeling. "Yes, it is."

"Okay, then. I guess I'll look at that horse in number five." Barley saluted Grant wryly and started to walk away, but stopped after just a few feet and turned back. "Seriously, though. My best advice? Don't let this one get away."

Grant raised his brows. For a guy like Barley, who was infamous for his unflappable detachment, this was the equivalent of jumping up and down and screaming.

"Okay," Grant said. "Message received. I'll think it over."

As he watched the little man stride away, the weaving gait of his bowlegs kicking up dirt, Grant tried to stay calm. No point letting wishful thinking run away with him.

The two truths weren't incompatible. Barley could be quite right about Golden Dawn's value, and Grant could also be quite right about needing to sell her.

But Grant was the only one who had the big picture. He was the only one who had seen both the horse and the solvency projections. All of his financial planner's clever graphs and charts showed Campbell Ranch nose-diving straight into bankruptcy if they didn't make their targeted income every month, rain or shine.

Without this sale, he didn't even come close to that target. And that was before he factored in all the extra expenses his broken arm would create. Not to mention the medical co-pays and deductibles.

If he tried to hold on to every good horse he encountered, instead of selling it, he might as well shut up the ranch now and head out to Memphis, where his father-in-law so desperately wanted him to be, in the job his father-in-law was dangling like a carrot.

He liked Ben Broadwell. And the job, heading up the foundation to help disadvantaged youths with after-school programs, literacy tutors and various kinds of mentoring, was a worthwhile cause. But...

But Ben Broadwell wasn't his father-in-law

anymore, really. Not since Grant's wife, Brenda, had died. And if Grant took that offer, it was as good as saying he would never be any more than a dead woman's grieving widower.

That might be true, in the end. But surely he hadn't reached the end yet. Surely there was still hope that he could build a meaningful life of his own.

So…he had to sell Dawn. Debate settled.

Or at least it should be. Still, he lingered by the paddock watching the filly romp and play awhile longer, even though his foot ached and a mountain of paperwork called.

"Hey, mister!"

He turned at the sound of Crimson's voice. To his surprise, she was only ten feet away, walking toward him. She wore soft, faded jeans and a loose shirt as blue as the columbines she waded through.

The sun brought out auburn highlights in her silky brown hair and gilded her cheeks, turning her to a kind of gold, just as it had done with Dawn. He felt his body react to her simple, unfussy beauty and had to throw up his guard in a hurry before it could show on his face.

As she drew closer, with Molly draped over her shoulder, and her classic mischievous smile on her lips, she showed no signs of feeling awkward—or sensing that he did. She held up a closed fist and shook it teasingly, the way a gambler might shake a pair of dice before rolling them.

"Can I interest you in some of the good stuff, mister? I've been watching you. You look like you could use some serious acetaminophen."

He checked his watch. He was at least two hours overdue. No wonder his foot was killing him.

"You're an angel." He accepted the pills and the small paper cup of water she'd been balancing in the hand that held Molly. He downed both pills in one swallow, realizing only afterward the cup was oddly soggy and bent around the rim.

He looked at the baby, who had swiveled in Crimson's arms and was now watching him steadily, a frown on her cherubic face. She held out one fat hand and uttered a demanding syllable.

"Oh, sorry, was this yours?" Smiling as he put two and two together, he handed the crumpled cup back. He scraped his lips between his teeth in exaggerated distaste. "Yum," he said. "Delicious."

Crimson grinned as Molly gummed the ball of wet paper. "In some cultures, baby slime is considered a delicacy. And speaking of dinner..."

He laughed.

"Marianne tells me you've asked her to cater dinner for you Monday night."

"Yeah." He wasn't aware she and Marianne chatted on a daily basis. "I've got a foreign buyer coming by. If he nibbles, it's a big sale, so a little wining and dining seemed in order."

And Marianne's dining was the best. She might call the place a "diner," but the swankiest place in Colorado could take a few pointers from her food. She'd become the go-to spot for catering lately, weddings and funerals, and everything in between.

A disturbing thought occurred to him. What if Marianne had run into trouble?

"Is there a problem? I know I didn't give her much notice, but Marianne said she could handle it. If she can't—"

"She can." Crimson shifted the baby to her other shoulder. "But the way she's handling it is to ask me to do most of the cooking. I've done that for her a couple of times, when she's been in a pinch. But this time the arrangement seems unnecessarily complicated, don't you think? I just thought I'd let you know, in case you'd like to eliminate the middleman."

"No, damn it." He frowned. "I deliberately didn't mention the dinner to you because you're doing too much work around here already."

And that was absolutely true. Not only did she take care of Molly, and spend hours driving to and from Montrose to see Kevin at the hospital, she'd taken over the cleaning, as well. And for these three days she'd cooked breakfast, lunch and dinner and sent it out to the stable office, where he often ate his meals while he worked.

Then, in the evening, when he was struggling with feeding the horses, she'd somehow materialized in the stables, with Molly in a backpack carrier, and pitched in there, too.

The extra pair of hands was a relief—a godsend, really—but it also made him uncomfortable. When he'd accepted her offer to stay here, he certainly hadn't intended to turn her into the full-time housekeeper.

And they hadn't talked about money yet, either. He hoped she knew he intended to pay her for everything. He hadn't forgotten she'd just been fired, and if she weren't stuck tending to Molly she'd probably be out there lining up a new job.

"For me, cooking isn't work," she said. "It's fun. I'm pretty good at it."

He'd discovered that months ago—everyone had, because her contributions to any get-together were always so delicious no one could believe she concocted them in an efficiency apartment's kitchen.

And since she'd been staying in his house, he'd learned firsthand just how amazing her skills were. And not just with food. With the whole domestic scene.

Because they'd met outdoors, doing manual labor for their outreach program, and, he had to be honest, partly because she was a straight-shooting, spiky-haired body modification artist, he'd never thought of her as the domestic angel type. But boy, had she surprised him. His half-renovated mess of a ranch house had never felt so much like a home.

Maybe that was partly why he was so wrong-footed around her these days. She was so different here…not at all the woman who deliberately preferred to be called Crimson Slash. In fact, it wasn't until he saw her in her robe the other morning that he'd noticed that her spiky, red-tipped hair was growing out in soft waves around her chin. And wasn't even red.

"If we're trying to impress this buyer, I've got a beef Stroganoff that'll have him on his knees." She wiggled her eyebrows suggestively. "And hey…if you've got a spare French maid costume lying around anywhere, I can guarantee a meal he'll *never* forget."

Grant's imagination served up a quick vision of Crimson in a flouncy black miniskirt and lacy apron. A quick sizzle shot through him—much like the one that had blindsided him that first morning, when he made the mistake of helping her arrange her bathrobe.

He squelched it as quickly as it appeared, as he'd been doing ever since that morning. Indulging even an unspoken attraction to this woman was wrong in so many ways. First and foremost: Kevin.

"Can't say I've got a French maid costume lying

around," he said, laughing easily to show what an innocent joke it all was. "Besides, if you're going to help with dinner, you're not going to be masquerading as an employee. You'll eat with us."

She was already shaking her head, but he didn't give her time to protest. "Seriously, Red, you'd be doing me a favor. He's bringing his girlfriend, and it'll be more comfortable if I've got a date, too."

She flushed, like a sudden sunburn, and he wished he'd bitten his tongue. Why had he used the word *date*? That wasn't how he meant it. He just thought that, in case Stefan was the jealous type, the man might prefer his host not to be conspicuously single.

Crimson wouldn't be a date. She would be his ally.

So dumb. But to be fair, when had conversation with Crimson become so touchy? Up until three days ago, she'd been the most comfortable female buddy he'd ever had. She was smart, sassy, straightforward and fun. Good-looking, but not hungry for admiration. Actually quite the contrary—with her spiky red hair and no-nonsense clothes, she seemed to be asking for some space.

Around Crimson, Grant could always just be himself. Easy, relaxed, uncomplicated. And then she'd moved into Kevin's room, and suddenly everything changed.

Well, maybe it was time to change it back.

"What's that scowl about?" He reached out his

good hand and tapped the furrow between her brows. "Since when did the idea of eating dinner with me become a fate worse than death?"

She laughed sheepishly, smoothing Molly's hair, clearly not wanting to meet his eyes. "It's not. It's just that I don't want you to think—"

"I don't think *anything*...except I'm not going to sit there pretending to be the cowboy king while you slave away in the kitchen. You're not my maid. You're my friend. Eat with us, or I'm sending out for burgers."

"Marianne's too busy even for that."

"Not Marianne's burgers." He tilted his head. "I was thinking maybe the Busted Button."

"No way!" Crimson's eyes widened in mock horror. The fast-food joint's real name was Buster's Burgers, but their billboard screamed "Fat and Happy—Guaranteed!" above a picture of a cartoon French fry with the top button of his blue jeans popping off, so no one in Silverdell ever called it anything but the Busted Button.

She narrowed her eyes, obviously well aware she was being played. "You'll never close the deal if you go to Buster's. Your buyer will be dead of a heart attack before dessert."

"Exactly." He grinned. "So. *Deal*?"

It was her favorite shorthand phrase, one she used when she was sick of debating.

She shook her head and rolled her eyes in that sardonic way he knew so well. He felt his shoulders relax. His good friend Red, who could dandle a baby, cook a gourmet meal and still call baloney when he tried to pull a fast one, was back.

"Deal," she said. "Now, if you'll excuse us, Molly and I have some grocery shopping to do."

MONDAY MORNING, CRIMSON went to visit Kevin much earlier than usual. The doctors had moved him to Montrose after the first day, which had been presented as a good sign, and she hoped it really meant there was hope.

Belle Garwood, from over at Bell River Ranch, had offered to keep Molly. Because Belle had a newborn baby herself, Crimson hated to impose often, but today, with the big dinner to prepare, she needed the help.

Though Crimson and Grant had both visited Kevin every day since the accident, they never went at the same time. Crimson had picked up a rental car, which made things easier. Even though going separately involved a tremendous amount of driving, especially now that Kevin was in Montrose, it seemed they both preferred it that way.

The schedule wasn't something they'd discussed much—beyond casually observing that it made sense to take turns. Tag-teaming covered more ground, they'd said. Alternating visits kept watchful eyes in Kevin's room more of the time.

Grant went in the daytime, mostly, when one of the hands could drive him to Montrose, piggybacking on some errand for the ranch. Crimson went in the late afternoons or early evenings, because it was easier to get a sitter for Molly. If they accidentally overlapped and ran into each other in the parking lot or in the hospital corridors, they never acknowledged that it was awkward.

It was, though.

At home, at the ranch, they'd been able to move past the geyser of sexual chemistry that had sprung up between them that first morning. They'd managed to settle down, even to recapture most of their old comfortable camaraderie. But at the hospital, with Kevin lying there in the dark loneliness of a coma, the memory of that moment seemed to hang over them like a fog of guilt.

This morning the large Montrose hospital was bustling with the usual flurry of early activity. Crimson had bought a colorful balloon to brighten up Kevin's room, and it bobbed foolishly beside her as she walked past the nurses' station.

"Cute." The RN standing at a cart dispensing medications into small cups grinned as she went by. "He'll love it."

Crimson smiled back gratefully. She loved the positive energy these wonderful ladies gave off. All of them talked to Kevin as if he could hear them perfectly, so Crimson did the same—even though she didn't always know exactly what to say.

So many topics were off-limits. Topics like how,

just before the accident, she had been on the verge of "breaking up" with him, or whatever you called it when the relationship hadn't ever quite gotten off the ground in the first place.

You couldn't Dear John someone in a coma. The fact that Crimson was caught in a romantic no-man's land was nothing—*less than nothing*— compared to the trap that held Kevin prisoner in this helpless half-life.

The door to his room stood halfway open, so she pushed lightly and entered, her smile still in place in case, miraculously, he'd opened his eyes and could see it. But he looked exactly the same as he had yesterday. Immobile and terrifyingly remote, as if some tether had been cut, and with every day he drifted farther away from the rest of them.

"I brought you a Donald Duck balloon," she said brightly, arranging the little cylindrical weight on the windowsill. She tied a bow in the string so the balloon wafted softly at eye level.

"I know you'll start doing your *oh boy, oh boy, oh boy* impersonation as soon as you see it." She pulled the guest chair closer to the bed, sat down and laid her hand lightly on his arm. "But you know what? I'll be so glad you're awake I won't even complain."

He didn't respond, of course. The IV continued to plink, and the monitor kept up its electronic hum and rhythmic beep. From just outside the door, voices and footsteps rolled down the hall like waves of energy. But Kevin was utterly silent.

"I wish you could have seen Molly this morning," she said, refusing to let herself be discouraged. "That front tooth has finally broken through, and she smiles all the time, as if she's showing it off."

More silence. But Molly was the one subject Crimson felt comfortable with. No matter how complicated everything else might be, she was certain Kevin would want to know his little girl was all right.

"She's sleeping better, too. I got one of those teething rings Grant suggested—" She broke off. Just mentioning Grant's name made her nervous. She didn't want Kevin to feel he'd been displaced as Molly's daddy…that she and Grant were the parents now. Even worse, what if some of her new feelings about Grant came through in her voice?

She imagined, sometimes, that even the way she said the syllable was different now. Huskier, leaden with tension and repressed emotions.

"Anyhow, I think there's less pain once the tooth cuts through. She seems much more cheerful now. And boy, is she eating! When I bought diapers yesterday, I had to get the next size up."

She chuckled, but the sound echoed eerily in the quiet room, and it felt out of place, like laughing in a church. She wondered why it didn't sound that way when the nurses did it. Probably because, when a nurse was in here, she didn't feel so alone.

She didn't feel so out of her depth.

"Oh! I took a video this morning." She pulled out her phone and thumbed through her pictures until she got to the right one. She pulled it up, hit Play and held the phone in front of Kevin's face, as if that made sense. As if he might just open his eyes and say, "A video! Great!"

On the phone's small screen, Molly waved her hands, grinned and let loose peals of giggles and hiccupping laughter. Occasionally, Crimson's thumb had covered the lens as she struggled to hold the phone out and the baby up simultaneously. It didn't matter, though. Because of course Kevin did not wake, did not open his eyes, did not show any signs of being happy to hear his baby's voice.

"Say, I love you, Daddy!" Crimson sounded like a cheerleader, urging Molly. "Say, come home soon, Daddy!"

And then…at the very moment Crimson said, "Come home soon, Daddy," Kevin's finger twitched. Crimson dropped the phone to her lap, staring at his hand. Her heart beat rapidly.

Do it again, she willed him. *Do it again*.

The light in the room changed as the door opened. Crimson looked up, her heart still pounding in her throat. It was Kevin's new doctor, Elaine Schilling.

"He moved his hand!" Crimson didn't leave Kevin's side, didn't let go of his arm, but she leaned toward the doctor eagerly. Her voice was tight and thin. "I was playing a video for him—a video of his daughter—and his finger moved. I'm sure of it!"

Dr. Schilling paused as she reached into her pocket to pull out the little light she used to check pupil response, an important indicator, Crimson had learned.

"Well…" The woman's hazel eyes were kind, but her thin, austere face didn't catch any of Crimson's eager enthusiasm. "It's certainly possible. But we must remember a person in Mr. Ellison's condition may exhibit reflex activities that mimic conscious activities. It's wise not to read too much into it."

Crimson stared stupidly, as if she couldn't understand the doctor's terminology. But she did understand. It was simple enough. Dr. Schilling was saying the twitch was just some involuntary misfiring of a neuron. She was saying it probably didn't mean anything, and Crimson shouldn't hope for a miracle.

But Crimson *was* hoping. She *had* to hope. Who could survive without hope?

She couldn't. She remembered how—almost fourteen months ago, just barely more than a year—she'd kept diving down into the cold, black water of the Indigo River, looking for Clover, telling herself it wasn't too late. If a passing stranger hadn't seen her there and jumped in to drag her to shore, she'd have drowned alongside her sister.

In many ways, drowning would have been better than giving up. She couldn't remember the man's face, but she'd never forget his voice, saying, "You have to stop now. She's gone." The words had fallen on her skin like razor blades.

So she *had* to keep hoping. She wanted to tell the doctor that, but she didn't know how to begin. She let her hand fall into her lap. She must have bumped the Play arrow, because suddenly Molly began to laugh again as Crimson again implored her to tell her Daddy to *come home soon.*

The doctor frowned, a stern but compassionate expression. She clearly thought Crimson had restarted the video deliberately, hoping to prove her point. She hadn't—truly she hadn't—but she couldn't help staring at Kevin's hand all the same. Maybe…

But this time Kevin lay as still as a wax mannequin.

And suddenly, Crimson's eyes began to burn. They stung fiercely, as if they'd caught fire from the inside. Was it possible he'd never wake up? That he'd never go home to his baby girl?

As she stared at that lifeless hand, scalding tears spilled over. She bent her head, and the tears fell against Kevin's skin. He showed no awareness of that, either.

Embarrassed, Crimson stood. The doctor needed to tend to her patient. Crimson was in the way here. She was making a fool of herself. She turned, but she could barely see which direction to walk. Everything was fractured by her tears.

As if she'd called for him, Grant was somehow there. He put his arm around her shoulders and murmured her name. She looked up at him, and even though his face was blurred, she felt a powerful magnetic pull, as if his shoulder was the only place in the world she could rest her head safely right now. The only place she could let these tears fall in peace, without feeling ridiculous or weak. Without exposing all the secrets she'd been hiding for so long.

"Come on, sweetheart," he said gently. His arm steered her toward the door. "Let me take you home."

She followed him out. But as they exited the dim room and emerged into the bright light of the hospital corridor, all she could think was...

If Kevin actually could still hear, how did it make him feel to hear his best friend call Crimson *sweetheart*?

CHAPTER FIVE

"I MUST SAY, Campbell, you are a lucky man." Stefan Hopler shoved his hands into the pockets of his elegant linen khakis as they slowly strolled back to the ranch house from the stables, a full moon lighting their way almost as clearly as high noon.

Grant wondered what Hopler meant exactly—if he meant anything at all. Was it just flattery—to soften him up for bargaining over the horse?

Somehow he didn't think so. The man's tone sounded genuine.

And why shouldn't it be? Hopler didn't know anything about Grant's history—he knew nothing about his dead wife, Brenda, or the little girl they'd once had...Jeannie.

Hopler didn't even know that Grant hadn't always been a rancher, that once, like Kevin, he'd been a young, ambitious lawyer—and that the career dream had died along with his family.

All Hopler knew was what he'd seen here today. The beautiful acreage of Campbell Ranch, greened by the rain and bejeweled with wildflowers. The renovated stables, the well-trained staff.

The extraordinary filly who exuded star power as Barley put her through her paces.

All of that did, indeed, make Grant a lucky man. Even so, he had an irritable feeling Hopler wasn't talking about any of those things. He'd bet good money Hopler was talking about the gorgeous woman who had just cooked them a gourmet dinner.

Hopler's date, Elsa, hadn't made the trip from California with him, after all. In fact, Hopler had broadly hinted that his couple days were over. And Elsa's absence meant he felt free to compliment Crimson effusively on everything from the Stroganoff to her perfume.

The flirting had been so thick it irritated the heck out of Grant. He'd had to bite his tongue a couple of times to avoid reminding Hopler that he was there to buy a horse, not a girlfriend.

Not that the compliments weren't deserved. Crimson hadn't been kidding about giving the man a meal he wouldn't forget. The food had been almost mystically delicious…and, beyond all that, she had presided over his table with so much wit and charm that by the time she offered them dessert, even Hopler, who was clearly a ladies' man, had looked a little dazed.

"Thanks," Grant said now, trying not to sound as tight-lipped as he felt. They'd left Crimson in the ranch house cleaning up after dinner while they walked out to give Hopler one last look at

Dawn. He was pretty sure Hopler was ready to close the deal, and he was determined not to spoil it now. "The ranch is a lot of work, but I love it."

"Oh, I didn't mean the ranch," Hopler said, smiling. "No, no, the property is beautiful and your horses are beautiful. But your real treasure is your woman. Is it serious between you?"

For a minute, Grant wanted to say yes. *Hell, yes. So back off.* He had an irrational urge to stake a Private Property sign on Crimson.

But he remembered her tears, streaming down her cheeks unchecked as she sat vigil beside Kevin's hospital bed this morning. She was private property, all right. But not his. The Keep Out sign applied to Grant every bit as much as it applied to Hopler.

Besides, she wasn't the easy-fling type—and Grant didn't have anything else to offer a woman. His heart had been hollowed out like a melon three years ago, when Brenda and Jeannie died. He'd come to Silverdell almost immediately after, driven by some instinct to carve out a new life. A physical, exhausting, completely different life.

And he'd done all right with that part. The ranch was distracting, the horses rewarding. He was too busy to mourn all day, too tired to grieve all night.

But when it came to things like love and family and forever, he was stuck in a frozen half-life as much as any comatose man in a hospital bed.

"No, we're not together," he heard himself saying instead. "She's a friend. She's actually dating a buddy of mine. Molly's father."

Hopler had met Molly earlier, of course. Crimson had put the baby to bed just before dinner, and miraculously persuaded her to sleep through all three courses.

"Molly's father." The man took a minute to digest that. "You mean the one who is in the hospital now?"

Grant nodded. He didn't like Hopler's tone. It sounded as if he were weighing his odds, and liked the news that his chief competition was in a coma.

"What time did you say your flight back to LA leaves?" Grant's bum foot caught on an oak tree root, and he grunted irritably as pain shot up his leg. Thank goodness he didn't fall. "We probably should talk about Dawn, if you're interested in buying her."

Not subtle, he knew, but that was too darn bad. He was tired, and he was hurting, and he wasn't feeling subtle. He was feeling pissed, actually.

His dislike of Hopler was irrational and unfair—he admitted that. The man seemed perfectly respectable, and naturally Grant had checked him out before inviting him to discuss the horse. His only sins were being too handsome, too rich and too acquisitive.

But damn it. Wasn't it enough that he planned

to take Grant's best filly away from Campbell Ranch? He had to start auditioning Crimson for a role in his cushy Hollywood life, too?

"Oh, I'm *definitely* interested," Hopler said, pausing as they reached the back porch.

Crimson was visible through the kitchen window. She stood at the sink, scrubbing a pot. She bent over her chore, her shoulders working rhythmically and a wisp of hair dangling into her face. Clearly annoyed by it, she pursed her lips and blew upward, trying to make the silky brown curl behave. The curl lifted, but it dropped into the same place no matter how many times she puffed.

Finally, she laughed. Shaking her head, she lifted her sudsy fingers from the dishwater, and tucked the lock behind her ear. When she lowered her hand again, a frothy dollop of suds remained, sparkling on her earlobe.

Grant could almost feel Hopler's heartbeat quickening.

"Wow." The man's voice was reverent, as if he'd stumbled on a unicorn. "Imagine. A woman who *looks* like that, *cooks* like that and then laughs while she's doing the dishes."

At first, Grant didn't respond. He found the description offensively reductive. Crimson was so much more than some Stepford paper doll. She was quirkier, more independent, more difficult and mysterious and real.

She was so much more *interesting* than some misogynistic millionaire's Donna Reed fantasy.

Hopler sighed. "I honestly didn't know women like that still existed."

Grant felt his nerves prickling. "They *don't*. She laughs only when she feels like laughing. When she feels bitchy, she cusses like a sailor and breaks the cups. Sometimes she just tells us to do our own damn dishes."

"Even better," Hopler said, unperturbed. He turned toward Grant, his expression quizzical. "But remind me again...which one of you is dating her?"

CRIMSON HAD KNOWN there would be a price to pay for Molly's long nap during dinner. And sure enough, at about 3:00 a.m. the baby began to squirm and whimper.

Crimson rose quickly, hoping to calm Molly before she began to cry in earnest. She knew Grant needed a good night's sleep.

She could use one, too—but that didn't seem likely. Though she'd been lying in bed for several hours, she hadn't been able to doze off.

The Hopler dinner had been both exciting and disturbing, and her mind was racing. Her thoughts circled restlessly until they tied themselves in knots.

So she was glad of a distraction—and the comforting warmth of the baby's body against her shoulder. Strange how much companionship an infant could provide.

And funny how not being isolated anymore could make her realize just how horribly lonely she'd been this past year. She'd been born two minutes before Clover, and those were the only two minutes in her life she'd ever been truly alone—until the night Clover died.

She hugged Molly tightly as she moved toward the changing table, which gleamed in the moonlight.

"Hush, honey," she whispered. "We'll get a clean diaper and a nice warm bottle."

Molly subsided, understanding the promise in Crimson's tone, if not her words. When Crimson laid her back against the cushioned plastic of the changing table, she kicked her feet a couple of times. She found her fingers and began to suck noisily.

Crimson moved quickly. She was learning Molly's rhythms, and she knew that, after about a minute or so, the baby would realize the fingers provided nothing to fill her tummy, and she'd start to fret angrily, as if someone had tricked her.

She had just finished heating the bottle when Grant appeared in the doorway.

"Hey," he said, rubbing his fingers across the stubble on his chin. "You must be exhausted. How about if I help with that?"

Her hand went instinctively to her hair, which

once again must be sticking out everywhere. All that tossing and turning...she probably looked as if she'd stuck her finger in a light socket.

"I'm fine," she said. "Sorry we woke you. I was hoping you could get some sleep. I know you've got an early morning tomorrow."

He yawned, as if in confirmation, but he moved into the room, anyhow. He wore soft blue-gray sweatpants and a gray T-shirt. His hair was tousled, too.

"I mean it. Let me help. I'm tired of feeling useless. If I sit in the rocker, I can feed her with one arm."

She hesitated, but he was already arranging himself in the mission-style wooden rocker over by the window. It was a large, manly piece of furniture, beautiful in its simplicity, and terrifically comfortable. When Kevin moved in, Grant had commissioned Jude Calhoun, a local woodworker, to make it to match the bedroom set already in the guest room.

When Crimson had first heard about the handmade rocker, she'd thought it sounded extravagant, especially since Kevin and Molly were obviously temporary guests, and Grant had no need for such a thing. But over the past week she'd learned what a work of genius it was. Quiet, roomy, with great back support and perfectly placed arms that helped support an infant for hours at a stretch.

Almost every night this week, both Crimson and Molly had fallen asleep in that chair.

"Surely she's in no danger," Grant said, glancing up at her with a smile that said he knew she doubted his ability to hang on to a squirming baby. "Not if I'm sitting down, and you're standing guard."

"Of course she's not…" But even so she waited, watching him brace his elbow on the rocker's arm. He let his casted forearm slant down toward his lap. That cast was as hard as a chalky rock, which she knew from bumping into it several times this week. No way Molly would fall asleep on a bed of unforgiving plaster.

"Maybe this'll help." She grabbed the little pink cotton blanket from Molly's crib, folded it four times and laid it over the cast. Jiggling Molly to buy an extra minute or two, she assessed the arrangement somberly.

Still not quite right…

Like a photographer posing her subject, she leaned over and carefully tugged Grant's arm out a little farther, creating a perfect Molly-sized nook between his cast and his chest.

"That should do it." She handed Grant the warm bottle, and then she slipped Molly into the cradle of his arm.

Molly gave Grant a wide-eyed, surprised stare. But when he touched the bottle to her lips, instinct took over. Closing her eyes, she began to pull intently on the nipple.

Grant leaned back, crossing his ankle over his knee. "Might as well get comfortable," he said with a tired smile. "See those fists? That means her fuel gauge is reading empty. We're going to be here awhile."

The only other chair was on the opposite side of the room, so Crimson sat on the edge of the bed. She looked at Molly, wondering what Grant meant. And then she saw it. The baby's tiny hands were fisted up near her chin, her arms rigid with concentration as she drank. Crimson had never noticed it consciously, but now she realized that, as Molly filled up, her arms would relax, and eventually her fists would open and fall limp at her sides.

That would be when the fuel gauge read "full."

She chuckled, but at the same time she registered, once again, that Grant seemed to be surprisingly knowledgeable about babies. He maneuvered the bottle like a pro, tilting it subtly first one way and then the other, tapping out air bubbles. When Molly's attention wandered, he gently stroked her cheek with his pinky finger, a move that automatically stimulated her instinct to suck.

Watching him there, sitting with his head back, his eyes shut, dark lashes brushing golden skin… if she hadn't known the truth, she would have felt certain he was the daddy.

She tugged on the hem of her nightshirt, suddenly uncomfortable with the intimacy of this peaceful, moonlit scene. The doubts that had been plaguing her all night returned full force.

"There's something I need to tell you," she said impulsively, choosing not to give herself time to change her mind.

He opened his eyes. The moonlight shone on him from the side, making the whites seem bright, and the dark brown irises almost black.

"Okay." His voice was calm but laced with caution. Obviously, he knew it couldn't be anything good. "What is it?"

"I just wanted to tell you… I'll probably be leaving Silverdell soon."

He didn't respond immediately. She knew she'd shocked him and wished she hadn't been so blunt. She should've eased into it more gently.

"I mean…not right away, of course. I know everything's pretty crazy right now, and I wouldn't want to leave you in the lurch. But it's time for me to move on. I hadn't ever planned to stay in Silverdell this long in the first place. So I'm thinking that…when Kevin…when Kevin wakes up…"

"I see," he said, as it became clear she didn't know how to finish the sentence. "Of course you've got to do what's right for you. But I'm sorry to hear it."

She nodded. "I'm sorry, too. I like it here. In

Silverdell, I mean. But…it's time. Even before the accident I knew it was time to move on."

And since the accident, since she moved in here, the danger had doubled.

And then doubled again.

She liked Grant Campbell. A lot. His friendship had come to matter way too much to her, and if she wasn't careful she'd start wanting more. She'd forget how to be comfortable alone. It would be so dangerously easy to settle into playing house, pretending she belonged with this lovely man and this sweet, motherless baby.

But she didn't belong with them. She didn't *want* to belong with them. She didn't want to care about anybody.

The silence stretched uncomfortably. The bottle was almost empty, and Molly's sucking slowed as she drifted back to sleep. With that same odd instinct, Grant seemed to know the exact moment he should ease the bottle away. Molly fretted a little but subsided quickly as he put his good hand behind her head and rotated her up onto his shoulder for burping.

Crimson was impressed. She wouldn't have thought that was possible with only one hand. It should make her feel better, knowing he was more capable of taking care of himself than she'd realized.

But it didn't.

She had the oddest feeling she'd hurt him. She

stared down at her hands, swallowing the urge to explain. He'd never understand, anyhow. Her compulsion to remain rootless and solitary since Clover's death wasn't a reasoned decision. It was a blind instinct. She was like an animal running from a predator that was all the more terrifying because it disguised itself as happiness, or love or joy.

She had no idea where she was running. She only knew that if she stopped, the danger would catch her. She'd shatter into a million, trillion pieces…and no one would ever be able to put her back together.

"Why?" Grant still sounded calm and clearly kept his voice low so he wouldn't disturb Molly. "I mean…why do you feel such a compulsion to leave right now?"

She searched her mind. What kind of answer could she give him? How much of the truth was it safe to share?

Sure, she'd been talking about leaving, even before the accident. But she hadn't felt this urgency. She hadn't felt quite this desperate, as if she couldn't leave soon enough to really be safe.

The bottom line was…something about today had frightened her. She'd found herself slipping back into her old skin. Feeling like herself again. Relaxing her guard.

Probably that was because she'd spent all day in the kitchen, creating her best dishes to help him impress Stefan Hopler. It had been a full year since she'd had access to such a beautifully appointed cooking space, and it was a kind of emotional orgy to use it.

A great kitchen had always been her happy place. The way some people lost themselves in dancing, painting or growing flowers, she lost herself in custards and pastries, in slicing fruits and sifting sugar, in violet and lemongrass and chocolate.

And oh, the kitchen she and Clover had planned for their restaurant…

It would have been glorious. Not that she absolutely needed all the frills. She'd made some great food in her efficiency apartment over the past few months.

But she was well aware cooking for Grant was especially gratifying. And the payoff…

When he bit into the fruit tart, and that look of shocked delight moved across his face, she practically glowed inside.

Which made her about as big a fool as ever lived.

"Listen, Red, I…" He hesitated, as if the right words were eluding him.

She waited, all too familiar with the dilemma.

"I should have said something days ago. I don't know why I didn't." He smiled. "But if you think you need to leave because I'm getting stupid ideas about us, you don't need to worry. That tension the other morning…it won't happen again, I promise. I wouldn't ever do anything to hurt Kevin. And I wouldn't do anything to jeopardize our friendship."

She felt her cheeks go hot. She wondered whether she could pretend she didn't know what he was talking about. But that was immature—and pointless, as well. He knew he hadn't imagined it. He knew the sizzle hadn't been one-sided.

"That's not it," she said. "We were both just exhausted, raw from what we'd been through. It didn't mean anything. I know that."

He didn't answer. But as long as she'd started, she might as well go on and finish what she'd originally wanted to say.

"Actually, I think you've got the wrong idea about Kevin and me. There hasn't ever been anything serious between us. We're really just friends, too."

He frowned. "I'm not sure Kevin sees it that way." He shifted Molly a little higher on his shoulder. "In fact, I have a feeling he thought it might go somewhere, even if you didn't."

"No, he didn't. Not really. He's still coming to terms with being a single dad—and obviously he had a pretty serious relationship with Molly's mother not very long ago."

She hesitated, thinking of how reluctant Kevin had always been to talk about Molly's mother. Crimson didn't know much more than her name,

Anne Smith, and that they hadn't ever been married, and Anne had voluntarily signed sole custody of Molly over to Kevin.

"Whatever happened with Molly's mother, it has to have been difficult. You've noticed how he refuses to discuss it."

Grant nodded.

"So he couldn't possibly be ready to be serious about anyone yet. And even if he thought he was, he knew from the start I wasn't in Silverdell to stay."

"Did he?" Grant's frown deepened. "I didn't."

She shrugged. She hadn't mentioned it to Grant because there hadn't been any need to. It had never occurred to her that it would bother him if he walked into Needles 'N Pins one day and discovered she was gone.

Kevin was different. Right from the start, Kevin had seemed inclined to take their relationship to a more physical level, and she'd needed to set some ground rules. No commitment. No sex, either, not with a guy who had recently split from his baby's mother and who was obviously desperate to build a new life, find a new woman, create a new normal. Kevin didn't have his heart on an even keel yet, and she had no intention of being his next emotional shipwreck.

"Anyhow," she continued, "I'm not talking about leaving immediately. But when Kevin wakes up—"

"What if he doesn't?"

She stared at Grant. In the days since the crash, neither of them had uttered those words. As if by unspoken agreement, they'd always pretended it was only a matter of time before Kevin came home and slept in this room again, feeding and changing and loving his own little girl.

But deep inside, they both knew better. They weren't fools. They were well aware every passing day made a full recovery less likely. The odds were already building against him.

"I've been thinking about that," she said, glad he'd been the first to speak the words aloud. She couldn't leave town without knowing Molly was cared for—and in order to do that, she had to confront reality. "I've been thinking about it a lot. I've decided what I need to do, and I'm hoping you'll help me."

He waited. Molly nuzzled his shoulder, her rosebud lips moving, as if she were dreaming of her mother's breast.

"I will if I can," he said. "What is it you think you need to do?"

She took a deep breath. "I need to find Molly's mother."

BECKY HAD APPLIED for every part-time job in Silverdell without getting a single callback, and she was starting to panic. Rory asked her about it every couple of hours, and each time she said, "Nope, no nibbles," his sneer got uglier.

"Guess being daddy's little princess isn't a very marketable skill, is it? Too bad you don't have a real tiara. At least you could pawn it."

His contempt stung. But she knew that, beneath all that nastiness, he was just as scared as she was. He kept applying for garage jobs, too—even some as far away as Montrose—but without a good reference, he couldn't get hired. And Joe Mooney wouldn't provide one.

Turned out, the reason Rory had been fired was, as he put it, that "the cash drawer wasn't right" several times. He'd implied the problem was just an arithmetic error. He'd raged against Mooney's unfairness. The cash drawer had been over as often as it had been under, he said, so what was the big deal?

Becky didn't see how that could be true. People didn't get fired for having *too much* cash in the drawer. But she didn't push the point.

The bottom line was their rent was due in a week, and they didn't have it.

She'd just about decided she would have to swallow her pride and go home to get some more jewelry to sell. She might not have any real tiaras, but she did have a beautiful sapphire her mother had left behind...

But as she walked from the bookstore to Donovan's Dream, where she picked up Fanny's lunch every day, she saw a Help Wanted sign in the window.

She froze in place, so thrilled her heart felt too big for her chest. She would love to work here. She'd be good at waitressing. People liked her, and she would probably get good tips.

And maybe, when she had learned the ropes, Marianne Donovan might let her help in the kitchen. That would be a dream come true.

She screwed up her courage and opened the door. The first four notes of "Danny Boy" rang out, and all the regulars sang, "The pipes, the pipes are calling" in response. Becky smiled. She loved the goofy tradition. It would be so much fun to work here.

Judy, the waitress who stood at the cash register, recognized her, of course. She'd been picking up this same meatloaf sandwich every Monday, Wednesday and Friday for the past two months.

"Hey, Becky," the woman said. "Hang on. I'll go ask Marianne if it's ready."

But she didn't go, because right then three customers lined up by the counter, checks and to-go bags in hand, clearly in a hurry to pay.

Maybe it was fate. Becky had been raised to follow the rules, but as her father always said, desperate times called for desperate measures. She sidled around the counter, hoping Judy wouldn't notice, and made a beeline for the kitchen.

When she pushed through the swinging doors,

Marianne looked up, clearly shocked to see her. But she was busy arranging strawberries and drizzling chocolate on a piece of pie, so she didn't shoo her out.

Looking at the thick white mounds of whipped cream, Becky's mouth started to water. She hadn't eaten much for the past couple of days. Whatever had made her sick earlier in the week hadn't quite passed, though it hadn't turned into a full-blown flu, thank goodness.

"What's up, Becky?" Marianne smiled, but her hands kept flying deftly between a bowl of fresh berries and the slice of pie. "Andy, can't you smell the casserole burning? Take it out, before we have to start over!"

"Damn it! Sorry!" The young man who had been standing at the stove wheeled around and pulled a baking dish out of the oven. "It's okay. No harm done."

"Good." Marianne turned her attention back to Becky. "Did you need something? Oh, that's right…you're picking up for Fanny. Isn't Judy out there? Andy, is that to-go meatloaf ready?"

"No, I'm not here about the sandwich," Becky said, her words tumbling over each other in her rush.

Marianne raised her eyebrows. "Fanny doesn't want her sandwich today?"

"No. I mean yes. Yes, she wants it. But that's not what I want. I mean, that's not why I came back here. I came back here because I want to apply for the job."

The flying hands finally stilled. "Which job?"

Becky bit her lower lip, embarrassed. The sign hadn't specified.

"Any job," she said honestly. "You know me, Marianne. I'm a very reliable employee. I've worked for Fanny for two years. I'm sure she'll give me a good reference. And before that, when I was in school, I worked at the college bookstore, too."

"Are you quitting Fanny's store? She won't appreciate it much if she thinks I'm trying to hire you away from her."

"No, I'm not quitting. I love it there. She just doesn't have enough hours to offer me. I've got an apartment now, and…well, my boyfriend got laid off, so I need a second part-time job."

From his position at the cooktop, Andy made a retching sound. "*Boyfriend?* Please. I'm going to be sick."

Well, that was rude. But he knew Rory, of course. In a town as small as Silverdell, everyone knew everyone.

Marianne shot him a reproachful look, but he had his back to them, so he didn't see it. "Well, I'm looking for a waitress, a dishwasher and a cook," she said. "Which one of those do you think would suit you best?"

"The cook," Becky said without hesitation. "I

love to cook. But I'll take whatever you've got. I really, really need a job."

"Do you have any experience? Have you ever done any restaurant work?"

"No."

"Who taught you to cook?"

"Roseanne." That was their housekeeper's name. Becky hadn't exactly had a mother to do the training. "My father's housekeeper. Roseanne is a wonderful cook."

Marianne frowned, but it wasn't an angry expression. It was more thoughtful. Sympathetic. Becky hated the idea of playing the pity card, but right now she would take any advantage she could get. She wanted this job more than she'd wanted anything in a long, long time.

"What is your specialty?"

Becky thought carefully. She wasn't sure she was good enough yet to have a specialty, exactly, but everyone loved her spaghetti. She was reluctant to say that, though. She had an uncomfortable feeling that spaghetti was too simple, that everyone could do it.

"Italian," she said, compromising. Andy made another rude snort, but at least he didn't say he was going to be sick, so she ignored him.

"I'll happily take the waitressing spot, though," she said, urgently. "It doesn't have to be the cooking job."

Marianne set the beautifully presented piece

of pie to the side and then plucked a big wooden spoon from a little bowl. Reaching around Andy's apron, she dipped the spoon into a stockpot that was simmering away on a back burner. When she pulled it back out, it was covered in a thick red sauce.

"Taste this," she said, holding it out toward Becky with a smile. "Tell me what it's missing."

Out of nowhere, as she stared at the spoon, Becky felt a horrifying surge of nausea. "I..." She swallowed desperately as her mouth began to water in the most disagreeable way. "I...I can't."

Marianne looked surprised, but even though Becky knew this was the end of her hopes, there was nothing she could do. One glance at the red sauce, lumpy with real chunks of tomato and speckled with flecks of basil, and her empty stomach had gone into full revolt.

"I'm sorry. I can't." She pressed her palm hard against her mouth and moved past Marianne, heading for the alley door.

She shoved it open with her elbows. She ran across the concrete service lane, toward a small grassy area at the back. When she reached it, she put one hand against the nearest tree trunk and tried to take a deep breath. But the Dumpster was just feet away, and the air was full of subtle scents from a hundred discarded meals.

She bent over at the waist and vomited into the mulch.

Just like the other day, the spell was violent, but brief. She heaved till her ribs hurt, bringing up almost nothing, and then it was over. Her knees trembled, and her eyes were wet with angry tears, but the nausea was gone.

And her chance of a job with it.

"Damn it," she said, fervently. "Damn, damn, damn."

"You poor kid."

Becky turned. Marianne Donovan was right behind her. The woman was probably only five years older than Becky was, but at the moment the label *poor kid* felt appropriate. She was so stupid…she'd been sheltered for so long she hadn't ever grown up properly. She didn't have any skills or experience…and now she didn't have any money, either. What a joke.

"Tell you what," Marianne said, studying Becky's face thoughtfully. "I'll hire you now, twenty hours a week. But you can spend the first few weeks practicing our recipes at home. Then, when you're better, you can come help me here in the kitchen."

Becky frowned. This sounded too good to be true. "What? You mean you'll pay me just to *practice* the recipes? You'll pay me to cook things at home?"

"Just for a few weeks," Marianne said. She put her hand on Becky's shoulder. "I can't have you tossing your cookies in the restaurant every day, now, can I? Not that great for business."

"I don't get sick *every* day," Becky said. "I don't know what's wrong with me. Just sometimes… just lately…I get these weird…"

"Right." Marianne smiled. Then she squinted. Her red hair caught the sunlight as she tilted her head. "Wait…you honestly don't know what's making you nauseated?"

"Well, at first I thought it might be something I ate. But I'm starting to wonder if it might be nerves. These days, Rory and I—"

"Nerves?" Marianne shook her head firmly. Her eyes were worried and kind. "I guess it could be. But…have you considered the possibility that it might be morning sickness?"

CHAPTER SIX

AT LUNCHTIME THE next day, Crimson stood in the kitchen, trying to decide how to use the rest of the fresh blueberries. Most of them had gone into the fruit tart she'd made for last night's dinner. That thing had been huge...designed to impress Grant's buyer.

She, Grant and Stefan had eaten just one small slice each, so she ended up putting the remains into the refrigerator, reconciling herself to eating leftovers for a month.

But mysteriously, though it was just barely noon, the empty tart pan was in the dishwasher now, as spotless and crumb-free as if it had been licked clean by wolves.

She smiled as she closed the dishwasher and hit Start. No chef ever minded when food disappeared quickly—it was, after all, the ultimate compliment.

"But we can't let it go to our heads, Molly," she cautioned the baby, who lay in her playpen on the far side of the kitchen, well away from sharp knives and hot burners. "On a ranch staffed by big, burly men, I bet nothing ever goes to waste. They'd probably have eaten rawhide and cheesypoofs from the convenience store, if the tart hadn't been hanging around."

At that moment, a lanky shadow fell across the tiled floor, and a deep chuckle rippled toward her as Grant strolled into the kitchen.

"Wow, Red," he said, grinning as he slapped a stack of mail on the breakfast table. "I never knew you were such a food snob!"

"No? Well, you live and learn." But she smiled, too, to show she appreciated his attempt at keeping things light after the heaviness of last night's odd conversation.

Being honest had been awkward, but she felt less claustrophobic today, for having spoken her mind. Ironic, wasn't it? Simply by expressing her feelings, and by having him acknowledge her right to *want* to run away, she'd made it possible to stay.

At least for a little while. At least until they found Molly's mother. Grant had promised to see what he could find out, and she didn't doubt for a minute he'd follow through.

As he thumbed open an envelope, he wandered over to make goofy noises at Molly. At six months, she was becoming verbal enough to respond with an eager volley of answering baby-babble. Soon the two were deeply engaged in a charming, idiotic dialogue that filled the kitchen with verbal sunshine.

Feeling oddly peaceful, Crimson reached into the refrigerator and pulled out the milk. She'd decided to make a blueberry crème brulée, even though she was fairly sure Grant didn't own either ramekins or a brulée torch. This gorgeous kitchen was actually about as well stocked as a movie set. It looked great, but the drawers and cupboards had been mostly empty when she arrived.

But in cooking, a challenge was part of the fun. She shut the refrigerator and turned to Grant. "Do you have a grill lighter, by any chance?"

He looked puzzled at first, before understanding dawned. "Oh. Yeah, somewhere. When I first bought the place, I pictured myself having great Sunday barbecues. That was before I understood how exhausting this horse gig would turn out to be."

She instinctively checked the depth of the shadows under his eyes. The sunny kitchen made it easy to judge. He was tousled from being outside all morning, and his sling hung loosely around his neck, unused. He'd stopped wearing belts for a while—with only one hand, buckling the things just took too much time—so his jeans rode a little lower on his narrow hips.

But he'd shaved, and the morning sun had painted his high cheekbones a rosy gold. His gold-flecked eyes were clear and bright.

Overall, she thought, he looked *much* better. He still looked tired, but it was a happy kind of tired, the relaxed exhaustion of a man who worked hard at something he enjoyed. He no longer had the drawn, strained tension of almost constant pain.

And he was walking without much of a limp, she noticed as he came back across the kitchen to where she stood, the bottle of milk half forgotten in her hand.

Maybe he was on the mend, even though it had been only a week since the accident. He was strong and healthy, and his body was already bouncing back.

If only Kevin would make some kind of progress, too. Maybe he'd move his hand again...or respond to stimulus when the doctor tested him. They were watching for any sign that he was, however slowly, rising up through the coma.

She closed her eyes briefly and said a prayer for something like that to happen today. Then maybe she wouldn't have to track down Molly's mother, which was a last resort, and might be a fool's errand, anyhow.

"I've been giving some thought to how we might find Kevin's ex-wife," Grant said.

She opened her eyes, blinking away her surprise that he'd seemed to read her mind.

"Yeah? Any ideas?"

"A few." He lifted the spigot to run water. Setting down the milk, Crimson automatically joined him at the sink to squirt some of the liquid soap into his palm—something they'd discovered was impossible to do one-handed.

"Good grief, you're a mess!" She had just noticed the washing wasn't routine this time. He must have been helping to feed the horses, because his hand was filthy. He'd never be able to scrub all that off—the back of the hand was especially hard to deal with.

"Here, let me." She took his hand between her own and massaged the soap in thoroughly for him. Then she held it under the running water and rubbed, even between his fingers, until all three hands were soap-free and squeaky-clean.

"Sorry to be so dirty, ma'am," he said humbly, giving her a dimpling half smile as he plucked the kitchen towel from the rack and flipped it over his hand. "Thank you, ma'am."

But he was just teasing. At first he'd been prickly about needing help, but his ego was healthy enough to get over that fairly quickly.

He had limits, of course. He dressed himself, even if it meant making little accommodations, like the belt thing, or wearing T-shirts instead of button-ups. He insisted on holding his toothbrush between his teeth to apply the toothpaste one-handed.

And she could only imagine what a struggle showering must be.

On second thought, maybe she *shouldn't* imagine that.

Shaking off the image, she moved away. In spite of these momentary lapses—especially considering how few days it had been—they'd found a good rhythm. She wondered how long till the doctors would remove the cast. A month, maybe?

Maybe, if she was careful, she could stay at least that long without getting too emotionally invested. Maybe if she just thought of it as a job…

"Kevin doesn't have any family," he said, and for a minute she couldn't remember what they'd been talking about.

Oh, right. Finding Kevin's ex. Anne Smith.

"Asking his family would of course have been the easiest way to track Molly's mother down. Failing that, I've done what I can with the documents Kevin keeps here. Her birth certificate gives us Anne's address at the time of Molly's birth, but she no longer lives there."

"Oh." Crimson wasn't surprised to hear that, actually. Whatever personality traits or difficult events made a woman abandon her infant daughter might easily have made her also abandon her home, her job, her life. Trauma could really change a person.

"I did a general internet search for her, but the name's just too common… I got half a million results. I tried the obvious things, like her landlord, forwarding addresses, work history, but she didn't leave much of a trail. I found a few of her neighbors and called them, but it's a huge apartment building, and they aren't exactly friendly. I had to leave voice messages with a couple of them, so we'll see if they call back."

Grant tossed the towel onto the counter, exchanging it for an apple from the basket. He pulled out a chair at the breakfast table and sat. "Kevin and I lost touch after college, so I don't even know where or when they met. We got Christmas cards from him, I think, but that's all."

"We?"

He had just taken a big bite of his apple. He raised his eyebrows as he chewed and managed a puzzled syllable. "Huh?"

We got Christmas cards, he'd said. Who was *we*?

She knew he already regretted the slip of the tongue. Ordinarily, he made absolutely no reference to his life before Silverdell, before Campbell Ranch. It was as if he'd been born three years ago, when he bought this place.

She knew one thing only—that he'd briefly been a lawyer in Boston. Kevin, who had been his law school roommate, had mentioned that fact one night when they were all out at dinner together. He'd seemed surprised that Crimson didn't know.

Grant hadn't reacted at the time, but he must have said something privately, because Kevin never brought Grant's past up again.

The conclusion that he'd probably been married and divorced was her own imagination at work—it just didn't seem possible that he hadn't been pursued to an altar by someone, somewhere.

"Nothing," she said, sorry she'd let herself get nosy. Again, she reminded herself she didn't poke around in people's private lives. It was only fair, considering she kept her own under lock and key. "It's nothing. Go on. You were saying you didn't hear much from him after college."

"No, it's okay." He swallowed the last bit of apple and smiled pleasantly, his posture relaxed. "I did say *we*, because I was married at the time. It's not something I talk about much, since it didn't last long, but it's hardly a state secret."

No big deal…though obviously it had ended. In divorce, or estrangement, or death? Though she was dying to know whether he and the wife-who-didn't-matter had any children-who-didn't-matter, she leaned back against the cool, rounded-granite edge of the counter and bit her tongue.

She could match his phony nonchalance, if that was how he wanted to play it.

"So what now? About Anne, I mean."

He shook his head. "Not sure. I wish I at least knew something about their relationship. It would make it easier to track her down." He ran his hand through his hair. "Hell, knowing what went on with them would make it easier to be sure tracking her down was the right thing in the first place."

"You two never talked about it at all? He never

said what happened, or why Anne left him with full custody of Molly?"

"Nope." Grant tossed the apple core toward the trash can and, even left-handed, dunked it perfectly. He grabbed a napkin from the holder and brushed it across his mouth. "I asked him early on after he moved in, but he just said it was ugly, that she was out of the picture, both legally and emotionally, and he'd rather not talk about it. He seemed pretty tense, so I let it go. Besides, we weren't exactly in the habit of having heart-to-heart chats about our love lives."

She shook her head. *Men.*

"Yeah?" He arched a brow. "Well, you don't know anything about her, either. And you're the one dating him. You never even asked?"

He had her there, of course. No, she hadn't. She hadn't asked because she, too, had sensed that he wouldn't want to answer. And because she didn't want to imply that their relationship was serious enough for confidences.

What a trio they were! Grant with his never-mentioned marriage—and inexplicable ease with babies. Kevin with his motherless daughter and mystery ex.

And Crimson with her ghost.

She obviously hadn't chosen to form friendships with these particular people by accident. It wasn't just that they'd shared the Silverdell Outreach work—that was a big, gregarious group.

Since she'd moved to Silverdell, she'd met at least a dozen people she liked very much, but she hadn't formed more than civil acquaintances with them, really.

She realized now that, ever since Clover's death, she'd instinctively been most comfortable with people who wouldn't pry. People who wouldn't try to break down her walls and expose her secrets. But locked in the selfishness of fresh grief, she'd never considered the possibility that they might also have walls, with secrets of their own crouching behind them.

"What about the custody judgment? Or the papers you signed for medical power of attorney? Anything there?" She thought she'd done pretty well, changing the subject without answering his question.

He shook his head thoughtfully. "Nothing particularly helpful."

"Did you have any mutual college friends who might have met her?"

"No…I don't think so. Not that I can come up with off the top of my head. But I'll keep thinking. Although, considering he came *here* when his relationship fell apart, and then named me as his health care surrogate and Molly's guardian…"

She nodded. That probably meant Kevin didn't have any other close friends. Or else it meant he'd wanted to get as far away from his old life as he could.

"The thing is," Grant said slowly, "I don't necessarily want to alert Anne before we know more about what happened. We don't know why they broke up. We don't know why she didn't want—or didn't get—even partial custody of Molly. I don't know why Kevin wanted to assign guardianship to me, and not to her. I didn't ask, because at the time it all seemed so remote."

Yes. No one ever imagined that a thirty-one-year-old man could one day be in perfect health, starting an exciting new job and raising his baby daughter…and the next day be lying in a hospital bed, unaware of the strangers coming in every morning to shine flashlights into his unseeing eyes.

"I just want to go slowly, if we can," he finished. "I'd like to find her and scope her out before we bring her into this."

Crimson had to admit Grant's approach made sense. Her instincts had told her any mother would want to know her child was in a stranger's care. She'd assumed that any wife—even an angry, estranged one—would want to know if her baby's father had been badly injured and might die.

But what did Crimson really know about it? If this woman had left her husband and her infant daughter without a backward glance, there was no reason to think she'd come rushing home for any reason…even to say goodbye.

"Do you think we should hire a detective?" She

felt silly even saying the words. Like someone in a TV drama.

But Grant didn't laugh. He nodded thoughtfully. "Maybe. Let me poke around a little more, and then we'll see where we stand. If we—"

His cell phone rang. The sound was loud and unexpected, and it broke the low hum of quiet conversation that had allowed Molly to drift off. The baby woke with a jerk and instantly began to cry.

"Honey, it's all right." Crimson rushed to the playpen and scooped the squirming little girl into her arms. She braced her against her shoulder and cupped the crown of her head with a soothing palm. "Shh…it's all right."

She moved out of the kitchen so Grant could answer the call in peace. For the next few minutes, she walked Molly around the open downstairs floor plan, passing from the renovated beauty of the great room to the half-finished chaos in the study, Grant's current project. From there, she circled the dining room, a shabby room he hadn't touched yet.

She liked the way he took his time with the renovations, and clearly would rather live with unfinished rooms than rooms restored in a careless rush. It said a lot about him…about patience and care and appreciation of work well-done.

She liked even more that when she'd met him, he'd been building walls for someone in need—putting his own plans on the back burner.

He was a good guy. He was a protector.

By the time they made it back to the great room, Molly had stopped crying. Crimson held the baby up to the picture window, where she could watch Dusty Barley working with Dawn, the beautiful Arabian that Grant was about to sell to that silly man from California.

She heard the murmur of Grant's voice as he finished his conversation, but she couldn't make out words. She was relieved when the murmuring stopped and was replaced by the sound of his footsteps crossing the kitchen and then coming through to the cypress flooring of the great room. Maybe the call had been one of Anne Smith's neighbors. Maybe they knew where she was now...maybe it would be that easy.

"It was the hospital." His voice was low. Somber.

Her heart hitched, and she clutched Molly tightly as she turned around. "Is it Kevin?"

"It's not bad news. I'm sorry, I should have said that first. In fact, it may be good news. One of the nurses thinks she saw him make a small, voluntary movement."

A small, voluntary movement.

"Like twitching a finger?" Crimson asked, feeling oddly numb.

"I don't know. Maybe. He's unresponsive again, so whatever it was didn't last. But apparently she says she heard him say something before he went back to sleep."

"He actually *spoke*?" Molly startled at Crimson's sharp tone, and Crimson took care to speak more gently as she continued. "What did he say?"

Grant moved closer. He rested his hand gently on Molly's back. The pear-like scent of the kitchen soap drifted up and filled her nostrils.

"Just one word," he said, looking intently at Crimson. "She thinks he called your name."

WHEN GRANT WALKED into Bronson's Books a couple of hours later, Fanny Bronson was on her knees by the cash register, unpacking a box of *Scenic Colorado* coffee-table hardcovers. He frowned. Fanny was pretty, and much brighter than her gossipy, girly mannerisms made her seem, but she often looked vaguely absurd. Like now. Her tight red dress emphasized her curvy rear end, and her ridiculous high heels stuck out behind her like red daggers.

How on earth did you run a business dressed like that? Unless your business was pole dancing.

But he didn't give a darn how Fanny, or any other woman, dressed. He was just in a rotten mood. When Crimson had heard about Kevin, she had left immediately for Montrose. She'd taken Molly with her, painfully certain that the presence of the baby would be the stimulus Kevin needed to wake up.

Grant had offered to go with her, but her expressive face had instantly registered an odd anxiety. "Oh. You can if you *want* to, of course..."

"No," he'd said quickly. "If you're okay alone, I've got a hundred things to tend to here." He had glanced outside, where Barley was once again working Dawn. "I'll drive over later this afternoon, when Barley goes to pick up the feed."

No reason he should mind. Now that his foot was better, he could drive. It was an awkward affair, requiring some maneuvering as he stretched his left hand to change the gears, but it worked.

And Crimson had her rental car. The two of them traveled over separately nearly every day already, because of their schedules, and to make sure Kevin got all the visitors and support he possibly could.

Besides, it was Crimson's name Kevin had whispered, not Grant's. It made sense for Crimson to go alone.

But watching her drive away had given him a sour taste in his mouth, and now he was in danger of taking it out on poor Fanny.

He stuffed the irritation down deep into his gut and reminded himself he was lucky Fanny was actually here. These days, he'd heard, her part-timers often handled the store in the early afternoons.

In fact, a young blonde woman was standing in the front bay window right now, her back to the store as she assembled a display of books about local flora, with flower-themed stationery and knickknacks thrown in for good measure.

Oh, yeah. The wildflower festival was this coming weekend. With his own world such a mess, Grant had forgotten about it—not easy to do in festival-obsessed Silverdell.

"Hey, Fanny," he called with as much enthusiasm as he could muster as the door shut behind him. "I got your message about Kevin's books. I thought I'd pick them up."

Fanny glanced up and immediately flushed. Her hands fluttered over her hair, smoothing stray ends. He didn't take the reaction personally. Fanny liked all men, but she had a well-known preference for the ones with fat wallets. Grant's bank account wasn't big enough to make her blush, but he did have an entire wall of bookcases in his newly renovated great room. She was eager to help him fill them.

Using the side of the cashier counter for leverage, Fanny pulled herself to her feet. Smiling, she tugged her dress toward her knees.

"I was just thinking about calling you! How is Kevin? I know they moved him to Montrose." Her pink lips folded in on themselves—an unconvincing attempt to look concerned. "That must mean he's worse?"

"Not at all." Suddenly, he was irritated all over again by the hunger for details he heard in her voice. Clearly, tragic gossip would be so much juicier than good news. "If they didn't think Kevin was going to come out of it just fine, they would have left him in Silverdell."

Actually, the doctors hadn't been even close to that optimistic. No one had promised Kevin would come out of it *just fine*. But transferring him implied real hope—Grant had to believe that.

It only made sense. Palliative care wouldn't require a move. The morphine in Silverdell was as good as any you could get in Montrose or Denver or even New York.

But recovery, with its surgeries and scans and rehab therapies…that was a different story. A story with a happier ending. And it required specialists a little town like this didn't have.

"Oh! Well, that's wonderful. I'm so glad." Fanny moved around to the back of the desk, her spiky heels clicking on the wooden floors. It sounded like someone typing on a noisy keyboard. "Let me see where I put those books…"

His tone had obviously been too curt. She seemed offended. *Darn.* He stared at the counter— she'd bent down and wasn't visible anymore as she hunted for Kevin's books.

Getting short with her had been rude, and counterproductive, too. Everyone knew Fanny was an avid gossip, though she was also relatively harmless. In fact, that was why Grant had come in today. She'd dated Kevin when he'd first moved to Silverdell. Just one dinner, but it was enough to ensure she continued to be particularly interested in his every move.

It had occurred to Grant that maybe she'd wormed some detail out of Kevin that night. Or in the two months since then. Even though they'd never had a second date, she and Kevin had remained friendly. She was first and foremost a businesswoman who needed all the local goodwill she could get.

"Hey, you don't have any of this year's wildflower festival posters, do you?" He glanced around the store. "I saw one in Marianne's café, and I liked it."

That was true, actually. The poster was pretty this year, and though he probably would have preferred to wait till his bank balance had recovered a bit, he would have bought one sooner or later. He had a lot of walls to decorate in that big, old ranch house.

Why not now, when a sale might smooth Fanny's feelings?

It worked. She rose smoothly, a couple of hardback books in her hand, and the smile had returned. "Oh, it is a nice poster, isn't it? Penny Wright—I mean Penny *Thorpe*—painted it. You know Penny, from over at Bell River Ranch?"

"Sure." The Bell River Dude Ranch was one of Silverdell's biggest deals. There were four Wright sisters, all married, several with kids, so they were a fairly impressive clan that held a good bit of power in town.

He couldn't have lived in Silverdell for three years without getting to know the Bell River sisters. They were gorgeous and spirited, every one of them larger-than-life.

Plus, they'd overcome a family scandal that might have destroyed weaker souls. In fact, their Greek tragedy made *his* tragedy look almost normal.

"In fact, the sisters have offered to help with Molly, which I really appreciate. With all the driving over to Montrose, and of course the ranch..."

Fanny nodded sympathetically. "It must be a heavy burden, having a baby land in your lap like that. I know Crimson is staying at the ranch and I'm sure she does her best, but..."

Fanny ran her palm over the cover of the biography Kevin had ordered. "But at a time like this, a child needs... I mean... Has anyone contacted her mother?"

Wow. That was easy. Grant had been racking his brain, trying to think how to bring up the subject without revealing too much. He should have known Fanny would do the work for him.

"Not yet. We're not entirely sure where Anne is right now." That was vague enough, he hoped, to keep Fanny talking, and to encourage her to offer whatever tidbits she knew.

But the look on her face wasn't promising. She

knit her brows and pursed her lips. She tapped her fingernails on the edge of the cash register.

"You don't know, either? That's so strange. I thought surely you… He never would really talk about her. I asked him, of course, but he always changed the subject." Suddenly, her eyes widened. "Oh. Oh, dear. You don't think she's…*deceased*, do you? Oh, the poor little baby. That would be just too terrible."

For once, she didn't look as if she was hoping for the worst. Grant liked Fanny better in that moment, when her expression was one of honest human compassion, than he ever had before.

"No," he said reassuringly. "She's fine. We're just having a little trouble getting in touch, that's all."

Fanny nodded, looking less troubled, but Grant could tell she would have liked to hear more facts. She wanted to be convinced. Unfortunately, Grant didn't have facts—just a gut feeling.

Wherever Molly's mother was, Grant had no doubt that she was alive. The one time he'd asked Kevin about her, he'd been surprised by the bitterness in his friend's face.

Kevin had started to answer, staring into his beer as if searching for the right words. "Molly's mother," he'd begun several times, only to let the sentence dwindle off.

Then, shrugging, he'd lifted a palm to wave the question away. "Anne's not in the picture," he'd said flatly. "It's complicated, and it's ugly, and I don't want to talk about it."

For Grant, that said it all. Death wasn't complicated. It was cruelly simple.

The door that led onto Main Street opened behind him, and a couple of new customers walked in. Fanny glanced toward them, brightening. "Melly! Joan! I'll be with you in a minute. I have some wonderful books set aside for you!"

She turned back to Grant with an apologetic smile. "I really wish I knew more," she said quietly. "I wish I could help you find her, but he would never say anything…"

"No problem." Grant gestured toward the books. "I know you've got other customers, so if you'll just—"

"I can ring these up for you, Fanny," a voice interrupted. "If you want to work with Melly and Joan, go ahead."

The blonde from the window display had joined them at the register. With a mild shock, he recognized her as the young woman who had been talking to Crimson in the hospital the night of the accident. Her black eye was now carefully camouflaged under makeup, and the swelling in her upper lip had gone down. Only the small, flesh-colored bandage across her nose remained.

"Thank you, Becky!" Fanny let the blonde slide in behind her and exited with another smile. She squeezed Grant's arm as she went past, and then tap-tapped across the floor toward the newcomers.

"Oh, Melly, you're just going to love the Egypt book I found!" Her voice was full of artificial enthusiasm as she led the women to the far side of the store. "Thirty-six color plates! It's amazing, and…"

In the silence left in their wake, Becky began scanning the barcodes on Kevin's books. Her shoulders were tight, hunched slightly toward her ears, as if she were nervous or embarrassed…

He wondered whether it made her uncomfortable, knowing he had seen her when she was black-and-blue. Maybe she wondered what Crimson had told him about her "fall."

"You look like you feel a lot better," he observed.

She glanced up, clearly surprised and wary.

He smiled easily. "We met at the hospital, the night I got this." He held out his cast. "You've recovered a whole lot faster than I have."

She bit her lip, as if she couldn't believe he'd mentioned that meeting out loud. But he'd always believed that little embarrassments were handled best by meeting them head-on. Only a very few subjects were so poisonous that they shouldn't be mentioned—and a tumble down the stairs wasn't one of them.

If, as he suspected, the story about a tumble had been a lie, she had even *less* reason to be ashamed.

A fall down the stairs might have been her fault, if she really was klutzy or careless.

But being assaulted by an abusive husband, father or boyfriend was *never* the woman's fault.

"Thanks," she said, and the tension of her hunched shoulders was reflected in her voice. "Makeup helps, I guess. I've tried to cover it the best I can."

He smiled again. He thought about trying to send her a subtle message that sometimes hiding the truth wasn't the best decision, but he decided against it. It might sound patronizing. She wasn't a statistic in a public service announcement about battered women. She was a real, live human being, and her situation was undoubtedly more layered and complex than he could imagine.

The young woman totaled the books quickly, took Grant's credit card and bagged everything while he signed. When he finished, he waited, expecting her to hand over the bag, but she clung to it, as if she were trying to prolong the exchange.

"Everything okay?" He smiled again.

She wasn't all that young, he saw now that he had a chance to study her. Definitely an adult, maybe early twenties. She only looked younger because she had such a sheltered aura...

Sheltered. The idea was oddly paradoxical, considering the black eye and broken nose. Was it her father, then, who pampered her most of the time, but grew violent when he was drunk, or frustrated by a show of defiance?

"Yeah, everything's fine. It's just... I wanted to ask..." She looked over her shoulder. "I mean, I wanted to tell you something."

"Sure. What's up?"

"It's just that...I heard you asking about Kevin Ellison's ex-wife."

He squinted slightly. He certainly hadn't expected this. He'd assumed Becky might want to send a message to Crimson, or to ask for help with whoever owned the fist responsible for that black eye.

"That's right," he said. "We're trying to find Anne, to let her know about Kevin's accident. Do you know her?"

She shook her head. "Oh, no. I just heard him say something odd once, and I got the impression he was talking about a woman he...a woman who had hurt him. I could have been imagining it...and, I don't know, it's probably nothing, but I thought, in case it helps..."

He had to work not to look too eager. "Anything could help," he said.

"Well, I was looking at this book about Las Vegas one day, when Kevin was in here with Molly. He came in a lot. He loved to read, Grisham and Ludlum and stuff."

Grant nodded. Very true. Kevin had a taste

for spy novels, even in college. He'd always been reading them when he should have been studying.

"Anyhow, he asked what my book was, and I showed him. I told him sometimes I dream about moving to Las Vegas. That made him laugh. He said he didn't recommend it."

"Why not?"

"He said he could assure me the advertising was absolutely correct. What happened in Vegas definitely *did* stay in Vegas—but that didn't mean it couldn't break your heart anyway."

CHAPTER SEVEN

ON THE WAY back from the hospital the next day, Crimson stopped in at Donovan's Dream. She was tired, but she'd promised Marianne she'd help bake cookies for the wildflower festival, and she didn't like to let her down.

It was three o'clock, the lull between lunch and dinner, and the restaurant was half-empty. But even so, when she opened the door and the "Danny Boy" notes rang out, half a dozen customers looked up, smiled and responded, "The pipes, the pipes are calling" before returning to their conversations.

Though she had been a little blue on the drive home, Crimson felt her spirits lift at the silly ritual. Marianne reported that the singing could get annoying, day after day, but Crimson hadn't reached that point yet. There was something charming about knowing you'd get the reliable group welcome, rain or shine, stranger or friend, good day or bad.

"Hey there!" Marianne came out of the kitchen with a to-go order in her hand. Her red curls were piled messily on her head, and she had some pink icing at the corner of her eye, like a beauty mark, but she looked happy to see Crimson. "I wondered if you'd make it. Fanny told me you'd been over in Montrose. Everything okay?"

Crimson set Molly's carrier on one of the empty tables nearby. Then she pulled out a chair and sat down beside her. The baby had fallen asleep halfway home, and with any luck she wouldn't wake until they got back to Grant's place and a warm bottle.

"It was all right." She shrugged, trying not to let her disappointment show too much. "Not as great as I'd hoped."

Frowning, Marianne handed the bagged food to her hostess, and joined Crimson at the table. "I heard he was awake. Was that just another of Fanny's crazy rumors?"

"No, it's true. Sort of. Yesterday, the nurse had been sure he was trying to talk. By the time I got there, he was asleep again. But he does seem to be less...or rather *more*..."

Crimson hesitated. She couldn't find the right words to describe something so subtle. "He's still unconscious, but it seems shallower, if that makes any sense. He reacts to loud noises. Just a flinch, or a twitch...but the doctors seem more optimistic. Or less pessimistic, anyhow."

She sighed, realizing how vague and uninspiring it sounded, but Marianne nodded eagerly. "That's wonderful news!" She reached out and took Crimson's hand. "That has to mean he's coming out of it."

Crimson appreciated the warmth Marianne gave so freely, not just to her, but to anyone she believed was in need. But once again, she had the feeling that her relationship with Kevin was being misinterpreted.

It was horribly awkward. She didn't enjoy accepting sympathy under false pretenses. And yet…how could you rush to distance yourself from a man in Kevin's position, a man who might not ever wake up, or who might wake to find himself brain damaged, unable to speak, paralyzed?

How could you suddenly start proclaiming loudly "We were just friends" without looking like a rat scurrying away from a sinking ship?

Oh, yes, she should have left Silverdell a long time ago. Every attachment, however casual, was a time bomb, waiting to blow up.

Molly stirred, raising her tiny hands as if reaching for something in her dreams. She moved her lips and then sank back into sleep. Extricating her hand from Marianne's, Crimson reached out to pull the soft pink blanket up a little higher, in case the baby was cold.

"It's just… It's Molly I worry about," she said, staring down at the peaceful heart-shaped face, so creamy and pink and perfect, like a china doll. She wondered whether Molly's mother was beautiful, too.

And she wondered how the woman could have walked away from her own newborn. People did it every day, Crimson knew that. But she still couldn't understand.

"Of course," Marianne said softly. "She's so little. But that might be a blessing. She won't remember any of this when she grows up."

That was true. It truly might be a blessing. Molly wouldn't be left with any harrowing memories, relived in dreams, or in the wakeful, empty hours before dawn. Tragedies could be endured. But spending the rest of your life haunted, and living in fear of the day another horror might arrive…

That was what sapped your strength until you were only half a person.

"Still. She needs her daddy." Crimson left the palm of her hand on Molly's tummy, a gentle, warm pressure she knew Molly liked. "They let me take her into Kevin's room today. I hoped that, when he heard her, it might…he might…"

Marianne nodded. "Of course. Did he?"

"No." She couldn't say more, because her throat suddenly was lined with fire. She felt as if she had somehow failed both Kevin and Molly. If the nurse was right, he had called for Crimson. Everyone else might assume that was a sign of his love, but Crimson knew better. They hadn't ever been "in love," so if he'd asked for her it was because he'd wanted her to do something.

It had to be Molly. If he knew anything at all, he knew Crimson was taking care of the baby. When she visited him, she talked only about Molly. She had put a picture of the baby by his bed, and she brought new photos, new videos, new funny stories, every day.

"I'm sorry," Marianne said. "I'm so very sorry."

Crimson looked up, stung by guilt. Marianne's face, ordinarily so lively and full of fun, looked wan. What had Crimson been thinking, sitting here wallowing in sadness and pulling everyone down with her?

She shook off her self-pity and mustered a smile. "Oh, don't listen to me. I'm just tired. Really, the news is good, overall. I'll try again tomorrow."

But Marianne's face didn't perk up. "I just wish there were something I could do."

"Don't be silly. I'm here because I'm supposed to be helping *you*! Have you decided which cookies you'd like me to make?"

That was the right question. Marianne apparently couldn't be glum while she was thinking about cooking. Crimson understood that.

"Yes. I was hoping you could do the macaroons. Mine are always a mess. I have no idea how you get the shell so shiny and smooth."

Crimson smiled. Marianne's macaroons were perfectly delicious, but she did sometimes struggle with the outer coating. "I'd love to. How many?"

"Umm…" Marianne pulled out a list from her apron pocket. "Last year I sold five dozen, even though the shells were a wreck. With you baking, I'm thinking we could sell six or seven easy. Think you've got time for that many?"

"Sure." Crimson would make time. It would be good for her. Baking was her therapy. "And I thought maybe I could—"

She stopped, her train of thought derailed by the sight of Becky Hampton coming through the front door, holding a large, foil-covered tray. She hadn't seen Becky since that night at the hospital, though she'd thought of her often, wondering if she should have said more.

The instant she'd caught sight of that black eye, she'd known Rory was responsible. No matter what Becky said, she hadn't fallen down the stairs at her apartment complex. At the very least, someone had "helped" her lose her balance.

She was relieved to see, now, that Becky's bruises were fading—and that no new ones had come along. In fact, Becky looked great. She was smiling ear to ear as she came up and extended the tray toward Marianne with a flourish.

"I did it!" She turned her smile to Crimson, to include her in the greeting, though it was obviously Marianne's approval she wanted. "I made the meatloaf, and it's terrific!"

Marianne laughed. She leaned forward and lifted one corner of the foil. A wave of spicy warmth rose from the pan. Shutting her eyes, Crimson inhaled thoughtfully. Onion and garlic, of course, and Worcestershire sauce. Beef, pork, veal...

Oops. Becky might have been a little too heavy on the cider vinegar. But not fatally. Crimson opened her eyes and smiled. "Smells divine, Becky. You're cooking for Donovan's Dream?"

Becky glanced at Marianne, apparently looking for permission to answer. Marianne smiled and nodded. She was busy unrolling a napkin full of cutlery to find a clean spoon.

"Not yet," Becky said, turning back to Crimson. "Right now I'm just learning the recipes, working on them at home. I've been cooking for two days straight, but the meatloaf is the first one that turned out well enough for me to bring it in. It's really good. At least I think it is. Rory said it was to die for."

She seemed to realize she probably shouldn't have offered Rory's opinion as the gold standard. "Rory's...well, he's not perfect, but he's very particular about his food."

"I bet," Crimson agreed mildly. Becky flushed, meeting Crimson's gaze defensively, but Crimson just smiled, inviting Becky to admit it might be true... Rory might be just a hair chauvinistic, just a tiny bit less evolved than the ideal man.

Becky hesitated, but finally she relented and smiled back.

"This isn't half-bad," Marianne said. She had trimmed off a spoonful from the edge of the loaf and was chewing slowly. Swallowing, she wound the napkin around the spoon and slipped it into her apron pocket. "Okay, let's get some comments. Take it back to the kitchen and tell Andy to let the staff know it's available for tasting."

With a small exclamation of triumph, Becky sealed up the corner and had just started to move away when Marianne reached out and snagged her sleeve at the elbow. Becky stopped and turned toward Marianne.

"You'll be okay back there, right?" Marianne frowned slightly. "I mean, they're cooking all kinds of things, all kinds of smells…"

Becky nodded. "I'm fine. I promise. Turns out it really was just nerves. Not the flu. Nothing serious at all."

For a few seconds, Marianne scanned her face as if she was looking for a sign. Crimson wasn't sure what passed between the two women, but somehow Becky seemed to reassure her boss that all was well.

Nodding with something that looked like relief, Marianne let go of her sleeve.

Crimson watched as Becky hurried toward the kitchen, holding her meatloaf close to her chest, like a baby. "I didn't realize you'd hired another chef."

"Yeah, well, she needed a job. And you keep saying no, so what was I supposed to do?"

Crimson laughed. For the past month or so, ever since she'd realized they shared a love of cooking, Marianne had been asking her to come work at the café. Crimson had never formally rejected her. She'd always just pretended it was a joke.

It had to be. No way she could allow herself to take it seriously. She needed to be free. She had to keep one foot on the road out of town.

In that respect, the job at the tattoo parlor had been perfect. Nothing but a paycheck and an interesting way to pass the day. Pete was a doll, but he wouldn't have missed her much, wouldn't have felt betrayed if she quit and moved on. And she wouldn't think of him six months from now, except as a nice guy she met once, somewhere, half forgotten.

Creating food in a kitchen, for customers, alongside a smart, generous-hearted woman who was looking for a reliable business partner, a creative comrade, a friend…

That wouldn't have been so easy to walk away from. Donovan's Dream, Marianne, the customers, even the four welcoming notes of "Danny Boy," would have seeped into her psyche, wound their way around her heart.

And before she realized it, she would have been caught like a bird in a cage. She didn't intend to take that risk.

"So…" Marianne checked her watch and then inhaled deeply as she wiped her hands on her apron, as if gearing up for the oncoming dinner rush. "No chance you're interested in buying a cute little Irish restaurant, is there?"

Her tone was so casual that for a minute Crimson didn't quite grasp the meaning. When she did, she could hardly believe what she'd heard.

"Why? Are you selling one?"

Marianne nodded. "I'm going to try."

"But…but why? You love the café. You *are* the café."

"That's the problem." Marianne leaned over to trace one gentle finger across Molly's forehead. "The café is my whole life. I think I might be ready for more."

Crimson was literally speechless. It was impossible to think of Donovan's Dream without Marianne Donovan behind it. And yet…it was also impossible not to feel the magnetic, dangerous tug of temptation.

Was Crimson interested in buying a restaurant?

A restaurant all her own…

Just as she and Clover had always planned, ever since they were little girls. Only a little more than a year ago, they'd been looking at properties, applying for small business loans, taking courses, experimenting with recipes.

Just a year. And then it was gone. Only the dull ache, the ghost of the dream, remained.

She squeezed the green-enameled shamrock around her neck until the metal grew warm and bit into the flesh of her palm.

"It's funny, really. It's as if I've outgrown the place." Marianne leaned back in her chair and gazed slowly around the café as if she were seeing it with fresh eyes. "I grew up in Silverdell. After my husband died, I came back because it felt safe. I threw myself into the work so I wouldn't have time to think about…anything."

Crimson nodded. She understood, though she'd dealt with her loss differently. Marianne had run home, to the familiar. Crimson had run away, to anyplace on the map that held no memory of the past.

Marianne took another deep breath. "I never thought I'd say this, but I'm ready to move on. I'm tired of hiding. I want to *live* again."

Her earnest tone was moving, and Crimson felt a prick of emotion behind her eyes. She forced herself to let go of her necklace. She had known Marianne was a widow, but she knew nothing beyond that. How long she'd been married, what their life together had been like, how he had died…

All too personal, the kind of thing she never knew about anyone anymore, because she never asked. She didn't want to get close enough to know.

Seeing the newfound peace in Marianne's face,

though, Crimson couldn't help being happy for her. If Marianne had really been able to step out of the shadow of her grief and turn toward joy, that was a tremendous victory.

She'd fought the darkness, and she'd won.

Before she could think about it, Crimson opened her mouth, and she almost asked, "How long did it take you to get past the pain?"

But before the first word emerged, she shut her lips in horror. The question was obscene. She might as well have asked, "How long do you think it will take me to get over my sister's death—how long until I, too, am free?"

Never. That was how long it would take. Crimson wasn't like Marianne. Marianne had carried the burden of a broken heart, which was painful and hard. But Crimson carried a terrible, insurmountable guilt.

And guilt wasn't a burden you ever had the right to put down.

"So…what do you think?" Marianne smiled. "Are you interested? I'd love for it to go to someone like you, Crimson. You are ten times as talented as I am, and you'd make such a success of the place."

Crimson was shaking her head before Marianne even finished talking.

"No," she said. "That's not possible, I'm afraid."

"Why not?" Marianne put her hands on the table, as if symbolically laying all the cards out, inviting an honest discussion. "If it's money, if you're not sure you could get a loan, I'm sure we could work something out. I'm doing all right. I could hold the mortgage for a while, until you figure it out. I wouldn't need the cash from the sale at once, because I'm thinking of going to cooking school and maybe working for someone else before I open another—"

"No."

At the sharp syllable, Molly began to whimper. Marianne leaned back, clearly startled.

Standing, Crimson blindly began to extricate the baby from the carrier, hoping she could focus on that and somehow control this weird, rising panic.

"It's not the money," she said, lowering her voice, hoping she hadn't sounded ungrateful—or crazy. "I mean, it's not *just* the money."

It wasn't the money at all, but she couldn't tell Marianne that.

Again, she thought of the check she carried in her purse, the check she'd been unable to force herself to cash for months now. Sometimes she thought she'd just burn the damn thing, but every time the thought formed she could hear her sensible sister gasping with half-horrified laughter.

"Silly Crimmy. Sometimes I worry about you. Don't you have even a *teaspoon* of common sense?"

No. No, she didn't. Everyone knew that. Clover had always been the levelheaded one.

So she wouldn't burn it, but she couldn't cash it, either. The number written on that piece of paper was so shockingly large. It was more money than Crimson "Slash" Slayton of Omaha, Nebraska, had ever had, or ever dreamed of having.

And yet, as payment for a human life, it was appallingly small.

"It's not the money or my credit," she said, pulling Molly up to her chest and taking a primitive comfort from the baby's peaceful, unquestioning, velvety warmth. "It's me. I mean, it's just not right for me. I appreciate the offer, but it's not something I would ever be able to do."

As she washed the dishes, Becky ran the faucet at a trickle and handled the plates gingerly so they wouldn't clatter against each other in the sink. The knives and forks were the hardest to control. They seemed determined to slip from her soapy fingers and clang together in a loud, metallic heap at the bottom.

Behind her, Rory was stretched out on the sofa in the living room, watching a car race on TV. He had already turned up the volume three times, his way of telling her she was making too much noise. Once more, and the neighbors would probably complain.

She didn't often get angry when he left the

kitchen cleanup to her. He hated it and was always cranky if he got stuck with the chore, so it was easier to do it than endure his foul humor. Besides, his idea of "clean" and hers were entirely different. She hated returning the next day to a sticky floor and a sink speckled with soggy food that hadn't made it down the drain.

But tonight the obvious imbalance of their workloads grated on her, and she couldn't seem to move past it. She had worked two jobs today, even if one of them was just cooking at home. And *he* had...

She had no idea what he'd done. He hadn't made the bed, that's for sure, or taken the dirty clothes over to the complex's laundry building. And he hadn't changed the bulb in the fixture over the sink.

She took a deep breath, disappointed by the sound of her own internal whining. Surely she wasn't going to become one of those cliché females who was always, as Rory put it, *chewing his ass* about petty household chores. Laundry, lightbulbs, sheets...

Did any of that really matter? Those were the things rich people hired handymen and housekeepers to do, not the things that made you fall in love.

And yet...

The zooming engines and the yelling broadcasters had begun to give her a headache. And her feet hurt. It was going to take her forever to finish the dishes if she couldn't even turn the faucet on properly.

Suddenly, she just snapped. She reached out and flicked the chrome spigot, sending a torrent of water gushing into the sink. The stack of dishes tipped over under the pressure, making such a clamor as they fell that even she could hardly believe the noise.

She held her breath, waiting for him to increase the volume yet again. He'd be superannoyed, and he probably wouldn't talk to her the rest of the evening. He might even go to sleep without saying good-night. He'd learned early on that she hated going to bed angry and had adopted it as his favorite punishment.

But tonight she didn't care. In fact, she was so irritated that if he *did* try to talk to her, she wasn't sure she'd answer him. Tonight, *she* might be the one who lay at the edge of the mattress and turned her back on *him*.

To her surprise, though, instead of the engines *vrooming* even louder, the sound suddenly stopped entirely. In the blink of an eye, the apartment went utterly silent, except for the aggressive whoosh of the kitchen faucet.

He'd hit the Mute button. Or else he'd turned off the television altogether.

The unexpected silence unnerved her far more than their childish war of noise ever could have.

As she stood there with her hands in the hot water, she found it difficult to breathe.

What was he doing? Was he staring at her from the couch? Or had he stood up?

She didn't dare turn around, but the skin from the small of her back to her nape prickled with anxiety. Stiltedly, she washed one knife, and then the next, and the next, instinctively returning to her earlier caution, never letting one piece of stainless steel touch another.

"If you've got something to say, princess, let's hear it."

Rory's voice startled her. It came from only inches away, though she hadn't heard him approach, and hadn't felt his presence. Plus, the timbre was so deep and cold it didn't even really sound like him.

It was a loaded question, of course. She shuffled through the possible responses, trying to find one that wouldn't inflame the situation. They all seemed too dangerous, and she couldn't force her mouth to open.

"You deaf, princess?" He put his lips against her ear. "I said. Let's. Hear. It."

A waterfall of shivers cascaded down the left side of her body. She kept her hands in the water and closed her fingers around a knife. It was only a dinner knife, a cheap stainless-steel utensil that struggled to cut a block of cheese, but at least it was something to hold on to.

She stared down at the water. Ordinarily, she took a child's pleasure in the pretty, rainbow bubbles, but tonight the suds were gray and dirty because there was no light above the sink.

"I'm sorry," was the obvious place to start. Then she might say her hand slipped on the faucet. Then she might offer to give him a foot rub while he watched the rest of the race.

But as his breath came hot against her neck, she smelled the beer he'd been drinking while he lounged on the sofa. The words stalled in her throat.

I'm sorry?

She wasn't one bit sorry. So to hell with pretending she was.

She lifted her chin, turned off the water and dried her hands on a dishrag. It seemed to take forever. All through those icy seconds, she could feel his hostility rising.

Finally, she turned around. Her face was only inches from his—so close she could see a couple of broken veins around his nose. He was going to be a full-blown alcoholic someday, she realized with a cruel clarity. He was lean and sexy now, at twenty-five, and his scruffy stubble was hot, but in ten years, fifteen at most, he'd look like a diseased, bad-tempered old man.

"Yes, actually, Rory, I *do* have something to say." She gestured toward the sink. "If you want these dishes clean, you're going to have to wash them yourself."

He squinted as if she'd spoken in some alien language he'd never heard before. He waited one second, two, three…as if giving her time to retract her statement.

When she didn't, his face hardened.

"You bitch," he said, and the word sounded wet, as if he had started to salivate.

"Call it whatever you want," she countered. "I'm tired, and I'm going to bed."

He tilted his head to one side slowly and pulled his lips back in a grimace. "No," he said softly. "No, I don't think you are."

He looked feral, she thought, and for some reason a simple, shivering disgust registered first… and the fear didn't arrive until a second or two later.

A second or two too late.

He took a step away, but only to get room to swing. His right fist rotated back, and then, as if it had been fired out of a slingshot, it arced forward and up.

In a flash of pain, his knuckles connected with her lower jaw. She heard a crack, and for a split second she was blinded by a constellation of red and yellow splintering stars. Agony streaked out in all directions, like a craze of lightning bolts.

When she could see again, through eyes that watered and stung, Rory was frowning at his hand, as if it had acted without his permission. And then he looked up at her, his expression pitiful.

"I'm sorry," he murmured. With a whimper, he reached out.

Maybe he intended to try to comfort her. Maybe he wanted to see if he'd broken anything, so that he could help. But her primitive lizard brain no longer knew the difference…and she ducked away from his hand as instinctively as if he'd been holding a knife or a gun.

"Becky, baby." He was shaking his head as if confused, as if he could make them both believe it had been a bad dream.

Well, in a way, it had. But she was awake now, and she was already out of the kitchen and halfway across the room. Oddly, though her brains felt loose in her skull, and her knees seemed to be made of water, she moved efficiently and quickly, and her mind was operating clearly. She knew exactly what she had to do.

She took her keys from the rack and, without making a show of it, she took his, too. She grabbed her purse from the end table by the door, and she was jogging down the stairs before Rory's beer-addled brain realized what was happening.

"Becky!" He charged to the doorway of their apartment, but then he just stood there, like a bewildered little boy. "Becky, let me explain."

She reached the bottom of the stairs. Her car

was parked right in front of their unit, but she didn't go to it. Instead, she found a nearby drain grate, bent over and dropped his keys carefully between the concrete slats.

The wet clank as they hit bottom was immensely satisfying, and it made her smile, even though smiling brought back the red, splintered stars. He would come after her, of course—he probably had a spare key somewhere—but at least this would slow him down and give her time to get away.

"Becky!" He was practically bawling now. He was going to rouse the neighbors if he didn't keep it down. But he didn't seem to have thought of that. "Becky, *baby!*"

"Shut up." She gazed coldly up at him as she opened her car door and tossed her purse inside. "I've got some bad news for you, *Roderick*. I'm not your baby anymore."

CHAPTER EIGHT

WHEN SHE GOT HOME, Crimson was surprised to see that Grant had company. She was even more surprised to discover it was Stefan Hopler, the California millionaire who had come to look at the horse Monday night.

Dusty Barley had apparently come in to join them, and the three men were comfortably ensconced in the kitchen, sitting at the breakfast table with half-empty beer bottles in front of them, chatting like old friends. Stefan stood when she entered and kissed her hand in a courtly piece of nonsense she found irritating.

She glanced at Grant, who had picked up his beer and was smiling down at it. He would, of course, guess that Crimson wasn't crazy about this kind of old-world theatrics. She tried to catch his eye. How were they playing this? What was Stefan's status? Were they still trying to impress him into making an offer on the filly?

And if they were…what on earth was she going to feed them? She mentally surveyed the dinner situation. What supplies did she have on hand?

She could whip up a carrot casserole in short order. And maybe, if she was lucky, some of the last pot roast had escaped the hungry staffers who, with her blessing, daily raided the refrigerator.

"We ordered pizza," Grant said pleasantly, as if he guessed her dilemma. He shifted his cast on the table noisily, to get more comfortable. "It should be here any minute. I got you pepperoni. Hope you're hungry."

"Sounds great." She smiled politely. "Grant, I'm sorry to interrupt, but could I get some help with Molly for just a minute, please?"

"Sure." Grant stood, obviously knowing she wanted to have a minute alone with him. "If you'll excuse me, Hopler? Dusty, why don't you see if our guest has any more questions about the filly?"

"Oh, no, I don't have any questions," Stefan interjected eagerly. "I'm well aware of the horse's virtues. Maybe I could help Crimson with Molly, while you wait for the pizza?"

Stefan smiled at Crimson as if helping her put a baby to bed was something he'd dreamed about all his life. "I'm very good with babies, I promise. I have eleven nieces and nephews."

He clearly expected her to agree. Obviously, he thought he'd maneuvered her into a position where she had to say yes or appear rude. She laughed internally. He must be used to dealing with nothing but well-bred millionaires' daughters. Crimson wasn't the least concerned about appearing rude.

"That's such a nice offer. Unfortunately, Molly has trouble sleeping unless Grant helps put her down." She beamed at him, well aware that Grant had done no such thing at their recent dinner, and yet Molly had slept angelically all evening. "Grant?"

The constraints of good manners could cut both ways. It would have been downright pushy for Stefan to continue to insist, so of course he deferred gracefully.

Grant followed Crimson up the stairs, chuckling softly.

"Ouch!" he murmured as soon as she shut the bedroom door behind them. "I believe that's check, Mr. Hopler...and *mate*."

She laid Molly on the changing table and started to unsnap her Onesie. "I gather we're no longer putting on the full-court press to wow this guy?" She slanted an amused glance his way. "And, just for the record, how many beers have you had?"

"Two." Grant planted himself in the rocking chair and propped one booted foot up on the window seat. He looked ridiculously comfortable, in spite of his cast. "I'm not drunk. I'm just having fun. I have a feeling Stefan is in for a bumpy night."

The diaper change finished, she handed Molly to him, laying her in the crook of his cast as they'd done the other night. Then she turned to get a bottle out of the minifridge and heated before the baby started crying.

"Why bumpy? Have you decided not to sell

Dawn, after all?" She hoped that was the case. She knew he needed the money, but he and the horse belonged together; anyone could see that.

"No, I'll still sell if he meets my asking price. I think the bumps are going to come from you. See, I'd be willing to bet the ranch Stefan came back tonight because of you, not because of the horse."

She scowled as she handed him the warm bottle. "Hogwash. What on earth would he want to see me for?"

Grant made sure Molly was comfortably cushioned over his cast, and happily drinking. Then he leaned his head back and shut his eyes over a playful smile. "Come on, Red. Don't play dumb. The man's got a crush on you, of course."

She was glad he wasn't looking at her, because she felt herself flushing—something she rarely did.

"Gawd," she exclaimed irritably, turning off the bottle warmer and then leaning back against the changing table with a sudden rush of tiredness. "What a nuisance. I haven't got time for rubbish like that."

"And that's why I said he was in for a bumpy night." Grant opened his eyes and grinned at her. "But don't worry. Be as prickly as you want. He lost his right to be wined and dined like visiting royalty when he decided to start treating the humans around here like horseflesh."

After that, they let the silence stretch on for a

few minutes. The only sounds in the room were the wet noises of the rubber nipple as Molly drank, and the occasional soft creaks of the chair, as Grant rocked gently with his foot.

"I called the hospital," he said after a few minutes. "You were gone a long time, and I wanted to be sure everything was okay. They told me Kevin was still pretty much out of it."

"Yes." She nodded, toying idly with the container of baby powder. They'd talked about Kevin briefly when she returned yesterday, but Grant had been busy, and she hadn't seen him much since then.

"It was disappointing," she said carefully.

"I know." He watched her for a little while, as if to gauge exactly *how* disappointing. His expression was so clear-eyed and steady that she realized she'd been completely wrong. He wasn't drunk at all...he wasn't even tipsy.

"The doctors seem encouraged, though," he said. "When I was there last night, I talked to Elaine—to Dr. Schilling—and she said she thought it was quite possible he'll make a full recovery."

"Did she?" Crimson ignored the *Elaine* reference and focused on the good news. None of the doctors had been that direct or that optimistic in her presence. "That's encouraging. Dr. Schilling's not exactly a Pollyanna, so that means a lot, coming from her."

Grant smiled. He looked down at Molly and then glanced at Crimson, raising his eyebrows to indicate the baby had fallen asleep. She reached down and gathered Molly up, resting her against her shoulder and patting her back lightly to get the burp she needed.

Grant hung on to the nearly empty bottle, watching in silence as Crimson settled the baby, flicked on the monitor and activated the night-light.

At the doorway, she paused to switch off the overhead fixture. He stopped, too, and cast a long glance back at the shadowed room. They stood close together in that narrow passage, close enough that she could feel a clean, citrusy warmth coming from him, as if he'd peeled an orange in the shower. Close enough that she could see the honey-colored stubble sprinkled among the dusting of darker brown.

She ought to move away, and down the stairs…

But she didn't. She couldn't. Suddenly, she couldn't bear the thought of not being close enough to Grant Campbell to smell his skin and count the golden flecks in his eyes.

She looked at him, and as if he'd asked them to, her lips parted. Her breath came shallowly, and her nerves began to sizzle and spark.

It made no sense. None at all. They stood in the worst possible spot for this, with a stranger at the bottom of the stairs and another man's baby in the room behind them, with unrevealed secrets lying in their pasts and no shared future at all…

It made no sense. But she wanted him to kiss her.

She was sure, electrically, shiveringly sure, that he wanted it, too. He let his gaze roam across her face, reading every inch of it. And then slowly, he lowered his head…

Below them, the doorbell rang. Her heart seemed to stop in her chest. They froze in their almost-kiss, their breath meeting and mingling even though their lips could not. She wanted to reach up and drag him into her, and yet she seemed to have no control of her own arms.

It was absurd. It was almost like a cartoon. A silly, unimportant pizza delivery man had rung the doorbell, and somehow that had hit the Pause button, causing her world to stop rotating. And now she had no power to move forward, to learn what happened next.

"Campbell," Stefan called from the foot of the stairs. "Campbell, there's someone to see you."

Slowly, as if it took great effort, Grant lifted his head and turned in the direction of the other man's voice. Crimson slumped back against the door frame and inhaled the deep breath she desperately needed. Her heart beat once more. The world began to spin again, and the moment passed.

"We should probably go down."

"Yes," she said, but when their eyes met, his looked as bewildered as she felt.

He stepped back, allowing her to pass through first, which she did, careful not to brush against him. She took the stairs in a quick, half-numb skipping motion, intensely aware of his heavier footsteps keeping time behind.

She had a feeling she was going to hold a grudge against pizza for a long, long time to come. Or maybe, when she came to her senses again, she'd be grateful for being prevented from making a terrible mistake.

Right now, with all her nerve endings humming, it was difficult to be sure.

"Let me get my wallet." Grant turned at the last minute, heading into the great room while she continued straight into the kitchen. "I'll be right there."

She was all set to apologize for keeping the deliveryman waiting, but when she entered the room she stopped dead in her tracks. The person at the door hadn't been the pizza man, after all.

It was Becky Hampton, dressed in sweatpants, a T-shirt and flip-flops, completely unsuited to a cool Colorado night. She looked so pale that Crimson wondered whether she might be about to faint. Crimson rushed over and put her arm around Becky's shoulders.

"Come," she said. "You need to sit down."

"No." Becky held herself stiffly. "No. Please. Just give me a minute. I can explain."

She tried to lift her chin and set her jaw, but something clearly pained her, and she cried out softly, lifting her hand to her face.

Bending close, Crimson moved the unsteady fingers away and had to bite back a gasp. An angry, purpling bruise was spreading up Becky's china-doll cheek and down her graceful neck, radiating out from a black-and-red impact point along her jawline.

Oh, dear God. The bastard had hit her with an uppercut. And he hadn't pulled the punch. He'd meant business. He could have broken her jaw.

He could, in fact, have killed her.

Crimson tightened her protective grip. She looked toward the doorway, where Grant now stood, watching silently. His face, too, was dark with an instinctive fury that anyone, anywhere, could do such a thing.

She loved him, at that moment, for being a born protector. She understood, without asking, that Becky could take shelter here.

"You don't have to explain," she said as the girl began to tremble. "You're all right, Becky. You're safe here."

"Mr. Campbell," Becky said, turning to Grant formally, as if she'd planned what she should say and, unable to regroup now, simply had to say it. "I'm very sorry to bother you, but I didn't have anywhere else to go. I'd heard that Crimson was staying at your ranch, helping with Molly. I could help, too, if only you…if she…"

She squared her shoulders, a heartbreaking attempt at a dignified courtesy. "If it's not too much trouble, could I please stay here for a little while?"

WHEN THE BELLS from the mission church near Grant's ranch rang at noon that Saturday, Grant figured he was probably the only person in Silverdell who wasn't at the wildflower festival.

Both Becky and Crimson were there, of course. They'd installed Becky in the manager's apartment off the barn—hardly swanky quarters, but clean and dry…and safe. She'd professed herself delighted with the accommodations, and she'd been a model tenant, frequently offering to help Crimson with Molly and cooking, but keeping to herself most of time, as if she dreaded making a pest of herself.

The two women spent all day yesterday making cookies for the festival, and batting away every ranch hand who tried to pilfer one—including Grant. "You can buy them at the festival like everyone else," Crimson had said, laughing.

But he'd known from the start he couldn't go. At least six women and two potential horse buyers had declared themselves sorry he couldn't come, but his Saturday mornings were dutifully set aside for paperwork. He'd been boxed up in the stable office for hours, updating records on all the horses connected to Campbell Ranch—especially to his breeding dam, Charisma Creek.

He'd bought Charisma three years ago, when he bought the ranch. She'd already had nearly twenty offspring even then. Those offspring now lived all over the world, where, in turn, they'd been bred or put to stud, and a new generation had come along.

That meant there were a lot of horses to keep track of, but it was critical to his business for him to know exactly how each one had performed in competitions and in show rings.

The better Charisma's progeny performed, the better her reputation would be—and his. Reputation translated into higher fees, which translated into a ranch that prospered instead of simply survived.

It was tedious work, but today, at least, there had been a payoff. May had been an excellent month for Charisma's line. At least six horses had done quite well in races—cups and trots and futurities that might not be internationally renowned but were big enough to get noticed.

Even better, one of the two colts she'd produced for him had just won a foal show and seemed poised to be an impressive horse.

Another win or two in June, and he might beat his projections by a mile. He stared at the spreadsheet. Did he dare to let himself hope? Well, he couldn't help it. Hope was already in the back of his mind, shining like a flashlight in the darkness.

Another win or two in June, and he might be able to keep Cawdor's Golden Dawn.

He scraped his chair away from the desk and stood with a yawn, stretching the kinks out of his back. The stable office had windows on both sides, and he could see the hands taking care of the noontime feeding. The horses poked their heads over the stall doors, eager for the socializing as much as for the feed. Arabians were affectionate creatures, and they enjoyed their human friends.

Dawn's golden head was the first, of course. She was the most alert and curious of them all. Grant strolled out of the office and down toward her stall. When he reached her, she bumped her nose against his shoulder and nickered softly.

She wanted to get out. Some horses could handle a lot of stall time, but others, like Dawn, needed freedom.

"I hear you, girl," he said, rubbing her muzzle. He flexed the fingers of his right hand, at least the part that extended from his cast, trying not to feel itchy with claustrophobia. But oh, how he wanted to get on horseback.

Not Dawn, of course. He didn't intend to let her carry any weight for another year, at least. But he had half a dozen horses that needed exercise, and he needed to ride the ranch, the way he used to do every Saturday to shake off the cobwebs after too much bookwork. He wanted the sun on his face and the wind in his ears. He wanted to feel like a rancher, not an accountant.

There were a hundred reasons he'd given up the law, but craving the outdoor life, a life of the body and not just the mind, was way up there at the top of the list.

"Hey, boss."

Grant looked toward the voice. Dusty Barley's unique silhouette was outlined in the stable door, backlit by sunbeams. He had a saddle hoisted on one hip.

"What're you doing here, boss? Shouldn't you be out on Elk Avenue buying some gal a columbine hair bob?"

Grant laughed, but in spite of himself an image of Crimson flashed into his brain. She would look amazing in one of those wildflower garlands they sold on every corner during the festival.

Although, she'd been there since early morning, so no doubt someone else had already bought her one. Hopler, maybe? The man was definitely interested. He'd left the ranch the other night just minutes after Becky arrived. With a bruised and weeping young woman standing in Grant's kitchen, even that determined California smoothie could tell he was in the way.

But Hopler hadn't liked being driven off, and

Grant knew the man would be watching for his next opportunity to make headway with Crimson.

"Seriously, boss. You're not even going to make a PR appearance at the festival? Talk up the horses? Drum up some business?"

"You could do the same," Grant observed drily. "Why are you still here? I thought I gave you the day off."

Barley harrumphed as he shuffled in, the heavy leather saddle causing his small frame to tilt deeply to one side. "I work for the horses, not for you. You just pay me."

Grant couldn't argue with that. He knew exactly what the old guy meant. Each day began when the horses started needing him, and didn't end until all the animals' requirements were met.

"So what's with the saddle? You taking somebody out?"

Barley nodded. "Keynote's restless. You know how the old goat is. He thinks we don't love him, now that Dawn gets all the attention."

As if he recognized his name, the black Arabian stallion in the stall next to Dawn poked his head over the door. When he spied the saddle, he strained to get as close to Barley as he could. His eyes sparkled, and he tossed his head with anticipation.

Keynote was twenty-three years old, and the sweetest-tempered horse on the ranch. All he ever asked was a daily ride and treat. Pitted dates were his favorite, though last year he'd stolen an ice cream cone out of a wrangler's hand—and liked it so much he still inspected that wrangler's jacket pockets every time he walked by.

Just looking at Keynote made Grant feel more frustrated than ever. A *child* could ride this obedient horse in complete safety. While he...

"Maybe *I'll* take him out."

With a short grunt, Barley hoisted the saddle higher on his hip. "Probably not a good idea," he observed unemotionally. "Better to keep solid ground under you till the cast comes off."

Good advice, no doubt. But a stubborn, rebellious streak had appeared out of nowhere. Why shouldn't he ride? What could happen—he might *break* something? Been there, done that.

Besides, this was lazy old Keynote, not the Tasmanian Devil.

"Ask Digger to saddle him for me," he said, ignoring Barley's frown. "You can take one of the other horses out, if you're really in the mood for a ride. Or *you* could go to the festival."

Barley snorted.

"Oh, and better bring the mounting block," Grant added.

"The *mounting* block?"

Grant smiled. Barley knew it wasn't his place to criticize Grant's decision outright, but he could make his tone communicate everything he wanted to say. The way he spoke, you'd think using a mounting block was as good as admitting you didn't know how to ride.

"Yeah, the mounting block. Keynote is fifteen hands. I can't get on him without it, not with only one arm."

"No, you can't. And maybe that should tell you something."

Grant laughed. "It does. It tells me I need the mounting block."

Barley chewed his lower lip, his eyes narrowed. He didn't like it, no doubt about that, but Grant thought it was possible he glimpsed a grudging admiration behind that disapproving squint.

The old man probably wouldn't have let a broken arm stop him, either.

"Aw, come on, Barley." Grant gave Dawn one last muzzle-stroke and then moved forward to open Keynote's stall. "There's no point standing there looking like you sucked a lemon. Get Digger, and get the blasted mounting block. My mind's made up."

CHAPTER NINE

"DANG IT, CRIMSON, why didn't you make more macaroons? They were gone by noon, and I didn't get a single one!" Mitch Garwood, his auburn hair gleaming in the setting sun, plopped down on the town square picnic table where Crimson and Molly were taking a rest from the festival. His wife, Belle, followed more sedately, pushing a stroller with their newborn son, Nick.

"Ignore him," Belle said, smiling at Crimson as she reached the table. "He doesn't need macaroons. He's eaten so many sweets today he's bouncing like a pogo stick."

"But not one macaroon," Mitch said, stretching his arms out along the wooden surface in mock despair. "Crimson, how *could* you?"

Crimson laughed. Mitch was just about the most adorable guy in Silverdell. She'd dated him a couple of times last year, when he and Belle had supposedly split up. But it hadn't come to anything, of course—not just because Crimson was commitment phobic, but also because…well, it might be easier to split an atom than to split Mitch and Belle.

They belonged together, and just seeing them

hand in hand gave people a little jolt of happy juice. Outwardly, they were complete opposites—Belle a brave, haunted heiress, who was almost otherworldly in her mysterious beauty, and Mitch a crazy cowboy, freckled, feisty and fun loving.

But beneath the surface, they were soul mates.

And of course, the entire population of Silverdell was holding its breath, waiting to find out what their baby would grow up to be like. A goofy cowboy or an elegant aristocrat? Or some fascinating hybrid that would probably be every bit as irresistible?

Belle bent over to coo at Molly. As a new mother, she was in the fiercest phase of baby craziness. "Look at you, Molly-dolly, sitting so quietly! You're such a good girl! Do you like the flowers, sweetheart? Nicky loves the flowers, too."

"He does not," Mitch said, frowning ferociously. But somehow that frown, turned on Belle, managed to say, "I adore you," just as clearly as if he'd been smiling.

"My big, strapping son likes the *horses*," he insisted, his brown eyes flashing with amusement. He loved to play the cliché. "See, Crimson? My little man is already wearing his cowboy booties!"

Sure enough, when Crimson craned her neck to see over the table, she spotted Nick's kicking feet. Someone had knitted tiny brown socks in the shape of cowboy boots. They were ridiculous and precious at the same time.

"Oh, brother," she said, shaking her head. "Indoctrination from the cradle."

"The womb," Belle corrected, but she obviously knew Mitch's macho-chauvinist attitude was all for show. He wouldn't dare adopt such an attitude seriously. Belle might look like a Botticelli painting, but she was a very tough, very independent woman who had single-handedly conquered more demons in her life than most people ever had to face.

"*Our* son loves the horses *and* the flowers," she added.

"*Everybody* likes flowers." Crimson chuckled. "And even if you didn't, you wouldn't dare admit it in Silverdell this weekend."

She glanced around, drinking in just how true—and how oddly wonderful—that statement was. Walking down Elk Avenue during the wildflower festival was like drifting inside a rainbow. Everywhere you looked, you saw color.

Garlands of wildflowers scalloped the air between streetlights. Tubs of phlox and columbine and daisies flanked every retail doorway. Booths lined the streets, selling wildflowers that had been crafted into every imaginable trinket and toy. Even the sidewalks seemed to have been carpeted in petals.

Half of Western Colorado must have come here

today, she thought. Silverdell's tiny population alone couldn't have accounted for the shoulder-to-shoulder crowds.

She'd been fighting those crowds all day. And though she'd been up late last night making the macaroons, and then awake again at dawn to deliver them to Donovan's Dream, she wasn't one bit tired.

It was about five o'clock now, and though she'd snagged this park bench only to rest her feet for a while before heading back to the ranch, she still wasn't eager to leave. The air was cooling, and the sky was a palette of pinks that deepened toward red and plum and purple with every passing minute.

Suddenly, the sound of music filled the air. She swiveled, looking toward the tiny band shell. A group of musicians had set up there, and, with only a cursory tap on the microphone to make sure the sound system was working, had begun playing an old children's song.

Daisy, Daisy, give me your answer, do.

Crimson recognized a few of the musicians, too. The old guy with the guitar was Barton James, the manager of Bell River Ranch and self-proclaimed "best cowboy poet and singer west of the Mississippi." Last December, she'd given him a tattoo of a Taylor guitar on his left shoulder blade, his Christmas present to himself.

"Daisy" ended to thunderous applause, and

they swung immediately into their next number. "My Wild Irish Rose." Obviously, they'd planned a flower-themed concert, appropriate for the day.

This time, a few people in the park sang along, notes warbling inexpertly but pleasantly on the crisp spring air. Halfway through, people even began to dance.

A white-haired couple got things started, executing some elegant twirls with courtly charm. Off to the side, a tall father balanced his little girl on his feet and traced a stiff-legged square on the grass. Then two teenaged girls with flower garlands in their hair jumped up and began to bob and circle together like wood sprites.

And couples...so many couples joined in. Some of them hardly moved, smiling into each other's eyes as they sang along. Others were tight knots of intimacy, with flower-crowned heads resting on broad shoulders...

Laughing, Mitch and Belle stood, as if pulled by invisible strings, and melded into each other. They never moved more than a foot or two from the stroller, but they managed to create an aura of twinkling romance, as if they were outlined by tiny golden sparklers.

Instead of feeling left out as she watched them, Crimson was filled with a sense of peace. Sure, the whole "festival" concept was fake—some of these dancing wood sprites would be reporting to jobs they hated Monday morning, and, though

Mitch and Belle were the real deal, she knew that some of these love-wrapped couples wouldn't last the weekend.

But even so…

There was something charming about the way everyone in Silverdell had agreed to set reality aside for forty-eight hours. Just for these two days, they'd agreed to pretend life was a flowered rainbow, and that everything was beautiful.

From her carrier tucked inside the stroller, Molly let out a happy squeal.

Crimson smiled down at the baby. "You want to dance?"

Molly waved her hands, and Crimson decided that was baby for "yes." She stood, and, bending over, she reached in and unhooked the safety strap. Molly squealed again, delighted that freedom was coming. When Crimson lifted her, all her muscles were rigid with eagerness, and she used her booties to prop herself against Crimson's rib cage so that she could better see the world around them.

Build Me Up, Buttercup…

Oh, she and Clover had always loved this song!

She began to dance. She was a terrible dancer, but so what? So what if she looked silly? So what if, deep inside, she still felt guilty, as if she'd stolen this moment from Kevin, who lay in his hospital bed, or Clover, who lay in her grave?

Even if Crimson Slayton didn't have a right to

be this happy, Molly Ellison did. She was only six months old. This was the age when babies were learning language and laughter, and discovering whether their world was going to be a place of sunshine or filled with sorrow.

Crimson owed it to Molly to open the door and let joy in.

And so, with one hand behind the baby's head, she bounced softly to the music. She spun Molly around until she giggled and buried her head in Crimson's neck.

As the song ended, Crimson dropped a kiss on the baby's ear. "Next time, you can go dancing with your daddy," she promised.

Brave words. A gust of wind passed through the square, tugging on the streetlight garlands until they rained gold pollen and pastel petals down on the park. Crimson hadn't prayed often in the past year, but she prayed now.

Let the words be more than brave. Let them be true.

"May I have the next dance?"

Crimson looked up, and to her surprise Stefan Hopler stood in front of her, his hand outstretched. She gazed at the long, elegant, manicured fingers—that hand would have proclaimed him a millionaire, even if the haircut, the linen suit and the chiseled nose had not.

She patted Molly's back. "*Both* of us?"

She didn't know whether he'd expected a threesome, but he was admirably graceful about it. His broad smile extended all the way to his eyes, as if it were genuine. "Absolutely! I'd be honored."

She couldn't say no to that smile, although the Wildflower Band, as she thought of them now, had just launched into a poignant rendition of "Edelweiss." Barton James was singing, and his cracked but beautiful baritone made the song almost unbearably sad and sweet.

Out of the corner of her eye, she could see Mitch and Belle watching curiously as she let Stefan fold his arms around her. But she consoled herself that they wouldn't remain interested in her for long. Their own magnetic connection would take hold of them, and, at least for the next few minutes, everyone outside their charmed circle would cease to exist.

Stefan was a good dancer—if you could even call this dancing. She hoped he'd assume her own clumsiness came from holding the baby, though if he'd been paying attention when she was "dancing" alone, he probably knew she didn't have much physical grace. When, at six, she'd told her grandmother she wanted to be a ballerina, Gran had almost choked on her lemon drop.

Stefan had been flirtatious from the first minute she met him, so she almost expected him to get too cozy. But he didn't. He didn't even try to squeeze her too tightly, which would have been hopeless, anyhow, with Molly in the way.

She relaxed a little. His manner was confident, and easy enough that he made it seem perfectly normal for her to be out here in public, holding someone else's infant and dancing with a man she hardly knew, while an old cowboy sang an Austrian song, and a chilly late-spring wind rained wildflower petals into her hair.

"I thought you were headed back to California," she said after a few seconds. Dancing in silence seemed too intimate.

"No…my plans are fairly open-ended." He smiled. "I had hoped to come to an arrangement with Grant about Dawn before I left. But the other night just didn't seem like the right moment."

She chuckled. "No. I can see that."

"How is your friend? Becky, wasn't it?"

"She's fine." Crimson was impressed, actually, by how calm Becky had been, once she got over her initial anxiety about asking for help.

"I suppose Grant said she could stay."

"Of course."

"I thought so." Stefan smiled. "He seems the type."

She looked at Stefan, hearing something odd in his voice. Offended and not even sure why, she felt her back stiffen a little.

The type? In her mind, Grant had been a hero. He hadn't asked any questions. He'd just offered Becky her choice of the third bedroom in the house or a small apartment just off the barn, where a ranch manager would live, if he could ever afford one.

Becky had eagerly accepted the apartment, insisting that she'd pay rent, and promising that it wouldn't be for long. "Just until I figure out what to do," she'd said.

"I'm not sure what you mean," Crimson said to Stefan. "What type?"

He lifted one shoulder. "The white-knight type. A beautiful young woman in trouble..."

Now she knew why she was offended. She flattened her lips. "It was the 'in trouble' part that he responded to. Not the 'beautiful young woman' part."

"Oh, of course. He would want to protect anyone who needed it, I'm sure. Obviously, after what happened to his wife..."

As his sentence trailed off, she fought to keep her face from reacting. He was fishing, clear as day. He wanted to know if she knew.

And she didn't.

But she'd be darned if she'd let him offer her this morsel of gossip as a present, the way a cat might proudly drop a dead mouse at her feet.

It wasn't his to give.

"I don't think his wife has anything to do with it," she said crisply. She meant to stop there, but she wasn't the meek type, and he might as well know it now. "And I hope you won't be discussing Grant's personal life so casually with everyone you meet."

His eyes widened. "Of course not. I didn't think of you as *everyone*."

He waited. Then, when she continued to bristle, he chuckled. "Goodness, it's awfully easy to misstep when talking to the two of you. Listen, I didn't mean to be intrusive. I know about his past because I do my research. Cawdor's Golden Dawn is a very expensive horse, and I don't do business with people I don't know."

That made sense, and she felt a little silly for overreacting. Molly had begun to wriggle, unsettled by Crimson's tension. She bent her head to kiss the baby and consciously forced the muscles in her back and shoulders to relax.

"Sorry," she said. "I shouldn't have snapped at you. We're going through a tough time, and I guess we're all a little on edge."

To his credit, he didn't push the subject any further. The song seemed endless, but finally Barton James finished with a flourish, and she pulled away as the crowd in the park began to applaud.

Awkwardly, she turned back toward the picnic table. And when she did, she saw that Grant was sitting there, chatting with Mitch and Belle.

He wasn't looking her way. She was grateful for that, because she needed a minute to compose her face. She had the strangest feeling that she looked guilty, as if dancing with Stefan Hopler somehow betrayed Grant.

Ridiculous. She frowned at herself. This was one of the reasons she needed to get away from this town. She was imagining all the stupid complexities that came with relationships, with lovers and boyfriends and commitments…except she didn't *have* any relationships.

She was just his friend's babysitter. And she was leaving as soon as Kevin woke up.

"Hello, Stefan," Grant said, turning around with a polite smile. "Hey, Red."

For a minute, when she first saw his face, her heart stopped. He looked amazing. His golden-brown eyes sparkled, and his cheeks were burnished, as if he'd spent the day outside, instead of in his office doing paperwork. She found herself glancing down at his right arm, as if she might suddenly discover the cast was gone, and he was healed again.

"Hi, Grant," she said in a studiously normal voice. She bent over to return Molly to her carrier inside the stroller. "When did you get here? I thought you weren't going to make it out today."

"Yeah, but I came down with cabin fever. Apparently, I'm not very good at being an invalid."

"I guess not!" Mitch groaned sympathetically. "Sitting around indoors all day is *torture*."

"And I'm afraid your son has inherited your

restless streak," Belle said, putting her hand on her husband's shoulder. "We need to go home, Mitch."

She'd stood and was pushing the stroller back and forth in front of her. Crimson recognized that as the "please don't cry" stroller waltz.

As if they'd rehearsed their timing, Molly immediately began to whimper, and Crimson stood, mirroring Belle. It was getting late—almost dark. White fairy lights in the park trees were just starting to be visible, as if the branches were full of iridescent moths.

"I probably should get Molly home, too. She's been a trouper, but she's out of gas."

To her surprise, Grant rose from his place on the bench. "Can I catch a ride? I came in with one of the hands."

"I'd be happy to give you a lift," Stefan put in with a smile. "I've been hoping for a chance to talk about Dawn a little more."

Grant eyed the other man coolly, and for the first time Crimson's discomfort returned. His expression wasn't exactly unfriendly, but it wasn't warm, either. If she didn't know better, she'd say he was annoyed with Stefan for dancing with her.

"Funny," Grant said slowly, "I thought it might be something else entirely you were interested in."

Stefan didn't respond right away. Though he was still smiling, his expression looked frozen, and a muscle in his jaw twitched ominously. But finally, after a few seconds, the set of his mouth relaxed, and his smile returned to a more natural curve.

"I have lots of interests," he said mildly. "It would be a boring life if we didn't, don't you think? But I can see that a night like this isn't made for doing business. Horse negotiations can wait until tomorrow." He tilted his head. "About ten sound good?"

Grant nodded. "Ten's fine. But I have to warn you, it might be a waste of time. I'm starting to have second thoughts about selling her."

"I understand. It would be difficult to part with something that rare, I'm sure."

Stefan didn't look the least bit fazed by Grant's comment, but Crimson was shocked to hear that Grant was reconsidering. He'd always insisted he didn't have the luxury of keeping Dawn.

"Let's meet, all the same," Stefan said equably. "Who knows? I might be able to come up with an offer that tempts you. And even if I don't, I'll still enjoy seeing her one last time."

GRANT CURSED UNDER his breath as he peeled a loose bit of old wallpaper from the dining room wall, only to discover another layer of old paper behind that. Flowers behind flowers, and all of them ugly. It was going to take forever to strip the room and prep it for new paint.

He backed down a step or two on the ladder, so that he wouldn't have as far to fall if he lost his balance. So much for the upbeat mood he'd found himself in this afternoon, after his long ride on Keynote.

As he'd jumped down off the horse, ignoring the lingering twinge in his right ankle, he'd felt fantastic. Fresh air was magic. He'd felt invigorated, in control of his life again for the first time since the accident. He'd been so high on freedom, so cocky from the small victory, that he'd decided to go find Crimson at the festival. She might need his help with Molly.

Yeah, right. Need his help? In the year he'd known her, Crimson had always had men lining up to do whatever she'd let them do—which wasn't much. She was the most fiercely independent gal he'd ever met, which naturally only made her more intriguing.

He'd watched her date a handful of guys since she moved to Silverdell. Never more than a few times each—that was her rhythm. The minute they got possessive or demanding, she ditched them without a backward glance.

And since he and Crimson were just friends, he'd always sat back and enjoyed the show.

So he had no idea why seeing her in Stefan Hopler's arms tonight had changed his mood so instantaneously and completely. It was like one of those elementary school science experiments, where you put red dye into water, drop in a chemical and watch the color disappear.

Poof! All that cocky euphoria evaporated, leaving behind a cranky feeling that was as unpleasant as it was illogical. And worst of all was the stupid, caveman way he and Stefan had tangled verbally, pretending to be talking about the horse, when they both knew they were really—

"Grant?" As if he'd conjured her, Crimson stood in the doorway to the dining room, one hand gripping the door casing. She poked her head in and glanced around the room, taking in the plastic drop cloth, the paint tray, the gallon-can of stripping gel.

"What on earth are you doing? It's two in the morning!"

"I could say the same about you," he said, "except I'm pretty sure it was Molly who woke you, right?"

She nodded. "Yeah, and then I decided to come see what kind of clumsy burglar was making so much noise in the dining room."

He smiled. "I couldn't sleep. I already counted the bumps on the ceiling, so I figured I might as well get something done."

She frowned, swiping at her hair to move the mismatched layers of silky brown locks off her face. "I thought you were going to hire someone to strip this old paper. Becky offered to do it yesterday, but I told her you had other plans."

"I did." He'd figured this was grunt work, not expensive to hire out since it didn't require any sophisticated skills. "But the finances are looking pretty good. I've been thinking that, if I just cut a few more corners, maybe I wouldn't have to sell Dawn, after all."

"Really?" Her eyes widened and lit up. She came into the room, her bare feet making almost no noise on the wooden floors. She wore a knee-length cotton T-shirt. It clearly wasn't designed to be sexy, and yet the way the well-worn, baby-blue cloth clung to her curves made his pulse race.

"Really?" She came to the ladder and, hooking her fingers over the brace, looked up at him, repeating the word in an awed voice. "Wow, that would be awesome! When you told Stefan you weren't sure you wanted to sell, I thought maybe you were…you were just…"

She twisted her mouth sideways, clearly trying to think how to say it.

He smiled down at her. "Just being a jealous ass?"

She gave him a quizzical glance. "No. I was going to say I assumed you were just playing hardball." She looked down at her fingers and toyed absently with the metal brace. "Besides, why would you be jealous? You know there's nothing between…"

"Between you and me. Yeah, I know." The words sounded harsher than he'd meant them to.

Crimson glanced up at him, her smile crooked again. "You know, Grant, you really should stop finishing my sentences, especially since you don't have a clue what I'm planning to say. I was *going* to point out that there's nothing between *Stefan* and me."

He took a deep breath, and then let it out in a chuckle. He loved the sassy way she called baloney on people. It was one of the qualities that had always made her such a good friend. When she was ticked, she didn't smolder and pout and give off smoke signals that were impossible to decipher.

She just informed you of your jerk status and expected you to shape up.

"Well, if there's nothing between you and Stefan," he said, returning to the wallpaper, "it's not for lack of trying on his part."

She shook her head. "Yeah, but... Come on. When was the last time you saw me date a guy with a better manicure than mine?"

She didn't wait for an answer. She moved toward the tools he'd laid out along the drop cloth and, bending over, studied them. "So...is it time to use that little thing that looks like a yo-yo with shark's teeth? Or are we still at the part where we peel loose bits?"

He had to force himself not to stare at the perfectly shaped, firm-pear outline of her gorgeous rear end. This was Red, damn it.

Sure, she looked great, especially now that she was letting that punk hairdo grow out and didn't always have a spiky attitude to match. But she was so much more than a pretty face or a sexy body. They'd first met at a playground-raising charity event for a Silverdell school that had money troubles. She didn't know much about construction—she tended to refer to implements like the scoring tool as "yo-yos with shark's teeth" or maybe just "gizmos"—but she worked harder and longer and with a better attitude than any professional he'd ever met.

"*We're* not anywhere," he said. "This is my project. You should go back to bed. You know Molly will be wide-awake, this time for good, in a few hours."

"And so will your horses. Come on, don't be stubborn. You *have* heard the story about the one-armed paper-hanger, right?"

She picked up a scraper and moved toward the west wall, where a couple of strips were lifting away from the plaster. He watched as she began nudging the paper free. She had deft hands, and the long ribbon of cabbage roses kept growing without breaking, curling around itself like a giant fern frond.

Her shoulders were squared in that determined way she had, so he knew she'd entered into hyperfocus. There was no point trying to argue with her, so he just shook his head and climbed back up the ladder.

They worked in silence for a few minutes. He

glanced over at her now and then and saw that her hair was spangled with little bits of chipped paper, and her wall was much further along than his. She couldn't get the highest areas, of course, since he had the ladder, but she was moving fast.

Two functioning hands and a laser focus really were an efficient mix.

"You know, Stefan said something tonight that was kind of…" She paused, raking her hair back again and trying to tuck it behind her ear. "Kind of weird. I thought you might want to know."

He dodged a cascade of dust from the wallpaper he'd peeled away, remembering at the last minute that his cast threw his balance off. Luckily, he steadied himself before he went crashing onto the drop cloth.

"Well, that depends. *How* weird?" He scraped some more, but he had a feeling he'd done all he could until he added the stripping gel. There were three layers of this crap, at least. Every single owner of this ranch house had clearly had an unnatural love of cabbage roses.

He grinned down at Crimson. "I'm not sure I want to hear anything *private* weird, if you know what I mean."

To his surprise, she didn't even smile at the feeble joke.

"No, nothing like that." She took a breath. "It was about you, actually."

Curious, he waited for her to continue.

"It seems he's been snooping around, trying to find out more about you. He says he researches everyone he does business with. So he's been looking into anything he can find about your ranch, your private life, even about your past…"

Ah. That answered his question. "Looking into it…and then sharing it with you?"

"No." She turned and gave him a frank gaze. "I think he would have, if I'd been receptive, but I wasn't. He just mentioned something about your wife. About what *happened* to your wife. I shut down the conversation by pretending I already knew."

He saw the tension in her white knuckles as she gripped her scraper. She didn't know, then. He'd never been sure. The story had made some newspapers and, with a little digging, could be unearthed in an internet search if someone was motivated enough.

But she hadn't dug, and now she wanted to know. That's where the tension came from. She wanted to know, and she wished she didn't.

A month ago—a week, even—he would have found some way to avoid this conversation. And he still wasn't crazy about the idea. In the three years he'd been in Silverdell, he'd confided in exactly no one, and denial had become a natural coping mechanism. He dealt with what had happened by pretending that it hadn't.

But if Stefan knew, it seemed ridiculous to try to hide it from Crimson.

He rested his scraper on the ladder's paint tray and backed down the rungs slowly. When he reached the drop cloth, his sneakers making the plastic rustle, he wiped his hands against his jeans.

"Let's take a break," he said. At the far side of the room, he'd stacked all the furniture together, to make space to lay out the tarp. He thought about trying to extricate a couple of chairs, but Crimson had already dropped her tools and arranged herself comfortably on the floor, her legs crossed in front of her, and her back against the wall.

He joined her there. He propped his right foot against the unopened can of stripper. Sometimes, when he'd spent too long on it, it still throbbed a little.

They were so close their shoulders touched. Once, she might have tucked her hand through the crook of his elbow, a companionable gesture that wouldn't have meant anything but an offer of emotional support. But that was before...

Before all this strange, prickly tension, this shimmering, uncomfortable *awareness* had developed between them. Now touching him was obviously out of the question.

That made him sad. He would have welcomed the warmth of a simple human connection right now.

And it reminded him why he hadn't ever seriously considered dating her. He hadn't wanted to risk a friendship that mattered…mattered more than he'd realized, in fact.

"My wife and daughter died three years ago," he said, deciding to start quickly, getting the ugliest parts out of the way first. Like ripping off a bandage, rather than inching it painfully across your skin. "My three-year-old daughter died of an extremely virulent strain of strep infection. My wife was killed a month later when she surprised an intruder."

She stared at him as if she couldn't believe her ears. He knew that expression—it was unmistakable. The eyes were wide, not in that playful, feigned shock people sometimes put on. In this look, the eyes opened at the same time the brows knit together, and the two muscle impulses together created a unique kind of strain.

For months after Brenda's death, he'd seen that face on so many people—on everyone he met, everyone who heard about his serial disasters. People had begun to avoid him—even the people who had stuck by him when Jeannie died. They didn't avoid him because they didn't care, but because they cared too much. He had entered the land of "other," where things too terrible to contemplate could happen.

It was as if he and the rest of the world no longer spoke the same language.

And, of course, he couldn't do much to help,

because he was locked in his own nightmare and didn't really even want to come out.

Eventually, it had been easier just to walk away. Away from Benjamin and Jeanette Broadwell, his in-laws, who clung to him as if he held their daughter's soul in his hands and their granddaughter's memory in his eyes. Away from his legal career, his house, his friends, his life. What was left of it.

Away from all the places he'd been with *her*. With *them*.

Out here, in this quiet little town, no one knew his story. No one had to struggle to find words. No one treated him like an invalid or an emotional cripple. He could begin to forget.

Or at least to pretend to forget.

"I'm so sorry," Crimson said quietly. "Both of them, within a month? That's the most heartbreaking double punch I could possibly imagine. I don't know how you got through it."

When he didn't answer right away, she took a deep breath and put her hand through his elbow, after all. "No, I *do* know. By not having any choice, that's how. The world doesn't stop turning just because it ought to, does it?"

"No," he said, relieved that she actually seemed to understand. Her simple expression of what he'd felt for so long made it possible to admit how grim it had been. How often he'd wished everything would just disappear. "No, it doesn't. Apparently, that kind of prayer doesn't get answered."

She nodded absently, as if she were processing the information, and finding it difficult to do so. Then, out of nowhere, she glanced up at him and smiled ruefully.

"I guess if the world really did stop turning," she said, "it would be pretty unfair to all the other people who happen to live on this rock with us. The ones who have no idea what that kind of tragedy is like."

He smiled, too. "The lucky ones."

She nodded again. "The lucky ones."

And then, as naturally as if they were some old, married couple, she dropped her head against his shoulder. The warmth of her moved through him, soothing. Comforting, as if she were made of medicine.

"Is that why you moved to Silverdell?" She spoke quietly, as if someone were nearby who shouldn't be awakened. "I know you've been here about three years. Was it just too difficult to stay in the house where they died?"

He wondered briefly how much detail to share, but then he realized he could simply talk normally. For once, their deaths weren't some strange, forbidden subject. He didn't feel that he had to pick and choose his words as carefully because they were booby-trapped.

"It wasn't the house itself, so much. Neither of

them died at home. Jeannie, our daughter, died in the hospital, but she'd been sick for about four days. Our pediatricians misdiagnosed it. They thought it was a stomach flu when really it was a strep bacteria she'd picked up when she cut herself on the playground."

"Oh." Her voice was very small.

"Yeah. She was miserable, but no one thought it was a big deal at first. I was at work—I was always at work—and Brenda was left mostly alone to take care of her."

He remembered the first couple of nights, when he finally got home from the office, and Jeannie was crying incessantly. Sitting at his daughter's bedside, applying a cool cloth to her head, he'd barked at Brenda to call another doctor, because this one was obviously a quack. But he'd gone to work the next day, anyhow.

And then, four days later, it had been too late.

"Anyhow, after Jeannie died, Brenda wasn't happy there. I worked way too much. That was my way of coping. She hated that—she said she was afraid, alone in the house. We lived in Boston, and not in the best neighborhood, because I was still paying off law school. So she went home to spend time with her family."

"Where was that?"

"Memphis. Her family's lived there for generations. The place was in her blood, and, looking back, I can see I probably shouldn't ever have asked her to move to Boston with me in the first place."

He could see Crimson's brows draw together. "But spouses follow each other to their jobs all the time. You didn't do a bait and switch, did you? She knew you were planning to live in Boston? When she married you, I mean?"

He nodded. "Technically, she knew. We married as soon as I graduated from law school, and I already had the job lined up in Boston. But I think she always secretly believed I'd change my mind and agree to live in Memphis instead."

"Without a job?"

"Her father has a law firm, one of the biggest in town. He'd made it clear there was a spot for me."

Boy, had Benjamin made it clear. To Grant, in his headstrong youth, the offer had looked like the gleaming, sharp-toothed jaws of a trap, set and ready to close around him.

"I should have taken it," he said.

She shook her head, a tiny movement, but he was keenly aware of every move she made. His skin was so sensitive to her presence that he could feel the tiny currents of warm air when she breathed.

"Nobody wants to be indebted to their father-in-law for their first job," she said defensively. "Surely she could see you needed to prove you could stand on your own two feet first. If only to yourself."

That was exactly what he'd told himself, back then. Now, though, he could see how selfish it had been. He wanted to prove his own worth—and he'd been willing to sacrifice Brenda's happiness to do it. He'd talked her into doing something she dreaded. He'd been dismissive of her need for her roots, so sure she'd get over it. So sure he knew better.

And of course he'd counted on her loving him enough to willingly tear away part of her identity, part of her soul, and follow him to Boston.

It might have worked, if it hadn't been for Jeannie. When Jeannie died, Brenda's heart had died, too. Her capacity for loving—at least for loving Grant—had been buried right alongside their little girl.

"Brenda's roots were deep, and she couldn't change that," he said. "It damaged her when I tried to transplant her. After Jeannie died, she went back to Memphis for an extended visit—I didn't know how long she planned to be gone. And then, one afternoon when she was alone at her father's house, two men broke in."

"Oh, no! You're saying something terrible happened to her, even in her safe, happy place?" Crimson's hand tightened on his upper arm. "She thought *Boston* was scary, but…"

"Yes. In the end, it was the historic Broadwell house that got robbed, not my shabby condo. And she just happened to be there. They knocked her down, probably just making time to get away. But she hit her head as she fell. It's a terrible irony, really, to think she died because the Broadwells were so secure, so well-off and well-known."

Crimson made a wordless sound. "Ironic? Maybe, but it's so, so much more than that. It's *brutal*. And it's viciously *unfair*."

He almost smiled at the innocence of her fury. They both knew no one had ever promised life would be fair. Like everyone else over the age of two, they'd heard that old saw a million times, and they'd seen it in action even more than that.

But at that moment, he loved her for the uninhibited passion in her voice. She'd never met Brenda, so she didn't realize what a beautiful, smart young woman the world had lost that day. And yet, Crimson cared. She cared enough to be furious on Brenda's behalf.

On *his* behalf.

"Why in hell is life sometimes so *cruel*?" She spoke more loudly now, obviously without realizing. Her knee twitched as if she wanted to stand up and challenge fate to a duel.

He squeezed his elbow against his side, pressing her hand against his ribs. He didn't have an answer, of course. No one did.

They sat in silence a long time. Gradually, Grant realized he felt lighter, as if he'd put down some invisible burden. It didn't make sense, because Crimson hadn't said anything philosophical or brilliant. She hadn't offered any insight about healing that made everything better.

But whether it made sense or not, it was true. He let his head fall back against the wall, and he shut his eyes. Her weight against his shoulder had changed, as if she'd fallen asleep. Her breathing was deep and regular.

His mind drifted back to the previous afternoon, when he'd ridden Keynote over to his ranch's little elbow of Bell River, one of the few tributaries that reached out this far into the fringes of Silverdell. The river was full from the spring's snowmelt, and it sparkled fiercely as it spilled over blue rocks, as if a thousand photographers' flash bulbs had been set off at once.

Crimson didn't ride, but maybe she'd like to learn. Maybe, when everything settled down, he could teach her, and he could take her out and...

His eyes opened. He was a fool. When everything *settled down*, she'd be gone. She'd already told him that.

He pressed his arm more tightly, as if that would be enough to keep her from leaving. It wouldn't be, of course—it wouldn't even be enough to keep her here in this room for another five minutes if she wanted to leave.

And the bottom line was, if she wanted to go, he had to let her. He'd learned the hard way... people had to make their own decisions. Whether you coaxed or coerced, reasoned or bullied, forcing them to go against their own hearts led only to disaster.

Suddenly, the sound of a baby crying filled the air. For a minute, he was disoriented. Because he'd been talking about her, Jeannie's memory was fresh. Everything inside him tightened and burned.

Drowsily, unaware of his inner paralysis, Crimson stretched and yawned. She patted her pocket, where suddenly he could see the outline of the little walkie-talkie-type baby monitor she always carried with her when Molly was sleeping. If he hadn't been so busy earlier, checking out her great backside, he probably would have noticed it.

"Oh, lordy," she said thickly. "Here we go."

He ought to offer to check on Molly for her. He could manage, in spite of his cast. If he could ride a horse, surely he could change a diaper. But as the crying escalated, reaching that faster pace and higher pitch that signaled real distress, he knew he couldn't do it.

Crimson knew, too. And, as usual, she acted as if there was nothing strange about a grown man who froze at the sound of a baby crying. She reached into her pocket and turned the monitor down, down and finally off.

The electronic amplification was gone, but he could still hear Molly crying in the distance. Somehow, that was even worse, because Molly sounded less like herself and more like…more like the ghost of a weeping child.

"It's okay," Crimson said with a sleepy smile. "I'll get her."

They both stood and he followed her to the door. At the last minute she turned.

"Thank you," she said.

"For what?"

"For telling me about Brenda and Jeannie. I know you don't usually talk about them."

What could he say? *You're welcome? Lucky you, I dumped my heartache into your lap?* He had a sudden guilty sense that perhaps he'd been feeling lighter because he'd transferred some of the burden of sorrow to her shoulders.

But Crimson didn't look sad or weighed down. She looked serious, yes, but kind. And strong. And very, very beautiful.

She stood on her tiptoes and, looking him straight in the eyes, she leaned in and kissed him on his half-open lips.

Just a butterfly kiss. A breath of sweetness, a flicker of heat. And yet his nerves caught fire, like a gas burner set to the match.

"Red," he said huskily.

But she was already gone.

CHAPTER TEN

SHE HAD THE dream that night.

She had hoped she wouldn't, even though she knew she was in the danger zone, given that her birthday was only a few days away.

She'd hoped she had finally moved beyond getting kicked in the gut by any of the painful anniversaries. She'd already lived through one birthday without Clover, and she'd lived through the anniversary of Clover's death, just two months prior.

It had been hard, but it helped that no one knew. So no one offered condolences or wanted to talk about the tragedy. On some level, Crimson had been able to pretend it wasn't happening.

On the dream level, though, it had been hell. All night long, she'd searched the cold water, calling Clover's name, in that weird way dreams had of making the impossible possible.

Last year, her birthday hadn't really registered all that much. The birthday had come only two months after Clover's death, and Crimson had still been in shock. She hadn't even remembered the day until weeks later.

Paradoxically, this year was much harder. This

year she wasn't numb, either for the anniversary of Clover's death or for this lonely birthday. Her mind had been filled with thoughts of Clover for weeks now.

And then, as she'd listened to Grant's story of loss and horror, his pain had seeped into her like ink into cotton, until she'd almost been able to see his little girl, lying in her bed, crying, while the doctors dithered and misdiagnosed and missed their chance to save her.

How unendurable that must have been! At three, Jeannie would have been talking in full sentences, and she would have been able to articulate her fear and misery. She might even have cried out for her daddy to make the hurt go away.

But he couldn't.

The minute he told her about Jeannie, Crimson had understood why he couldn't tend to Molly when she screamed. Crimson was no psychologist, and she had no idea if there was a term for that kind of emotional paralysis, but she knew, as clearly as she knew the sun rose in the east, that Grant Campbell couldn't bear to hear Molly cry because he'd heard too much crying already.

He couldn't comfort Molly, because he hadn't been able to comfort his own baby girl.

So, though it was full light by the time Crimson fell asleep, she woke gasping for breath and clawing at the sheets, as if they were the dank weeds under the river. She sat up, her heart in her throat, and tried to calm her breathing before she woke Molly up, too.

All in vain. Apparently, babies could sense distress even when it was silent. As Crimson sat in bed, fighting to steady her heartbeat, Molly began to fidget, whimper and finally wail.

"Morning, sunshine," Crimson said, putting her feet to the cool wooden floor and managing a smile. "We meet again!"

She dressed them both quickly. By the time she got downstairs, it was only nine-thirty, and the house seemed quiet. She glanced out the window toward the drive, where Becky's car was usually parked, wondering if their guest was sleeping late. But the car was gone, and when she went into the kitchen she saw a note on the table.

It was from Becky, and it said she would be helping Marianne at Donovan's Dream if anyone needed her.

"Looks as if we've got a few minutes to ourselves, pumpkin," she said. Molly gurgled happily.

But then, with a rush of irritation, Crimson remembered that Stefan had said he'd be dropping by at ten.

"Rats." She grabbed a hard-boiled egg and a cup of coffee, hoisted Molly onto her shoulder and hurried out to find Grant.

She'd assumed he'd be in the stables, and he was. He was in the office, talking to Dusty Barley.

The two of them were huddled together over the computer screen, their faces lit by the LED display.

They looked fully absorbed. Somber. She frowned, hoping it wasn't bad financial news.

At the thought, the check in her purse seemed to glow as if it were radioactive. She glanced behind her, toward the stables, where Dawn's honey-colored head was peeking over the stall door, checking her out.

Though she wasn't exactly a horsewoman, she had to smile. That animal was so amazing. If Grant lost Dawn, it would be the world's worst injustice. She wasn't at all sure she could sit by and watch it happen. So, she could either go poke a hole in all four of Stefan Hopler's tires, or...

"Red!" Grant looked up from the screen and smiled. "What're you doing up and out already? I hoped you'd sleep late."

"I did," she said. "Almost *too* late. I ought to go check on my apartment. I know my plants are gasping for water, and that trash is probably pretty ripe by now. After that, I'm heading to Montrose. I didn't get over to see Kevin at all yesterday."

The elevated office was too small to accommodate all three of them comfortably, so she remained on the stable level, just a step or two below.

She gave Dusty a smile, too, wondering whether he knew Stefan was expected any minute. "And I might look at cars, too. So I'll be gone awhile."

The insurance check had arrived for her car, which had, of course, been totaled, but that check was sitting in her purse with the other one. She hadn't had time to go car shopping, nor was she interested in it, to be honest. The rental was cheap, and it got her wherever she needed to go.

"Bottom line…I just really want to get out of here before your company arrives."

"You don't want to be around when Stefan comes?" Grant raised his eyebrows in mock innocence. "He'll be crushed."

She glanced at her watch, bouncing Molly to keep her contented. "Seriously. It's quarter till. I'm gone. Anybody need a lift to town?"

"I don't," Grant said. He looked at his wrangler. "You need a lift?"

"Naw." Dusty shrugged. "I'm not going anywhere a horse can't take me."

"Okay, then. But what am I going to tell Stefan when he asks where you are?"

"Tell him…" She glanced at the baby. "Nope. Can't say it in front of little ears. Why don't you improvise?"

He chuckled. Then, to her surprise, he scraped back his chair across the rough-hewn wooden floor and stood. "Barley, can you double-check these numbers? And maybe call the Brittons, and find out how Desert Rose did in that futurity. If she even placed…"

"Yep. Will do." Dusty dropped himself onto the

chair with a puff of saddle dust and began to study the screen. "Go'n now. Let me think in peace."

Grant came out of the office, took the two steps down to the stable floor with only the slightest hitch in his gait and reached out to pinch Molly's cheek gently.

"Come on," he said. "I'll walk you to the truck. I've got news."

As they emerged into the sunshine, she watched his face closely, trying to read whether the news was good or bad...and what it involved.

She assumed it wasn't about Kevin's condition. The doctors rarely called until midday, and sometimes weekend days offered little official communication. If she and Grant wanted to know how Kevin was doing, they had to go see for themselves. Which was what she planned. She was feeling slightly guilty that neither of them had made it over yesterday.

It was the first day since the accident they hadn't visited his room. It was as if they'd both maxed out at the same time and needed a break.

And it was just coincidence that, on the same day, Grant had finally broken his silence about Brenda and Jeannie.

It meant nothing that, on the same day, she'd kissed him...

"It's nothing bad. It's about Anne," he said. She wondered if her anxiety had been visible on her face. He seemed eager to set her mind at ease.

"What about her?" She knew he'd had a tip that Anne might have connections in Las Vegas—might even be living there. He'd nosed around and found a woman of the right age who seemed to fit the description.

"Well, I'm thinking…now that we have a solid lead, maybe I should hire someone to check into her. There's an investigator I know. He's pretty good. He's not cheap, but he gets results fast, so you don't end up paying for as many hours. He's discreet, too. I thought he might do some digging. You know…find out where she lives now, where she works, what kind of person she is…"

He stopped abruptly and turned around, realizing he'd left her behind. She'd slowed and then stopped as if her feet had been caught in the dirt.

"What? You don't think it's a good idea?"

She adjusted Molly, who had drooled a wet spot the size of a tennis ball on her shirt. "*An investigator you know?* Who knows investigators?"

"Lawyers." He smiled. "Former lawyers."

"Oh." Slowly, she started walking again. Lawyers probably did need to know PIs. It seemed weird, at least from a dessert chef's perspective, to have your own PI buddy in every state, but she supposed it made sense. Lawyers dealt with all sorts.

"Okay. Yeah, sure. I think it's a fine idea. I'll pay half, of course."

He turned to look at her again, but kept walking. She thought, for a minute, that he might refuse, but he seemed to reconsider.

"Sure," he said. "That's great. I'll let you know what he says."

They'd reached the rental car. The air around them smelled green and sharp, and somewhere in the distance someone was running a lawn mower or a tractor—something that was shredding the grass and making it fill the air with its hint of summer to come.

The hood of the car winked under the bright morning sun. A sun that was definitely climbing high. She looked again at her watch. Nine fifty-five.

If Stefan came early…

"I really should go." She opened the passenger door of the backseat and began to settle Molly's carrier into its seat belt restraints. As she lowered the baby in, she glanced over her shoulder at Grant.

"When he locates Anne…" She wasn't exactly sure what she had been going to say. "What do you think we should do?"

"Depends on what Tarleton learns," he said. "If she's not in prison, or insane or the madam of a bordello, we'll probably get in touch with her."

He sounded so casual. So sure everything would work out all right in the end. Crimson hadn't ever been swoony about patriarchal men, hadn't ever longed to hand her problems over to some big strong guy to solve, but today, with so much at stake, Grant's steady gaze and easy smile were reassuring.

Even Molly liked the soothing rumble of his voice. The baby reached her hand toward him and cooed. He obviously knew what she was asking for. He responded by holding out one finger, which Molly immediately claimed as her new chew toy.

She guided it slowly toward her mouth, and, instead of withdrawing, he leaned closer, so that his arm would reach.

"It'll probably take him a day or two to scope things out," he said as the baby gummed the tip of his finger. "And then…I don't know. Call her? See if she wants to meet? Or we could just go and check her out ourselves, if that seems best. But that would mean an overnight, probably, if she's really still in Las Vegas. Do you think we ought to take Molly?"

Crimson glanced in at the baby, still gnawing on his finger so innocently, unaware that they were discussing her future.

"I don't know. Maybe not. It's all pretty touchy, isn't it? So hard to know exactly what Kevin would want."

He nodded. "Well, I guess we can play it by ear when we get Tarleton's report."

"Good idea," she said. But she wasn't really thinking about the PI anymore.

Her mind kept repeating that one word. *Overnight.*

She looked at him, her mouth suddenly dry. He was smiling, and the gold flecks in his eyes made it look as if he were made of sunlight.

She swallowed, but her throat was dry, too, and she realized she'd been breathing quickly, through her mouth.

Oh, she was a fool. *Worse* than a fool. But a flare had been lit in the pit of her stomach, and it was going to take more than a lecture on common sense, or a sermon on restraint, to extinguish that fiery glow now.

BECKY STOOD IN the bay window of Bronson's Books, packing away the columbine-decorated notepaper and teacups hand-painted with violets. She loved this display, which was set up to look like a Victorian living room.

She'd been surprised when she got in this morning, and Fanny had asked her to break it down. She'd thought surely they could leave it up for a few days, at least. It was so pretty. The customers loved it. It had sold a ton of wildflower books and gewgaws.

"Can't. Father's Day is in less than two weeks," Fanny had said briskly. But probably because she felt sorry for Becky and her bruised jaw, she tried to make a joke out of it. "Besides, wildflowers are so *yesterday*, don't you think?"

Yesterday. Literally. It was Monday morning. The festival had ended at six last night, not even twenty-four hours ago, and it was already irrelevant.

Becky supposed it was a bit like Christmas. All the fun was in the lead-up, in the preparation and anticipation. Once the day itself was over, people could hardly wait to pull down the tree, vacuum up the needles, and get their living room back to normal.

She wrapped tissue lovingly around her favorite bookends, which were shaped like bouquets of roses. Just like Christmas. Or like a love affair. All the fun was in the beginning…and when it was over, you couldn't get away fast enough.

She touched her jaw absently. Then she shook her head and decided to dwell on something else.

Spices. She'd think about spices. Did she dare add a little extra basil to Marianne's lentil soup recipe? It might taste awesome…but on the other hand there might be a reason Marianne had limited it to half a teaspoon.

Absorbed in the question, she moved carelessly in the crowded space. Her hip rammed into the table, her elbow bumped the silver tea tower and before she knew it the whole thing tilted over. She yelped, reaching out to steady the table with one hand, and, with the other, catching the crystal vase of peonies just before it fell.

But not before it splashed water all over the big, expensive volumes of *Colorado Wildflowers* stacked beside it.

"Oh, no." She grabbed the lacy napkin and swiped at the top book, pushing the water to the side, where it sank harmlessly into the tablecloth. "Oh, damn."

She picked up the damp book and shook it. Wouldn't you know it? The bouquet of peonies was the one real prop in the display. Teapot, empty. Teacakes, plastic. But peonies, real—and placed in real water.

And the book cost a hundred and twenty-five dollars. It was as heavy as an anchor, filled with beautiful color pictures, and if she'd ruined it…

"Need any help?" Alec Garwood, who had been sitting in the children's nook reading to his baby sister while their mom shopped, stood just below the elevated platform, staring at her. He held his sister, Rosie, on his bony hip, which couldn't have been comfortable. But surprisingly, Rosie sucked placidly on her two middle fingers, as content as if she were sitting on a cushy throne.

As Becky had learned since working for Fanny, Rosie Garwood was infamous on Elk Avenue, the main commercial street in downtown Silverdell. She was about a year and a half now, and she was the most beautiful little princess baby you could imagine—all glossy black curls and huge green eyes and lips so puffy and pink you'd swear she wore lipstick.

But wow, did that kid have a temper! The only person who could calm her down was Alec, which was kind of funny, considering he was just a young boy himself. Rowena, Rosie's mom, tried, but she had a temper, too, so it was more like watching stags lock horns.

Mostly, shop owners like Fanny prayed Rosie wouldn't tag along when Rowena came into town.

"No, thanks. I'm okay." A little embarrassed, Becky put down the soaked napkin and used the hem of her T-shirt to work on drying the book. Alec might be only about twelve, but he was tall and confident, and he seemed older.

"Just a heads-up." He had a mouth full of chewy chocolate candy he'd just dug out of his jeans pocket, but he still enunciated clearly. "If you were thinking about trying to just shove it on a shelf and hope nobody notices, that's a bad idea."

Becky scowled at him. "I wasn't thinking anything of the sort."

"Good. Cause somebody *always* notices, and then they try to pretend the real problem is that you were trying to hide what you did. Better to tell Fanny now, but remember to look really sad, like you feel terrible about it, because that's absolutely key."

"Oh, is it, *really*?" Rowena appeared behind

her stepson's back, her arms full of books. Her voice sounded stern and disapproving, but Becky could see her face, and she was clearly fighting back laughter.

Alec's eyes widened. Then he recovered smoothly. "I'm just telling the truth. I thought I was *always* supposed to tell the truth."

"Alec Garwood, take your sister outside and wait for me on the bench."

"*What?* What did *I* do? Rosie and I were just—"

"Hush! You. *Go.*" Rowena pointed her index finger at him, and then, comically, Rosie did the same.

In an adorable baby lisp, she echoed her mom. "Hush! You! *Go!*"

Alec glowered. "Why, you little traitor!" But he went, obviously recognizing when he was outnumbered.

Rowena set down her armful of books and reached out to touch the cover of *Colorado Wildflowers*.

"May I look?"

Becky didn't know what to do except hand over the book, the pages of which were already beginning to swell from the moisture.

"Oh, this is the exact book I was hunting for! I'll take it! Fanny seems to be in the back. Do you have time to come ring me up?"

Becky tried to reclaim the book. "I'll be glad

to, but let me get you a fresh copy. I spilled some water on this one—"

But Rowena wasn't letting go. She folded the book against her chest and raised her eyebrows. "I'll take this one. At the dude ranch, with a hundred people a week manhandling it, I promise you no one is going to notice if it's a little damp."

Becky knew she shouldn't let her, but she didn't see how to prevent her without making a huge fuss. She climbed down from the elevated bay and rang up the order, which took forever, because Rowena kept seeing things she wanted to add.

A bunch of bookmarks, a stuffed pony, half a dozen board books, practically the entire *New York Times* bestseller list in hardback...

The Bell River sisters were always good customers. Bell River Dude Ranch had to keep its guests amused 24/7, and having good books around probably wasn't a luxury. But this was... like...serious overkill.

It wasn't until Becky was bagging it all up that she noticed Rory had come into the bookstore, too. He stood off to her right, pretending he was reading a magazine. For a minute, she froze, unable to make her arms move. She felt her cheeks grow cold, as if a wind had passed over them, and she knew they must be pale.

Which would just make her bruise stand out more vividly than ever.

"Everything okay?" Rowena frowned. She

began turning her head, looking around the store for the source of the problem. When her gaze landed on Rory, her jaw set in a hard, square line.

Becky hadn't ever noticed what a strong bone structure Rowena Wright Garwood had. She was pretty famous in Silverdell and all—their family story, with their dad killing their mother years ago and dying of a brain tumor in prison, was everyone's favorite topic in a gossip-fest, even all these years later.

So yeah, everyone knew Rowena was a firebrand and a beauty and a force to be reckoned with, but suddenly Becky understood that Rowena's beauty wasn't the most important thing about her.

The strength was.

Casually, after she dug out her credit card and handed it to Becky, Rowena also took out her cell phone and began typing a text message. While her thumbs flew across the keys, she kept up a running chatter about how she was "simply a menace in bookstores," she was always catching heat at home, she was probably going to be in "so much trouble…"

It sounded weird, all wrong for Rowena, who obviously was the boss of Bell River Ranch and wouldn't take any garbage from anybody about what she bought. But Becky just murmured noncommittally, glad that someone else was keeping the conversation going.

She wasn't sure she could have. Her throat had gone dry, and her heart was beating too fast. She didn't really believe Rory would do anything violent in public, but still…just the sight of him…

"Oh, oops! I think I'm going to have to have that darling Madeline doll, too!" Rowena reached over to what Fanny called the "impulse section" and grabbed a small box that held a little Madeline figurine, based on the children's book. "Rosie will love it."

While Becky rang up a whole new order, Rowena kept texting.

Suddenly, Fanny came out from the break room and stood at Becky's side without saying a word.

Before Becky could quite register what that meant, the front door opened and Sheriff Garwood, Rowena's husband, walked in. His gold star winked sharply as he moved from the sunlight to the shop's fluorescent overheads.

Even little Alec Garwood, his son, returned from banishment. He headed straight to Rowena, handed Rosie off without a word and went to stand beside his dad. He must have been on tiptoe, because he looked almost as tall as the sheriff.

And then Becky finally understood. Rowena had texted out her SOS, and brought in the marines to protect Becky from Rory.

She ducked her head self-consciously, caught between gratitude and shame. It was so embarrassing. Did everyone in town know what had happened? Was everyone gossiping about how she'd been shacking up with a smooth-talking creep?

Did she have a reputation now as a pathetic, battered girlfriend?

Something about that was offensive to her, on a very deep level. She wasn't weak, and she wasn't a victim.

But then she realized something shocking. No, she wasn't weak. No, she shouldn't be written off as a victim.

And neither should any of the *other* battered women in the world.

The important thing, once again, was not that she'd been knocked down, but that she'd gotten up again. The important thing was the strength.

She wasn't going to let this one bad decision— the decision to choose Rory—define her forever. She thought about that momentary scare, when she thought she might be pregnant, and realized she'd never be foolish enough to put herself in such a dangerous situation again.

More important, she wouldn't put any child of hers into that situation.

Summoning all her courage, she lifted her head and met Rory's gaze. "What are you doing here?"

She was glad she sounded firm, though she knew she might never have found her voice at all, if it hadn't been for Rowena's reinforcements.

He frowned. "I need to talk to you."

"No, you don't," she said. "You need to leave."

He didn't like that. Not at all. His brows came together.

"Becky, I *said* we need to talk." He took a step forward.

Instantly, Sheriff Garwood was between them, blocking Rory's view of her. "You hard of hearing, son? Ms. Hampton said she wants you to leave. Ms. Bronson would like you to leave, as well." He tilted his head. "And to tell you the truth, so would I."

Rory chuckled, though it sounded a little stiff. "Why? I can buy a book if I want to. I haven't done anything wrong."

"Haven't you? I wonder what Ms. Hampton would say if I asked her about that bruise on her jaw."

"She wouldn't say anything," Rory returned calmly. He sounded utterly confident, as if Becky were a puppet, and he was the ventriloquist who could make her say whatever he pleased.

She knew she had only herself to blame for that. Crimson had tried to warn her. Crimson had spent hours, that first night at Grant's ranch, trying to talk her into filing a complaint against Rory. But Becky had refused. She had just wanted it all to go away.

It wouldn't go away, though. She understood that now. The minute she'd agreed to pretend she'd fallen down the apartment steps, instead of telling the world he'd knocked her down, she'd helped create this monster. And the monster would grow bigger and bolder every time he wasn't held accountable.

"She'd tell the truth...that she fell down. Wouldn't you, Becky? You think I'd ever hurt her? You don't know me, Sheriff. You don't know *us*."

Becky recognized that wheedling tone. That tone was meant for her. Rory hoped it would turn her heart to mush. And her brain along with it.

"She wouldn't tell lies about me," he insisted. "She loves me, and she knows I love her. So yeah, go ahead. *Ask her*."

Sheriff Garwood glanced over his shoulder at Becky. "Ms. Hampton? If this man hurt you, you have every right to file a complaint. Would you like to do that?"

She glanced at Fanny, who was staring at Rory, her expression stony with disgust. Then she looked at Rowena, who had her palm protectively on Rosie's head, but was watching Becky. As their eyes met, Rowena smiled and gave Becky one subtle incline of her head.

"Yes," Becky said, suddenly erupting with all the fury she'd been repressing. "Yes, I would like very much to file a complaint."

"Becky!" Rory's voice rose. "Becky, goddamn it, don't let this guy—"

"Hush!" Rosie, that queenly little tyrant who looked so deceptively like a china doll, was suddenly in a rage, disliking Rory's tone. Her shouted, lisping command was loud enough to silence the room. "You! *Go!*"

CHAPTER ELEVEN

TUESDAY MORNING CRIMSON was surprised to learn that Grant had to go to Memphis for a couple of days, to join his former in-laws for some event that involved a foundation they'd set up in Grant's daughter's memory.

He was on the board, which he insisted was a nominal position, but it meant he couldn't shirk this duty. He seemed hazy about how long he'd be gone—the main event was that night, but sometimes the Broadwells had set up other meetings with donors, and they always hoped he'd attend.

He promised he'd keep the visit as short as possible. He seemed genuinely apologetic about leaving Crimson with full responsibility for Molly and Kevin—especially after the dust-up at Fanny's bookstore yesterday. Becky would help, of course, but with her two jobs she wasn't able to do much in the way of babysitting.

Still, the event had been planned long ago, and he didn't want to disappoint the Broadwells. Crimson understood that.

Before he left, Grant called someone out to install a security system at the ranch. Rory had been charged with third-degree assault, but he'd bonded out this morning. Becky said she hadn't heard from him, and didn't think she would, especially since the judge had issued a temporary protection order.

But the *protection order* was, in the end, only a piece of paper. Crimson didn't know any statistics on the matter, but her gut told her it was a dangerous time. Obviously, Grant felt the same way.

The installer was still working when, around noon, Grant took a taxi to the airport. As they said goodbye, she wanted to try to pin down whether he'd be back tomorrow, but she stopped herself.

It didn't matter. In fact, she thought as she watched the taxi bump slowly down the front drive, raising a trail of dust behind it, maybe it was better if she spent tomorrow alone.

Tomorrow was her birthday. She hadn't mentioned that to anyone, of course. The last thing in the world she could tolerate would be some well-intentioned celebration. Without Clover, the birthday was an ugly, mutilated thing. A piece of debris from another life.

She just needed to get through the day in her own way. But no matter how hard she tried to ignore it, she'd undoubtedly be rotten company.

Grant was lucky he wouldn't be here to endure it.

By late Tuesday night, though, Crimson found she missed him far more than she'd expected to. Far more than made sense. It wasn't as if they spent every waking hour together. Often, even when he was at the ranch, he was so busy she didn't see him for the entire day.

But at least he was nearby, and that made the whole world feel different. Near enough that sometimes, as she stood in the great room looking out the picture window toward the pond, she could see him walking the field with his men. Near enough that she could hear him come in late at night and get ready for bed. His bathroom adjoined her bedroom, and she could sometimes hear the cute little half profanity he growled as he tried to immobilize his toothbrush with his cast long enough to put toothpaste on it.

"Friggin'…"

It had become her signal that all was well. Everyone was inside, safe and accounted for. She'd smile into her pillow and, finally relaxed, she would drift off to sleep.

But not that night.

As she lay there, remembering how he'd told her his father-in-law was always lobbying to get him to move back to Memphis, she had a sudden flash of fear. She knew he was having money troubles—that was why he had considered selling Dawn in the first place. What if, while Grant was in Memphis this time, his father-in-law made him an offer that was too tempting to refuse?

What if he never came back?

Well, that was dumb, of course. He'd have to

come back, if only to settle things here, sell the ranch and get his things. But that wasn't the same as *really* coming back. That wasn't the same as coming back to *stay*.

Given that she, herself, didn't plan to stay in Silverdell long-term, it seemed odd to be so disturbed by the idea of Grant giving up the ranch, but she was. If he went back to Memphis, he would be forever trapped in the role of Brenda Broadwell's widower. He'd lose his hope of finding a new dream.

And Campbell Ranch was the right dream for him. He belonged here. If she'd ever met a man who came alive in the out-of-doors, who understood animals with something approaching magic…

If she'd ever met a man who should *not* be cooped up behind a desk…that man was Grant Campbell.

She had so much trouble sleeping that, at one point, she even considered going out to the manager's suite in the barn to talk to Becky. But she wasn't sure the baby monitor would reach that far, so she stayed in the main house, alone, and peeled wallpaper. Maybe if she helped him make a little progress on this dream, he would find it harder to abandon.

The hours ground by slowly as she fought with the ancient, gummy layers.

It became Wednesday when she wasn't looking.

When she finally realized, glancing casually at her watch, the moment was strangely anticlimactic. It was their—her—birthday.

She'd made it through another year.

But…so what?

Nothing had changed. Stupidly, she'd been counting off the passage of the days, weeks, months, the way a prisoner might scratch days into the stone walls of his cell. But the prisoner's scratches made sense—he was marking time until he was released.

Her three hundred and sixty-five days were over—and then some.

She'd done the time. She'd faced the emotional landmarks, dreamed the dreams, rebuilt some rickety semblance of a life. She'd survived the first birthday without Clover…and the first Christmas. Then the anniversary of the day she died…

And now the *second* birthday without her.

It wasn't ever going to end, was it? Because, no matter how many anniversaries and birthdays passed, Clover would always still be dead.

The only thing this birthday marked was the beginning of the *next* three hundred and sixty-five days alone.

And that made Crimson feel so hollow inside she was suddenly afraid the slightest movement might cause her to break into a million pieces. She carefully put down her scraper and climbed the stairs. Without even wiping off the bits of soggy wallpaper that clung to her skin, she sat in the wooden rocker and stayed there all night, watching Molly sleep.

Her own sleep came in snatches, in choking breaths that tasted of river water and twitches that made the rocker sway like an undercurrent.

When she woke, she went through the paces of living, like a zombie. The baby, the feeding, the changing, the cooing and playing and pretending. The drive to Montrose, where Kevin still slept, and only the beeping machines proved he was alive. The cooking, the cleaning.

At one point, she took out a map, covered her eyes and let the tip of her ballpoint pen fall onto a random spot, trying to decide where she would go next, when she left Silverdell.

Anything for distraction. She even considered scraping more wallpaper, but the smell made her feel sick. That smell would always remind her of the moment she'd seen the hands of her watch pointing to midnight. Pointing to the beginning of her empty forever.

So when she saw a taxi come up the drive late Wednesday afternoon, just before sunset, her heart leaped in her chest, as if someone had put defibrillator paddles to it. She rushed to the front door and threw it open, hoping it was Grant.

But the man who got out of the car was a stranger to her. Or…

No, he was a stranger. Wasn't he?

He was paying his driver, so she couldn't see his face. He was almost as tall as Grant, but not quite as muscular. No gold in his brown hair. And he wore a city suit, city wingtip shoes, a city maroon-and-navy-striped tie that fluttered in the stiff spring breeze.

He turned, and her hand tightened on the door frame.

It was Martin Geary. The man who had once been engaged to Clover.

The man who had turned to Crimson, that first night, while she was still dripping dirty river water, while she was still coughing mud from her lungs, and cried, "It was *you*! *You* talked her into this, didn't you?"

He'd apologized later. A hundred times. But he'd thought it, he'd said it and, as the saying went, no one could unring that bell.

Besides, she knew he was right. She'd talked Clover into jumping off that bridge. It would be fun. A lark. A little final crazy mischief to celebrate the graduation to adulthood, responsibility and the future as partners in "Crimson and Clover," an upscale restaurant in San Francisco.

Clover wouldn't ever have done it on her own. Clover wasn't a risk-taker. She wasn't a fool.

Crimson was.

After the funeral, she and Martin had parted on civil terms, but there'd been no misunderstanding about the future. She didn't want to have any contact with him, not ever. And the feeling was mutual.

So she couldn't fathom what he was doing here.

It couldn't be a coincidence that he showed up on this date. And yet, he hadn't come or called last year. He hadn't even called on the anniversary of Clover's death.

So why now?

Surely he knew better than to think she'd be interested in wallowing in their loss together. If he suddenly, belatedly wanted to get maudlin about Clover's birthday, he could do it alone. She certainly didn't intend to hold hands and tell funny stories about her sister. She had no interest in group hugs, or crying on each other's shoulders and pretending that would make the pain go away.

She *prayed* he knew better than that.

But if not to mark the birthday...then *what*?

She couldn't even bring herself to smile a welcome at him as he walked toward the door. He *wasn't* welcome.

He didn't seem surprised by her lack of warmth. As his taxi peeled away and retraced its path down the drive, he just kept walking stolidly toward her.

At least he didn't have a suitcase in his hand. Whatever he wanted, he expected to be able to get it done quickly.

He stopped at the foot of the front steps.

"Hi, Crimmy," he said soberly. "It's good to see you."

She cringed. *No.* She wanted to shout the word. *No!* Not *Crimmy.* Everyone who had the right to call her that was dead. Her grandmother had invented the name when Crimson and Clover were orphaned, at only three years old. But her grandmother had died long ago, too old already when she took the girls in to have any real chance of seeing them to adulthood.

So by the time they were seventeen, only the twins had remained, and they had to be everything to one another—parent, grandparent, sister, friend.

When Martin was engaged to Clover, maybe she'd granted him the right to use their pet names. But Clover was dead now, too. All connection was severed. Crimson Slayton and Martin Geary were nothing to one another.

She wouldn't dream of calling him Marty anymore, either. Not in a million years.

"Hello, Martin."

"You look terrific, Crimson," he said, making a point to adjust the name.

Good decision. She smiled grimly. No one had ever said Martin Geary was stupid. Clover would never have loved a stupid man.

She wondered if he meant it, about how she looked. Around here, people gushed about how her beauty was blooming, but that was only because she'd finally stopped doing such weird things with her hair.

Martin had never seen her that way—when she looked more like an anime character than a real person, her head covered in red-tipped hedgehog spikes. He'd never met Crimson Slash, the pool-playing tattoo artist.

He'd known only "silly Crimmy," the fun-loving, slightly reckless, wildly outspoken pastry chef in training, who wore her long brown hair halfway down her back, just like her sister's.

"Thank you," she said, deciding not to believe it. "You look well, too. But I have to admit I'm surprised to see you. What are you doing in Silverdell?"

He glanced toward the interior of the house. "I was hoping to talk to you."

"About what?"

"Crimson." He raised one eyebrow, calling her bluff.

Suddenly, out of nowhere, she had a terrible, primitive urge to slap him. To slap that look off his face. She remembered so well the nights the three of them had sat around the sisters' apartment, drinking cheap wine and tasting their newest concoctions, while she and Clover tried to master that cool eyebrow trick.

Crimson had learned quickly. Clover was still trying to get the hang of it when she died.

But the gust of primal rage blew out as fast as it blew in. Crimson wasn't going to slap anybody.

And she wasn't going to keep him standing out here like some pushy magazine salesman.

It was going to be a chilly evening. She folded her sweater over her breasts, and her arms over that, but in spite of the rebuff of her body language, she tried to smile. She was going to be a civilized human being. She was going to be kind, because Clover would have wanted her to be.

"Why don't we talk inside?" she said.

Nodding, he climbed the stairs. He followed her in, glancing around curiously. "Nice," he said. "Great old house. It suits you."

"It's not mine," she said. "It belongs to a friend."

It occurred to her, belatedly, to wonder *how* he'd found her, but she didn't want to waste time on that. What difference did it make? Someone knew something, someone had said something. Heck, maybe he even hired a detective to find her, just as she and Grant had hired one to locate Molly's mother.

The important question was *why*? What did he want?

From the beginning, she'd offered him part of the insurance settlement.

But Martin had adamantly refused. He was fine, financially, and he knew Clover had intended for Crimson to have the money, if it were ever necessary to carry on with their restaurant dream alone.

Was that it? Was he here to ask her why she

hadn't followed through? Maybe he felt that, since she hadn't opened the restaurant, he deserved some of the money, after all.

Fine. Her purse was within reach, and if he said one word about the insurance, she'd whip out the check and toss it in his lap. It would be a relief to have the matter finally settled.

Wordlessly, she led him toward the kitchen. She could at least offer him something to eat. He'd always liked her blueberry pie, and if the ranch hands hadn't finished it off while she was in Montrose, she should have a piece or two left in the fridge.

Molly was napping upstairs, so she'd assumed she wouldn't have to discuss all that. But as they passed the living room, where the empty playpen was set up and littered with toys, he stopped in his tracks.

He turned a brilliant smile her way. "You have a *baby*?"

Whatever trail he'd followed hadn't included a lot of details, then.

"No," she said flatly. "I told you, this isn't my house. And it's not my child. I'm…" She didn't feel up to explaining the whole wretched mess. "I'm babysitting, essentially. Look, are you hungry? I think I have some pie."

"Yes." His smile was conciliatory. "That would be great."

She let him sit at the breakfast table and made

him a cup of coffee to go with the pie. She sat, too, and she managed to make small talk long enough to let him get about half of the slice down. But when he started offering effusive compliments on her baking, she ran out of patience.

"Martin, that's very sweet of you, and it's nice to see you, really. But I've got a lot to do today, and I can't just sit and socialize. It's time to tell me why you're here."

Nodding, he wiped his mouth slowly. Taking a deep breath, he turned a level gaze her way. "I came because I wanted to be the one to tell you. I'm…"

Finally, he blinked, and she knew he'd reached the moment this whole thing had been leading to.

"I've met someone, Crimson. Her name's Margaret. She's wonderful. I think you'd like her." He blinked again. "I think Clover would like her."

He thought Clover would like her? Ice water moved slowly through Crimson's veins. Everything, from her pulse to her thought processes, seemed to slow.

"And?"

"And I'm in love. It's not the same as it was with Clover, of course. It couldn't be the same, because there's no one like Clover—there could never be. But Margaret is a good person. She's beautiful, inside and out."

He paused as if he were trying to sell her something and wanted to find the perfect hook. "She's a doctor, a pediatrician. She loves dogs, and the Beatles and…" He smiled. "And, for some reason, me."

She didn't smile back. *"And?"*

A pulse beat in his jaw. But there was no avoiding it anymore.

"And we're getting married next week."

GRANT HAD BEEN so glad to get home he almost didn't notice the taxi pulling into the driveway, immediately behind his own. It was dark, and he was busy trying to just extricate his folded wad of bills from his wallet, much less count them accurately with one hand.

It wasn't until he emerged and spotted the stranger leaving from his front door that he realized what was going on. His shoulders tightened, but he quickly saw that, whoever this guy was, he wasn't Rory. So he lightened up a little.

Still…who the hell was he?

The two men met each other on the walkway. Grant, his garment bag slung over his shoulder, and his cast in the sling for a change, because his arm had been aching, stopped and gave the other man a smile.

"Were you looking for me?" he asked politely.

"No." The stranger gave him a curious once-over. "Well…wait. Is this your house?"

If Grant hadn't been so tired, that might have struck him as funny.

"Yeah," he said. "Grant Campbell, of Campbell Ranch. And you are…?"

"Martin Geary." The man started to offer a handshake, but realized just in time that Grant's right hand was encased in plaster. "I'm…"

He frowned, as if he'd forgotten his lines. "I'm a friend of Crimson's."

"Okay…" Grant heard the tension, the odd clutch when Martin said the word *friend*. What was that all about? Was *friend* a euphemism? Was he an old boyfriend? A *current* boyfriend?

No. Crimson didn't have a current boyfriend. Not even Kevin, as he—and everyone else—had assumed.

She'd been telling the truth when she said that she and Kevin weren't an item…not romantically, not physically.

Even if Kevin might have hoped for more, she'd never promised him anything like that.

If she had, she wasn't the kind of woman who would… She wouldn't have…

Wouldn't have what? Kissed him the other night? Why not? It had just been a thank-you kiss, a peck on the lips between friends.

Hadn't it?

"Speaking of Crimson, where is she?" He glanced toward the house, but there was no sign of anyone at the door, or even at a window, waving goodbye. The house was strangely dark. "Is she inside with Molly?"

"No." Martin Geary cleared his voice. "She left a little while ago, with the baby. She said she had to drive to Montrose. I had called a cab, but she... well, she seemed in a hurry, and she wasn't able to wait till my taxi got here. She showed me how to lock the door."

Grant was frowning, finding this hard to believe. He hoped she hadn't given this guy the security system code.

Geary gestured toward the checkered cab. "But it seems my ride is here, unless you came home in two taxis just now." Smiling, he edged around Grant. "Well, I'm sure the meter is running already. So I guess I'd better get going."

He walked a couple of steps, and Grant decided to let him go. Any questions he had, he'd ask Crimson. But when Martin was no more than a couple of yards away, he stopped and turned back, silhouetted in the beams of the taxi's headlights.

"Campbell," he said.

"Yes?"

"Just..." The silhouette jammed his hands in his pockets and shrugged. "Just be nice to her."

Grant cocked his head. That was an odd, and oddly irritating, statement. Who was this guy to instruct him on how to handle Red?

"I usually am," he said.

"I mean...be extra nice to her *today*. Birthdays...anniversaries...I'm not sure what you even call days like this. Whatever the right word is, milestones are hard."

"Anniversaries? Birthdays?"

A surprised hesitation. "Oh. *Wow.* She hasn't told you about her sister?"

Grant shook his head, but on some deep level he wasn't really shocked. Around here, apparently, no one told anybody anything. They might as well have been cloistered, living under a vow of silence.

"I didn't even know she has a sister."

"Had. She… She… *Damn it…"* Martin ran his hand through his hair, looking frazzled, as if it were all too complicated to unravel with a stranger, especially with the two taxis idling impatiently behind them—his cab waiting for him, and Grant's cab blocked by the second car and unable to make an exit.

"Crimson *had* a sister. An identical twin. Clover died just a little over a year ago. Today is her… today is *their* birthday." The taxi driver honked, flashing his lights irritably. Martin waved, signaling he'd be right there. "I probably shouldn't have told you, but…"

"It's okay," Grant said. "I'm glad to know."

The other man nodded uncertainly. He shrugged again and loped off toward his cab, a jogging shadow flickering through first one set of headlights and then another.

Grant watched him go and then went into the

house to turn on the lights and set down his suitcase. The fact that she hadn't even waited to see Martin safely off painted a disturbing picture of Crimson's state of mind. She hadn't just left. She'd fled.

He had planned to take a short rest, maybe grab some food, before going out to visit with Dawn. He'd been looking forward to it.

Suddenly, none of that appealed to him.

From the foyer table's cluttered drawers, he unearthed the keys to an old, battered Chevy. He rarely used that car, because it was one gasp away from needing a new transmission. But it was the only vehicle on the ranch right now that wasn't a stick shift—and his arm really was aching.

Before he left, he called Crimson's cell phone, but it went to voice mail. So he made his way to Montrose as fast as the old rattletrap could take him. Maybe her phone was off because she was still in Kevin's room. Maybe Grant would get lucky, and he'd find her there. Even if she told him nothing about her sister, or why today was significant, he still wanted her to know she wasn't alone.

He parked in a no-parking spot, not caring about any ticket he might get. When he reached the lobby, he pounded repeatedly on the elevator button with the heel of his left hand, as if he could bully it into descending faster.

He didn't stop to talk to any of the nurses, a couple of whom looked surprised and disappointed. But when he reached Kevin's room, no one but the sleeping man was in it.

"Were you looking for Crimson?" The pretty red-haired nurse appeared in the doorway. "She left, oh, I don't know…maybe half an hour ago?"

"Was she okay?"

The nurse frowned. "I guess so. I mean, she looked fine. I'm not sure exactly what—" She raised her shoulders helplessly, and then moved to steadier ground. "Mr. Ellison is doing very well," she said, her voice bright, as if she were glad to offer him the news as a consolation prize.

"He is?" Grant looked toward the bed. It all looked the same to him. The same thin, immobile stretch of anonymous human outline beneath the institutional blanket. The same whirring, beeping machines. The same glistening drip of what might well have been the same plastic bag of nameless fluid from the IV stand.

"Oh, yes." The nurse came in briskly and went over to plump Kevin's pillows. "The doctor was very pleased. We opened our eyes today, didn't we?" Still bent over the unconscious man, she shot a smile toward Grant. "Twice!"

And so, of course, Grant couldn't just indulge his own selfish desires. He couldn't simply run out the door, as if Kevin weren't a real person, as if the unconscious man didn't need care and friendship, maybe even more than Crimson did.

Grant's burning instinct to find her, to be with her...all that had to be set aside for a little while.

He pulled up a chair, sat down and started telling Kevin about his day.

By the time he made it back to Silverdell, and to the ranch, it was almost midnight. The birthday, if that's really what it had been, was nearly over.

Crimson's rental car stood in the driveway, its engine cold when he laid his palm on it. Crimson had been home a long time, then.

He let himself into the house quietly, determined not to wake her if she'd been lucky enough to get to sleep. The house was quiet, so he assumed she had. He moved through the house toward the kitchen. He was almost dizzy with hunger and weariness, and he hoped the men had left him a crumb or two.

But as he passed the great room, he paused. A slender form stretched out on the sofa, and he turned toward the sight, his body recognizing her even before his brain did.

Crimson. Her soft blue nightshirt glowed a little in the moonlight, and, below it, her long legs stretched out like pale stalks.

He moved closer, and the details gradually took shape. She was sound asleep. The graceful oval of her face looked very young, without the strong-willed determination that shone from her eyes when she was awake.

For a minute, as he saw the unnatural darkness under those beautiful eyes, he held his breath...

Had Geary hurt her? But then he exhaled roughly. It was only mascara, smeared from too much crying.

One slim arm was tucked under her head, and the other was folded against her chest. Her hand was fisted tightly, clutching a crumpled white tissue.

He let his gaze slowly take in the rest...the other wrinkled white lumps dotting the floor, as if the ceiling had rained tissues. The baby monitor on its side, its amber light glowing. And next to it, washed with a sepia brown in the monitor's weak light—as if it were a relic from a hundred years ago—lay a small picture of Crimson.

But also somehow *not* Crimson. He bent closer. The girl in the picture smiled, but her smile was demure, shy, a shadow of the vibrant grin he knew.

This must be Clover. Her sister. Her lost twin.

A wave of sorrow moved through him. She'd endured this day all alone.

He knelt beside the sofa, awkwardly, because of his cast. With his good hand, he reached out to move the tangled brown hair from her face. Her lips were open...she must have cried so long she couldn't breathe through her nose anymore.

He bent his head, following instinct, not logic. He had no delusion that his kiss would work some fairy-tale magic. He was no prince. He was just a man who desperately longed to show her that he cared.

And he also had no delusions anymore about just how much he *did* care. She was still Crimson...still his friend. But she was so much more than that now.

Maybe she had always been more than that...

He had almost reached her. His lips had met the warm current of air from hers.

And then he heard the first squawk from the monitor. She twitched in her sleep, but her eyes didn't open.

Instinctively, he reached down and spun the volume dial so the crying wouldn't startle her. Molly was clearly waking in one of those rare fits of wretchedness—maybe from a bad dream, maybe a painful tooth—in which she didn't work her way up to a scream. On nights like these, she woke up already in full throttle.

Even with the volume down, her wailing was as loud as if she were right there in the room with them. The high-pitched, piercing sound rolled down the open stairwell in waves of misery.

And yet, amazingly, Crimson slept on.

He had never seen her this exhausted. She was limp, in a sleep deeper than sound, utterly spent.

Molly screamed on.

Grant stood. His heart thudded angrily in his chest, demanding to be removed from the noise, but he ignored it. He grabbed a quilt from a nearby chair, shook it open and spread it over Crimson's bare legs. He tugged it up to her chin.

And then he made his way to the stairs. He braced himself against the memories that cascaded over him.

He could do this. This wasn't Jeannie. It was time he stopped letting himself off the hook. He didn't have a monopoly on tragedy. He wasn't the only person in the world who was drowning in pain.

He wasn't even the only one in this house.

Crimson needed one thing from him tonight, and it wasn't a kiss, or any kind of sexual consolation. It wasn't even love.

What she needed was for him to step up and be an equal partner in this mess.

It seemed to take forever, but in real time he probably reached Crimson's bedroom door in a matter of seconds. In the glow from the night-light, Molly was red-faced and wet with tears. She'd rolled to her stomach and was trying to sit up. Her cries were weaker now, interrupted with hiccups and struggles for air.

At the sight of her, something squeezed painfully inside his chest. She was just a baby. Just a helpless baby who had no mother, and no father... and who had no idea that she reminded Grant of anyone else.

He reached into the crib with his good hand,

using his cast as a brace for her head, and lifted her gently.

"It's okay, sweetheart," he said, in the voice he'd always used when Jeannie was teething or colicky…or dying. "It's all right. I'm here."

CHAPTER TWELVE

CRIMSON HAD BEEN to several Bell River Ranch parties, and the Wright sisters always did things up right. But at this particular party, Alec's twelfth birthday celebration, Crimson had a whole new perspective.

This time, the Friday of what probably had been the toughest week of her life—at least since Clover—she decided that the best part of the Bell River dude ranch's operation was that they always offered first-rate babysitting.

The party was out here by Cupcake Creek, where the preteens could raise hell without driving the Bell River guests crazy. But all the babies and toddlers were back at the main house, lovingly tended by a team of young staffers hand-chosen by Rowena for the job.

"Frankly, I attribute all of Bell River's success to the babysitting," Rowena said, laughing as she leaned back against her husband, Dallas. She stretched luxuriously to celebrate being Rosie-free for a couple of hours. "Nothing ruins a family vacation faster than having to spend every single minute with your family."

Everyone at their picnic table joined in her

laughter. No woman on earth adored her kids more than Rowena Wright Garwood—but Rosie was as tricky to handle as a stick of dynamite.

The sun had set hours ago, and for the past twenty minutes or so, Crimson had been telling herself she ought to go home. One part of her missed Molly terribly. She missed the baby's warm cuddles, her infectious laughter and those adorable cooing sounds she made.

But another part of her hated to leave this little haven. It was a relief not to be responsible for anything or anyone, just for a few hours. The past week had been...

Well, it had been tough.

Even though Becky had her own quarters, having her living at the ranch was stressful—not because she was unpleasant, but because she was so profoundly unhappy. Crimson tried to include her in anything she did, like cooking, or outings to the park with Molly. And every time they were together, Crimson could feel her internal struggle.

Becky never admitted she regretted filing a complaint against Rory, but she was obviously torn. She'd loved him, and she wasn't the type who could turn that off like a spigot.

Crimson's unacknowledged birthday, and seeing Martin, had been unsettling, too, of course. And then there was Kevin. The early promise of the twitches and the eye movement hadn't turned into anything yet. When she'd gone to Montrose this morning, the doctors had admitted he wasn't much better. If anything, the initial hope was fading.

Plus, Grant was expecting to hear from his PI any minute now, and that anxiety was taking a toll, too. What would Anne Smith be like? How would she react to the news? Molly's future seemed to hang in the balance.

So, though she hated to admit it, Crimson was emotionally wiped out. An evening of being catered to and waited on by the well-trained, cheerful Bell River staff was sheer heaven.

Around the edge of the big glamour tent—where Alec and his friends would camp out tonight—Crimson caught a glimpse of the sparkle of starlight on the creek. The peaceful beauty of it called to her, a rare occurrence since Clover's death, so she set down her punch and stood.

Belle, who sat next to her, looked up with a question in her glance. "You're not leaving already!"

Shaking her head, Crimson smiled. "I just feel like moving around a little."

Belle nodded. Though her feet were on her chair, with her knees tucked under her chin, she tried to lean forward enough to scan the grounds.

"I think I saw Grant a few minutes ago...maybe over by the moon walk? I think he had shoe duty."

Crimson glanced at the big red inflated bounce house. Sure enough, Grant was standing guard, counting heads and making sure the children who entered remembered to remove their shoes. Right now he was laughing as he tried to help a little boy tug off a pair of cowboy boots that were more than he could handle.

For a minute, watching him, Crimson could barely breathe. His smile, his eyes…they seemed to sparkle with starlight, too.

"Yep, there he is, probably hoping some kind soul will come and rescue him." Belle's voice was oddly arch. "Poor guy. Maybe you should go see if he'd like to take a break."

Crimson glanced at Grant one more time. In some ways he was just another emotional complication, wasn't he? When they were together, she couldn't stop feeling things that didn't make sense…

So she decided to enjoy the creek by herself.

To avoid him, she took the long way, skirting a cluster of kids screaming with pleasure as they raced around in a game of tag. She recognized it as the preteen version of courtship. At twelve, this was the best the boys could do when they wanted to show a girl they were interested.

And vice versa, apparently. Little Katie Landringham was like a heat-seeking missile, her arms always reaching for Alec. And she wasn't the only one. Blond, blue-eyed Alec had that special combination of a pretty face and a badass attitude that made preteen girls swoon.

Crimson kept walking until the shrieking faded. She followed a small bend in the creek, and then, realizing she was surrounded by silence, she stopped.

Above her, the clear, starry night seemed immense. A line of ancient pine trees crowded the horizon, on both the eastern and the western sides of the creek. Though she knew the dude ranch was just beyond the trees, it seemed a million miles away. She couldn't even see the lights of the cabins through the maze of leafy branches.

Slowly, she relaxed. The week's tension drained away, until she felt light…almost hollow, in fact. As if she were an empty room that had been swept clean.

Out here, with no one looking, she had no facade to maintain, no feelings to hide, no decisions to make. It was odd, how different she felt once those things were gone. Without guilt, tension, stress and pretense, who was Crimson Slayton?

Apparently, she was no one. Here in the darkness she felt like another shadow, a wisp of mist. She felt as insubstantial as if she were a floating bit of dandelion fluff. Almost invisible…

It should have felt fabulous and free. Instead, it felt strangely frightening, as if she might truly disappear, might fade from translucent to transparent, like a ghost. As if she might blow away and never be missed.

She folded her arms over her chest, clutching

her elbows just to feel the reassuring solidity of her own skin. And somehow, finally, she understood that this life she'd chosen was no life at all.

Clover was gone, and all the dreams she and Clover had shared were gone, too. She couldn't change that. But whether she liked it or not, whether she thought fate had made a terrible mistake or not, *she* was still here.

And unless she wanted to waste decades as an empty, papery husk, useless to the world and tossed about by every wind, she was going to have to find something meaningful to do with her life.

She was going to have to find a new purpose, a new goal. Not a person...never another risk like that. But a cause, a mission—that would be safe enough.

Yes. Just the idea seemed to restore substance to her body, seemed to anchor her feet more securely to the ground. When she left Silverdell, which, God willing, would be very soon, she wouldn't simply drop a pen blindly onto a map. She would find some worthwhile cause she could dedicate her energies to—without risking her heart.

"*There* you are! I was beginning to think you'd been abducted by wolves."

At the unexpected voice, she turned her head sharply. Grant was walking toward her, his footsteps crushing the flora, sending the scent of honey flooding into the night air. "I've been looking for you everywhere. If Belle hadn't happened to notice you heading out this way…"

"Oh. I'm sorry. I didn't realize I'd been gone so long." She made a show of checking her watch. "I was just about to go back to the party."

Oh, Belle, she thought inwardly, *what are you up to?* Matchmaking? It surprised her. Most people assumed Crimson had been getting serious with Kevin before the accident.

But maybe Belle had been a little more perceptive than "most people." She was a quiet woman, but she was always watching.

Besides, people in love were notorious for trying to partner up everyone around them.

Belle, please. Don't. That was such a dangerous game.

"I'm sorry to drag you out all this way to find me," she said politely. "You should just have texted me that it was time to go."

"Go? I didn't come out here because I want to leave. I came out here to be with you."

She opened her mouth. Then she closed it. She couldn't think of an answer that didn't sound rude…or encouraging. She was too emotionally wrung out to walk that fine line.

He didn't seem to expect an answer, though. With his hands in the pockets of his jacket, he gazed contemplatively over her shoulder, down toward the creek.

"I love this river," he said. "I looked at a dozen

properties when I was ready to buy. I think what sealed the deal was realizing one little sliver of one little offshoot of Bell River ran through the acres I bought."

She nodded meaninglessly, only half sure what he'd said. Inside her brain, alarms were going off. They should leave. Go back to the party. Immediately.

Looking at their surroundings through his eyes, she suddenly saw that this secluded nook of the creek cried out for romance. It had been made for skinny-dipping, and then for making love, soaking wet and moon-washed, on the wildflower-dotted grass.

She folded her arms across her chest and tightened her lips. She wouldn't indulge in fantasies like that. She didn't want to be out here with him—she didn't want these feelings.

It was the starlight, she told herself. But she knew that wasn't true. By Molly's crib, in the kitchen, out in the pastures under a noonday sun... it was all the same. She felt this way whenever Grant was close enough to touch.

"Come on. We're here. It's gorgeous. Let's stay awhile." He smiled. "You can't really want to go back yet. Surely you've had enough whooping, squealing kids for the moment?"

She smiled. She didn't say yes, but she couldn't quite say no, either. Her brain and her heart wouldn't agree on the appropriate answer.

But silence was its own form of acquiescence, and he obviously knew that. He moved a few feet to a level spot and then took off his jacket and spread it on the ground. The tall, thick grass bunched under the fabric like pillow stuffing. He gestured toward it, and after a moment's hesitation she sat, sinking down as if it were a featherbed.

Even stretched out, the jacket wasn't wide enough to let them sit very far apart. When he joined her, their shoulders touched, and the scent of him seemed to surround her—slightly citrus, with a sweet hint of sawdust. It mixed with the honey from the white clover beneath them to create an unforgettable perfume.

He settled back on one elbow with a sigh, as if his foot still pained him a little. His right leg was cocked up, and he let his cast rest on his knee. The effect was that his body tilted slightly toward her, and a shiver passed down the side of her body where they touched.

They sat without talking for several minutes, just watching the creek. The moonlight on the water was sharp, glassy, as if the tumbling stream were full of diamonds. It turned the large, wet stones to gleaming chunks of black opal.

"So," he said suddenly, breaking the silence. "Stefan finally made an offer on Dawn."

She turned toward him, a quick flash of dismay streaking through her like adrenaline. As if her

body were responding to a fight-or-flight stimulus. "He did?"

Grant nodded. He bent over to pluck a small
white flower from the grass. Then he twirled it
in his fingers, first one way and then the other.

She frowned, tightening her arms across her
chest. "Don't play games. He made an offer...
and?"

He grinned, the starlight reflecting in the whites
of his eyes as his laugh lines shifted. "And it was
way too low. I rejected it."

"Rejected it outright? No counter offer?"

He shook his head. "No counter offer." He took
a deep breath that sounded as if it came from a
very satisfied man. "I'm keeping her. Financially,
it'll be touch and go for a while, but if all the stars
align I should be okay."

She let out a breath. "Oh, I'm *so* glad," she said.
"She's one of a kind. You two belong together."

"Yeah." He still looked at the creek, but he was
nodding slowly. "The thing is, I finally decided...
what's the point of monetary success if you have
to give up everything you care about to achieve
it?"

She smiled wryly. "I wouldn't know much
about monetary success, at any price. Maybe you
should ask Stefan."

He chuckled, of course, as she'd intended him
to.

"I would, but he went back to California this

afternoon in a bit of a huff. Apparently, he thought his offer was just opening the negotiation, not ending it. I had a hard time convincing him I wasn't playing hard to get."

He slanted a glance at her. "The guy isn't very good at taking no for an answer."

"No," she agreed. "But then, he probably hasn't had much practice."

Out of the corner of her eye she could see his amused smile, and suddenly she felt the gloom lift just a tiny bit.

Grant had found a way to keep Dawn…

Finally, something had gone right.

A large dark bird flew past them, its wings beating the scented air. Its silhouette skimmed the surface of the creek gracefully, the tips of its wings gleaming.

Grant stood as if he wanted to watch its progress. He walked a few feet down the sloping bank, drawing closer to the burbling creek. She stood, too, and joined him there.

They watched together, transfixed, as the bird beat on, following the creek bed, tracing every looping curve of the long ribbon until, finally, it disappeared from sight.

Oh, the independence in that wingspread! The self-determination in that flight!

Impulsively, Crimson bent over and slipped off her shoes. Holding them in her hands, she moved toward the water, where the rocks offered a natural stairway down to the creek. Maybe she'd wade in at the edge. Just for a minute…just to prove to herself that she could.

It had been so long…

But the instant her toes touched the cold water, her lungs turned to lead. Her heart throbbed wildly in her chest. Seen from this close, the creek was black and much deeper than she'd realized. She felt the mud of the bank give under her toes, and she smelled the familiar organic musk of vegetation. She tasted the metallic bitterness of mud and fear…

She couldn't. The water… *She couldn't.*

She scrambled backward, like rewinding a film, leading with her heels, retreating blindly up the bank she'd just descended.

She was a fool. She should have known she wouldn't be able to do it.

She hadn't been in any water deeper than a bathtub since Clover died. What on earth had made her even consider this?

Confused, she began to put her shoes back on. Coming out here had been foolish. *Staying* out here, in this intimacy with Grant, had been a huge, huge mistake.

She hadn't been wrong. She did need to change her life. But she had to be careful—baby steps… nothing but baby steps or she might find herself in over her head once again. She might find herself waking up from nightmares with pieces of her broken heart in her hands.

Grant came down to her, to where she was wrestling with her shoe. Her wet foot didn't seem to fit inside it anymore.

"Are you okay?" He seemed perplexed by her sudden clumsy hurry. He put his hand under her elbow, as if he feared she might fall.

She nodded, swallowing hard and fighting to keep her breathing normal. "I'm fine. It's just... It's just..."

"Too cold?"

"Yes." She snatched at the excuse. "Yes, it's much too cold."

"I should have warned you," he said. "Last year, my little tributary wasn't warm enough to wade in till at least August."

She nodded, but she didn't dare speak. She needed to get out of here. She hoped he would think her change of mood was just what he'd said...that the water was like ice.

He still had his hand under her elbow. She could feel his thumb grazing the edge of her breast. Shivers cascaded through her, raising goose bumps, making her nerve endings thrum.

This was dangerous. The way he made her feel was dangerous. Without even realizing he was doing it, he'd find a way to make her take risks... to wander down to the dangerous bank of passion, of caring...of love.

No. And no, and no again. She needed a direction—not a lover. A purpose, not another tragedy. She didn't want to *feel*…she wanted to *do*. She needed purpose. Tasks. Noise and strangers and more work than she could handle.

"I should go now," she said. Her voice was thin and tight.

"No," he said softly. "Please don't." He tightened his hand on her arm. "I wanted to say…I am so sorry about your sister. I wish you'd told me. The other night, when I told you about Brenda, you could have—"

She jerked her head back, as if he'd slapped her. "How do you know about my sister?"

"The man who came to visit the other day… Martin something?"

She nodded warily.

"He was leaving as I got home, and I think he felt awkward. So he explained why he'd come. He told me it was your birthday, and that the day probably be difficult for you, because your sister was gone. He said she was your twin."

She nodded. "Yes." She had to say something. She had to offer something, or it would seem unforgivably rude. He was being very kind. "Clover. She…she died. But it was more than a year ago. So really. There's no need to—"

But Grant wasn't buying that. He began to stroke his thumb across her skin, and she felt it tingle warmly.

"Red, it doesn't matter how long it's been. It's always going to be difficult. And I want you to know that I really do understand. And I care."

She looked at him, and she realized she was shaking her head.

"It's not the same. What happened to your wife…what happened to my sister…it's not the same."

"Isn't it?"

"No," she said. "Or if it is, it doesn't matter. It doesn't change anything. It's not as if we can…"

"Red. Don't."

She wasn't sure what he meant, but somehow the word made her stop talking.

She could hardly bear to keep looking at him, and yet she couldn't look away. His expression held such a compelling, strangely erotic mixture of tenderness and fire.

His hand tugged softly, easing her toward him. Her muddy, cold toes stumbled slightly on the slick rocks, and that only brought them closer together.

He was going to kiss her. But first his eyes… he seemed to be reaching inside her and trying to find her soul.

And she felt strangely helpless to stop the probing.

He was too…too powerful. Everything female in her strained toward his masculine sexuality.

It would have been so easy to surrender. So easy to pretend they were just two normal people about to kiss on the bank of a beautiful, star-lit creek. So easy to pretend they were just two normal people hovering on the brink of a beautiful love affair.

So easy…and so *wrong*.

"No. Stop. I don't want to do this."

He tilted his head, and she knew he didn't believe her. He was obviously reading signals that weren't being expressed in anything as simple as words.

But he didn't pull her any closer, obviously aware that, whatever he believed her body was saying, if her words said no that was the only thing that mattered.

"Okay," he said softly. He studied her face, and those questioning eyes seemed to demand an explanation.

She frowned, wondering how to explain. "Look, Grant. I know you imagine we'd make a good couple because…because we're both broken."

"Imagine?" He smiled a little. "Am I really just *imagining* that?"

"Yes. And you have the idealistic, poetic notion that if you put two broken things together, somehow, as if by magic, they'll make each other whole."

He raised his eyebrows. "Isn't it possible I'm right?"

"No." She shook her head over and over. "No, no, no."

"Crimson, you know we…" His thumb was warm against the inside of her elbow. "There's just no point denying—"

"I'm not denying *anything*. I see what's happening between us. We're both lonely. And we want to believe that two wounded people could come together and heal each other. But it won't work like that. It won't heal us any more than putting two blind people together would suddenly make them able to see."

He was shaking his head now, too. "You're trying to use logic, because being analytical instead of emotional makes you feel safe. I understand that. But what's happening between us isn't—"

"No." Roughly, she pulled her arm free. She had to break the magnetic hold he seemed to have on her…before it was too late. "Don't you see? Even if I weren't leaving Silverdell the minute we find Molly's mother, we'd still be the worst possible people in the world for each other."

"Why?" His brows were low over his eyes. "I honestly *don't* see. *Why?*"

"Because…" She stared down at the dark creek, which no longer held even a sliver of starlight. "A person who can't swim can't save someone who's drowning. Trying to isn't just stupid. It's suicide."

THE PACKAGE FROM Tarleton came by courier around noon the next day, just about the time

Grant had given up and resigned himself to waiting until Monday to get any news.

When the truck drove in through the gates, Grant was behind the stables, standing between two paddocks. He had been alternating between watching Barley work Dawn on his right, and keeping an eye on the new foal, still nameless, on his left.

When the courier loped across the grass toward him, Grant felt a frisson of excitement. The Anne Smith they'd pinpointed had turned out to be the right one, and Tarleton had specific news. The PI always communicated "nothing yet" by email, but he used a courier when he had something important to share. He was old school and didn't like to send sensitive information over the internet, which he insisted was "as leaky as a spaghetti strainer."

Too impatient to wait until he got back into his office, where he had a sensible letter opener, Grant tipped the courier and sent him on his way. Then he took the edge of the packet between his teeth and tore.

One day, watching him peel off a work glove with his teeth, Crimson had accused him of going feral, becoming part animal, part man. But Grant had just laughed. He'd found that a strong set of teeth compensated nicely for his useless right arm.

Spitting out the nasty, gluey bit onto the grass beside him, he tucked the envelope under his cast and extricated the papers with his good hand.

Tarleton was always thorough, so there were at least a dozen pages of text. Even more photos. He read enough to get the general idea. Then he curled the whole collection up as if he intended to swat a fly and started walking away.

"She's out in the barn," Barley said. The older man had obviously been watching every move Grant made, even though he'd appeared focused on the horse. "With the little blonde."

"Thanks." Grant waved the papers over his shoulder. "I know where she is."

Behind him, he heard Barley chuckle. "Well, of *course* you do."

Grant almost stopped to ask him what he meant by that, but why pretend? He knew what Barley meant. Awareness of Crimson had become almost like some kind of sixth sense for Grant. No matter what else was going on, one part of his brain was always conscious of where she was and what she was doing.

He was just surprised that Barley had noticed it. He smiled wryly to himself as he walked, hoping the old man wouldn't start lobbying for Grant to keep Crimson, too. It was bad enough that the old man felt free to give Grant advice about horses. At least the horses were under Grant's control.

"Keeping" Crimson wasn't his call. She'd made that crystal clear last night.

As he approached the barn, he heard laughter coming from the manager's suite, followed by the chortle of a happy baby. He inhaled, smelling something sweet and tart, like apples. Were the two of them cooking in there? He knew how barebones that tiny kitchen was, but he also knew that Crimson could probably create a feast with nothing but a square of tin foil and a Bunsen burner.

He rapped his knuckles sharply on the door, hoping to be heard over the laughter. He didn't usually interrupt when she was with Becky—well aware that her company was like therapy for the unhappy young woman. But Crimson would want to read Tarleton's information right away.

Becky answered the door with a bright smile. Her bruises were fading, and she looked as if she might have added back one or two of the pounds she'd lost in the first few days after leaving Rory.

"Hey, Grant! Come on in. You're just in time for apple cobbler!"

"Sorry," he said, sincerely. "I'm not going to be able to stay. I just need to see Crimson a minute. Barley said she might be with you."

"I'm here." Crimson came around the corner of the kitchen wall, her hands still encased in oven mitts. She smiled, but it was guarded. Though their encounter at the creek last night had ended without ugliness, they'd been stiff and formal with each other ever since.

"Hi." He did his best to sound natural. He still wasn't convinced that her logic had made sense last night, but he knew that wasn't the point. It didn't matter whether he believed it. What mattered was that she did.

"I wondered if we could talk for a few minutes." He lifted the papers so that she could see how extensive they were. "I've had a report from Tarleton."

She began pulling off the oven mitts instantly, her eyes wide. "Of course." She glanced back toward the kitchen, biting her lower lip. "Darn. The cobbler won't be ready for another twenty minutes. And, Becky, you said you have to leave for work soon, right, so you can't watch it?"

Becky looked from one of them to the other. Clearly realizing something important was happening, she smiled reassuringly.

"Actually, I ought to leave right now, so why don't you guys talk here while the food finishes? I mean...it's your apartment, after all."

She scooped up a black leather shoulder bag from the end table nearest the door. She hugged Crimson quickly and bent down to Molly's blanket to give her a goodbye kiss on the nose.

At the door, she turned back with one last grin. "Be sure to save me some of that cobbler, though! Don't you guys dare eat it all!"

When she was gone, Crimson eagerly held out her hands for the report. She began reading even as she made her way across the small living room toward the well-worn sofa that had been there when Grant bought the ranch…and probably decades before that, too.

"Oh, Anne is lovely!" Crimson sounded surprised…and relieved. He knew she wasn't using *lovely* in the sense of *good-looking*. She meant that Molly's mother looked normal. Modest, sensible, sane. Maybe intelligent enough to talk sense to.

As she lowered herself onto the sofa, Crimson almost sat on one of Molly's teething rings, absorbed in her reading. Grant snatched it out of the way just in time. It was cold and wet, frozen a few minutes ago but thawing quickly, and would have given her quite a shock.

He reached down and handed it to the baby, who ignored it completely. Molly was far more interested in a square of sunlight on the blanket, with dust motes swimming in it.

Crimson read a few more paragraphs. She glanced up at Grant with her mouth slightly open. "Oh, good Lord. She's so *young*!"

"I know. Just turned nineteen when Molly was born, right?" Grant took a seat beside her on the sofa, though the old springs creaked in protest at their combined weight. He hadn't taken time to read the report thoroughly out in the pasture, so he sat close enough to look over her shoulder.

He read the date on the first page. "No…she was still eighteen then. She turned nineteen about a month ago."

"So…when Molly was conceived…"

"Right."

God, what a mess! Grant could have kicked Kevin for being such a fool. Kevin was Grant's age—thirty-one. What on earth had he been doing, romancing an eighteen-year-old girl and getting her pregnant?

Crimson's face was thoughtful as she flipped through the several pages of pictures of Anne Elaine Smith. She looked at every one, and then went through them all over again.

Grant wasn't sure what Crimson saw, but to him, the most remarkable thing about Anne was how *un*remarkable she was. She looked more or less like every other healthy, middle-class American female. Attractive enough, he supposed. Trim. Curvy without making a fuss about it. Bright-eyed. Good teeth and a great smile.

To Grant, she looked like one of those generic coeds a state university would feature on the cover of its brochure. Pretty enough to subliminally promise the boys a full social life, but meek enough to assure their parents it would all be okay.

The second time through, Crimson stopped at one photo and stared at it a long time. The shot was dated just yesterday, which made it seem particularly alive and relevant. It showed Anne in front of a dental office, dressed in a set of brightly colored scrubs, printed all over with smiling cows. She was holding the door open, but had squatted down to console a little boy who was crying, clearly afraid to enter the office.

She looked sweet-natured and good with kids. She did *not* look like a young woman who had recently abandoned her newborn daughter.

"She isn't at all what I was imagining," Crimson said softly. She ran her fingertips over the bouncing brunette ponytail, the kind of healthy, glossy, perfect hair one associated with cheerleaders and beauty queens. "Not even a little."

"No, me, either. When you say *pregnant Vegas teenager*, or *runaway mom*, my mind conjures up a very different image. Big bras, big hair…at the very least big makeup."

He glanced down at Molly, who seemed to be falling asleep on her blanket. "Sorry to talk about Mommy that way," he said, grinning. Then he transferred his smile to Crimson. "That's probably an unfair stereotype, huh? But the real Anne busts *all* the stereotypes."

Crimson nodded. "I agree. So…what do you think happened?"

"Well, these addresses indicate she moved away about the time she would have started to show." Tarleton had been extremely thorough, providing every known address for Anne Smith during the period between Molly's conception and today. He'd even provided the name of the dentist she'd worked for in Price, Utah, the small town where she'd lived while waiting for Molly to be born.

"And she seems to have moved home, to live with her parents, right after the birth. Tarleton didn't find any sign that she contested custody. She seems to have relinquished Molly willingly."

Grant still couldn't wrap his mind around it, actually. And apparently neither could Crimson, who kept staring at one picture of Anne after another, as if she were looking for clues.

"Do you suppose she ever even told her parents?"

"Hard to be sure," he said. "But it doesn't seem so. Looks as if she went back to Vegas after the birth and took up her life right where she left it. The dentist she works for now—the one whose office is in that picture—was the one she started working for right after high school." He ruffled through the edges of the pages, skimming them one more time.

"We can sit here all day, trying to figure it out, but it seems to me it's time to act." He leaned back against the sofa, tired of letting the pictures and facts and documents substitute for the real thing. "I think it's time to talk to Anne Smith ourselves. Don't you?"

Crimson let the papers drop onto her lap. "Yes," she said eagerly. "Your PI provided a cell number. Shall we call her now?"

He nodded. "I'd be glad to do it, but do you think she might find it easier to talk to a woman?"

Crimson seemed to see the logic of that. She extricated her phone from her pocket, glanced down at the papers from Tarleton and began punching in numbers.

She looked nervous…as if entering those digits into her cell terrified her. Then, putting it to her ear as she kept her gaze locked on Grant's, she gripped the cold rectangle so hard her knuckles went white.

It was intensely anticlimactic when, after seven or eight rings, he could just barely hear the distant sound of a voice mail message begin.

They should have thought of this. They should have prepared a script.

"Anne," Crimson began haltingly. "This is Crimson Slayton. You don't know me, but…"

She hesitated. She frowned at Grant, who nodded carefully. He knew she'd be circumspect. They'd never thought it was a good idea to spring the whole story at once, at least until they met her face-to-face and could make more informed judgments about her character.

"But I'd like to talk to you, if you could call me back. It's…it's about Kevin."

She swallowed, and then she recited her number, though of course it would already be in Anne's incoming call list. Grant knew she just needed something to say.

When she was finished, she swallowed again. "Thanks," she said. As if on impulse, she added, "I know this must be a surprise. But…it's important. I really hope you'll call."

CHAPTER THIRTEEN

SHE DIDN'T.

Crimson had been afraid of this, actually. Something in that perky, well-modulated voice seemed so determined to sound normal. To be normal. To be just another nineteen-year-old dental assistant, and not a secret unmarried mother.

They waited all day... Crimson called again. Grant did, too. But Anne never picked up, and she never returned their calls, no matter how many messages they left.

They debated whether they should phone the dentist's office, in case she was at work, though that seemed unlikely on a weekend. Or maybe they should phone her parents' house.

Ultimately they vetoed all of that and decided, instead, to make the trip to Vegas themselves. Maybe Anne Smith would find it more difficult to ignore them if they were standing right in front of her.

It was a full day's drive to Vegas, so they left early. It didn't take long to get ready. In addition to her own traveling bag, she'd kept a bag ready for Molly, complete with instructions for Marianne about feeding, her favorite toys, the position in which she found it easiest to fall asleep. But there were a hundred little things in a baby's life that were used on a daily basis and couldn't be packed away in advance.

They would drop Molly at the diner, which had the added benefit of giving them a chance to talk to Becky, who was filling in as waitress for early Sunday brunch today. Crimson wanted to be sure Becky wasn't nervous about being alone on the ranch all night.

When they arrived, Becky dismissed their concerns. Marianne, who had Molly in her arms, ready to go home and babysit while her staff ran the restaurant, assured them that Becky could spend the night with her, if she felt uncomfortable in any way.

Bristling like a kid told she's not old enough to climb a tree, Becky had insisted she was fine. She wasn't an infant, for heaven's sake. But over her head Marianne and Crimson had exchanged a knowing smile. In many ways Becky did seem like a child to them. Until she'd moved in with Rory, her life had been relatively sheltered. And even getting punched by a nasty boyfriend wasn't the most terrible thing that could happen to a person.

Horrible, no question, but not the worst. Not if everyone came out alive.

So they went, confident that they'd left everyone provided for. They had to pass Montrose as they headed west, and that slowed them down, too, because Crimson had a powerful feeling they should stop and see Kevin before they left.

Grant was wonderfully patient and didn't even comment on how silly it was to treat *feelings* as if they were prophetic omens.

She dashed into the hospital alone, while he waited in the car. When she got to Kevin's room, her compulsion to see him did seem absurd. His coma felt very deep today…particularly impenetrable and discouraging.

But she sat on the edge of his bed and held his hand tightly as she explained where they were going.

"We want to tell Anne you've been hurt," she said gently. "We think maybe, if she knows Molly doesn't have you at home right now, she'll want to come help."

She massaged his cold fingers, wishing he could give her some sign that he'd heard, and that he approved. But he didn't, and so she had to fill the void.

"Look, Kevin. I don't know how you really feel about Anne, or whether you'd actually want us to do this," she admitted helplessly. "But my gut tells me it's the right thing. For Molly's sake. And I know that's what you'd want us to do. Whatever is right for Molly."

No response.

Finally, she kissed his hand, and she left him

there. It was many hours to Vegas, and already they couldn't be certain they'd arrive before dark.

They made great time, though. The western sky was still blazing with sunset when finally, at about seven, they pulled up in front of the solid stone house that belonged to Paul and Marjorie Smith, Anne's parents.

It was probably dinnertime. Not ideal, in Emily Post terms, but at least a moment when the odds of finding the family at home were good.

When Crimson eased the car to the curb in front of the house, she waited a few seconds before turning off the engine. It was such a big step, confronting Anne. She still felt it was the right move, she still felt the woman had a right to know her daughter might lose the only parent she had.

But something about those unanswered calls made her feel strange.

"This is it," Grant said. It sounded like the kind of "filler" statement people made when they just needed to close the gaps of silence.

Conversation had been easy through most of the ride. They had agreed, tacitly, to put the awkwardness of the riverbank behind them, and, besides, they had so many comfortably neutral subjects to discuss. The report on Anne. Possible explanations for what had happened between the young woman and Kevin. And, of course, working out what to say when they found her. All relatively safe topics they both cared deeply about.

But as they neared the address, the car had fallen silent, conversation limited mostly to announcements from the GPS recorded navigation, which sounded like a sultry Brit who thought making left turns was sexy.

Crimson wasn't sure what Grant was thinking about, but her own brain had begun to move past the strategies of finding Anne and convincing her to come with them.

She'd begun to think about the "after."

She'd begun to realize how wrenching it would be to turn Molly over to someone else, even her own mother. And Crimson would have to move out of Grant's house, because of course it was ridiculous to think she could stay once the baby was gone. It wasn't as if he needed a keeper. He'd developed so many brilliant work-arounds for that broken arm that he was almost as independent and active as ever.

She still helped him button his cuffs, if he ever wore a dress shirt. But no one—especially no *rancher*—needed a full-time, live-in personal button assistant.

"Ready, Red?"

She turned toward him. "Ready as I'll ever be."

His face looked calm, his smile steady and reassuring. "It'll be fine. The worst she can do is tell us to scram…but somehow I don't think she will. She didn't look like that kind of monster to me."

Crimson knew what he meant. But she also

knew that sometimes monsters came in ordinary packages. "Still…I brought about a hundred photos of Molly, just in case. And not only on my phone. I printed them out, so we could leave them with Anne if she says she wants time to think it over."

Grant smiled as he opened his door and prepared to step down. "Diabolical," he said. "Poor woman doesn't stand a chance."

As they walked up the front walk, Crimson noticed how perfectly maintained the little squares of lawn were. Short-clipped, thick grass without any sign of weeds or bare spots. Flower beds crisply edged, full of showy pink peonies. Someone here was a gardener…and she thought she might sense a touch of OCD, as well.

The Smith family believed in presenting a tidy, bourgeois face to the world. In her experience, no one's life was as squared off and perfect as this exterior suggested. Did that mean they had something to hide?

Or was she just letting her nerves get away with her?

Her purse was an over-the-shoulder hobo bag. She pressed the bag against her hip so hard she could almost feel the outline of everything in it— her lipstick, her cell phone, her wallet, her keys… and, of course, the packet of baby pictures.

As Grant knocked on the door, she took a breath so deep it went all the way down to her toes. She arranged her face in a pleasant expression and double-checked her posture.

"Red. Relax." Grant angled a wry grin at her. "I doubt she'll make her motherhood decision based on whether you can balance a book on your head."

She let her shoulders fall more normally. He was right. Thank God he was here with her, to provide a note of sanity.

It took a minute, but finally the big front door with its gleaming brass horse-head knocker opened. The man who stood there was without doubt Anne's father. Though it all looked different on a male of nearly fifty or so, he clearly had the same gentle features, the same shining chestnut hair.

"Yes?" He didn't open the door very far. And he didn't smile very wide.

Crimson wondered whether they looked like door-to-door missionaries.

"Mr. Smith?" Grant offered his most irresistible smile, and in spite of his obvious distrust, the older man couldn't help but smile back.

"Yes?"

"My name is Grant Campbell. This is my friend Crimson Slayton. We were wondering whether we could talk to your daughter, Anne."

The man's smile dropped from his face so fast it might have been attached to an anchor. Behind him, a woman's voice could be heard.

"Who is it, Paul? What do they want? Tell them it's a bad time."

Crimson felt illogically cranky, just hearing the knee-jerk negativity of that voice. *Tell them it's a bad time?* Before they'd even heard what this was about? What if she and Grant wanted to tell Anne she'd just won the whopperball lotto?

"Mr. Smith," she began. "We're sorry to interrupt, if you're busy. But it really is important. If you'd just tell Anne we're here—"

"I'm sorry," he said in a quiet monotone. "I can't."

He couldn't? Why? Because that shrew in the background wouldn't *let* him? Crimson made an irritated sound and inhaled hard. "Listen, Mr. Smith, that's just—"

"Red." Grant nudged her, his cast chilly and firm against her bare forearm. She subsided reluctantly. She really did need to work on her temper. Clover had always said so. *Crimmy, you're always fighting dragons you've invented in your own head.*

"You can't tell her?" Grant's tone expressed only polite surprise, and an honest disappointment. No hostility. Crimson had to grudgingly acknowledge it was a much better approach. "Why not?"

"Because Anne's not here. She's gone. She moved out this morning."

Suddenly a shadow fell over Mr. Smith as his

wife finally joined him at the door. Mrs. Smith was probably only about forty, with black hair and blue eyes and a very expensive dress covering a very well-tended body. She would have been stunningly beautiful if her expression had been even one degree less sour.

"God, Paul," she said, her words whipping out like a lash. "Why did you tell them that?"

Her husband's shoulders had stiffened when he heard his wife's voice. "Because it's true," he said quietly, without turning around, without even leaning a fraction of an inch in his wife's direction.

Grant kept his gaze firmly focused on the husband, obviously the more receptive of the two. "Do you have a new address for her? We've tried her cell. We've left messages, but—"

The woman sputtered, as if the comment were impertinent. But the man shook his head. "She left her phone here. She wouldn't take anything we pay for. And she wouldn't tell us where she was going."

"Paul, for God's sake. Are you just going to air our dirty laundry to anybody who comes to the door?"

"Mr. Smith," Grant interrupted quickly. "I understand. But if you hear from Anne, will you give her a message for me, please?"

"We *won't* hear from her," Mrs. Smith said

waspishly, and put her hand out to close the door, as if that ended the discussion.

But her husband held the door open with an iron grip.

"*I* might," he said.

The expression on his wife's pretty face when she heard that was so comically shocked Crimson thought she might just lean over and kiss the man.

Ah, yes, Mrs. S. The worm has turned!

"What do you mean, *you* might?" Mrs. Smith's eyes were narrow. "Why would *you* hear from her?"

Finally, her husband deigned to cast an expressionless glance over his shoulder. "Because *I* didn't call her a whore. *I* didn't tell her she'd disgraced our family. And *I* didn't say I never wanted to see her again. So why don't you go finish your dinner, Marjorie, unless you think we should discuss the situation at even greater lengths with our guests?"

Judging from the black fury in Marjorie Smith's face, Crimson suspected there would be hell to pay later. But right now the woman was apparently too stunned by her husband's mutiny to do anything but stalk away.

Paul Smith shut his eyes for a second, as if he were counting her footsteps. After about five seconds, he opened them again.

"If you have a message for Anne," he said, letting his gentle gaze flick from Grant to Crimson, and back again, "leave it with me. I don't know how long it will take, but I'll make sure she gets it if she calls."

THE EVENING SEEMED endless to Grant, and he could only imagine how long it seemed to Crimson. They were going to have to head back to Silverdell in the morning, so if Anne didn't call tonight...

He'd had a note ready to go. He'd tried to provide for any contingency, including the possibility that Anne wouldn't be available when they showed up—or just wouldn't talk to them. If they hit a dead end, and she still wasn't returning the calls, they'd have to get the news to her somehow.

Not ideal, and definitely a last resort.

But last resorts were where they stood now.

His note had been simple and honest. *Kevin has had an accident and is in a coma. Hospitalized in Montrose, CO—prognosis uncertain. Molly needs you. Please call Grant or Crimson as soon as you can. We'd like to help.*

He'd included both their cell phone numbers next to their names.

They'd chosen to stay the night at a conference hotel just outside town, a well-appointed place where they could book large, adjoining rooms and a restaurant that had great online reviews.

Neither of them was terribly hungry, and they felt too deflated and low-energy after the disappointment at the Smith house to celebrate finding Anne, but they went to dinner, anyhow. All through the meal, they kept their phones on the table, in plain sight.

When her salad came, Crimson double-checked that her ringer was at top volume. Ten minutes later, when her chicken showed up, she checked it again, as if it might mysteriously have reset itself.

But Anne didn't call.

After dinner, Grant suggested a stroll out back, where a pretty patio overlooked a decent-size lake. But Crimson glanced once at the glassy water and, tensing visibly, countered with the suggestion that they could sit in the lobby for a while.

So that was what they did.

A wedding reception was going on in one of the hotel's meeting rooms, and overdressed young men and women in color-coordinated shades of violet kept slipping in and out, giggling and flirting and clearly making full use of a free bar. Every time the double doors opened, a swell of electronic dance music swam into the lobby and then was choked off again as the doors swung shut.

In another room, a conference of pharmaceutical reps was doing pretty much the same thing, without the violet corsages and boutonnieres. And without anywhere near as much joy.

The lack of privacy and the constant noise made chatting down here almost impossible. They ended up doing more people watching than anything else, occasionally remarking on some element of the decor or, that old, awkward fallback, the weather.

It was awful. And yet, neither of them even mentioned the possibility of going upstairs, where they could talk quietly in one of their suites. After last night, any kind of intimacy didn't seem like a good idea.

Eventually, as it drew close to eleven o'clock, they reluctantly accepted that Anne wasn't going to call tonight. Putting her phone back in her pocket, Crimson yawned.

"I think I might go upstairs," she said with an artificially casual air. "I'll probably take a hot bath. And then I suspect I'll just pass out."

If she'd surrounded herself with an electrified fence and hung a neon sign over her head that said No Trespassing, she couldn't have made it clearer. She did not want company.

As if she hadn't already made that clear enough last night. She must have been afraid Grant was slow on the uptake. She'd probably known a lot of men in her life who thought "no" meant "probably not." Or maybe just "not now."

But hey. In this one respect, anyhow, Grant was her dream guy. He would never, ever push a woman to do anything she felt ambivalent about. He wouldn't even press Crimson to try the French toast at brunch tomorrow if she wanted the waffles.

So there was exactly zero percent chance he'd try to talk her into *sex*.

Not in this lifetime. Not even if he burned himself up with wanting her.

"Good night, then," he said, standing politely and offering her a light smile. "I'll stay down here awhile. I'm not sleepy yet. And besides, I'm pretty sure one of those bridesmaids was flirting with me."

She laughed, but he could tell her heart wasn't in it. She glanced at the elevator and then back at him. "If Anne calls you..." she began.

"I'll let you know right away."

"No matter how late it is?"

"No matter how late it is."

She nodded punching the button to call the elevator. It must have been already waiting on the lobby level, because the doors opened immediately on a swoosh of scented air.

Just as the doors were about to close again, she abruptly put out her hands and stopped them. "Grant, wait." She smiled awkwardly. "I just wondered... What time did you want to get going in the morning? Since I won't see you again tonight, I probably should know our timetable."

He almost laughed out loud. How many different ways was she going to warn him that she didn't want to have sex tonight?

"Nine sound okay?"

"Sounds great." She released the door and hit the button for their floor. "Night then."

When she was gone, he finally went out to the

patio. He needed the open sky over his head, and he needed it now.

It was a pleasant night, and the view was nice, with the hotel curving along one side of the lake, and its lights reflected in the water. But the tipsy wedding guests and the morosely drunk sales reps had poured out here, too, and there wasn't anywhere for him to sit.

He walked the grounds for a while, hoping the night air would make him sleepy. He walked until his ankle ached. He walked until he was sure Crimson would be asleep.

And then he went to his room, intensely aware of the silence wafting out of hers. He stared at the doors that joined the two rooms. He unlocked the one on his side, just in case she needed him. He hadn't slept less than twenty feet from her for the past two weeks without learning about her restless, muffled nightmares.

He got in bed, and he set his phone alarm for seven, though he was fairly sure he wouldn't sleep.

BECKY ATE THE whole apple cobbler. The whole thing.

Gah! She'd resisted it all day, and even after dinner she'd made herself settle for a healthy pear for dessert. Then, around midnight, *boom.* Her willpower just went up in a puff of smoke.

Afterward, she sat on the couch, feeling like a

beached whale in bunny slippers, and stared in horror at the empty dish.

Sometimes she couldn't eat a thing…and then something like this would happen, and she'd eat like a hog.

What was wrong with her?

Good thing she'd already had definite proof she wasn't pregnant, or she might start to believe Marianne was right about morning sickness.

Thank goodness that horror hadn't come to pass. It wasn't that she didn't want—she always had. She'd dreamed about it when she was younger, imagining how she'd be the perfect mother, nothing at all like her own mother.

But she knew that if Rory was the father, she would have been having this one alone. And that terrified her. It would be pretty hard to be the perfect mom with no husband and no money.

But thank goodness that wasn't going to happen. She couldn't blame tonight's pig-out on hormones or pregnancy cravings. She was just a fool.

She wondered whether she could make a replacement before Crimson got home tomorrow. Could she remember all the ingredients, all the nifty little tricks Crimson had used? If only she'd taken notes…but she'd been having too much fun.

Still, she could try, and if it didn't turn out right she could always pretend that…

Oh, to heck with all that. Why should she pretend anything? It wasn't as if she'd stolen the thing. Crimson had left the cobbler here because she *expected* Becky to eat it.

As she did about twenty times an hour these days, she congratulated herself for leaving Rory. He was a firm believer that his women couldn't possibly be too rich or too skinny. If he saw her pigging out like this on apple cobbler, he'd probably drag her by the hair into the bathroom and make her puke it up.

Selfish, controlling son of a...

Just thinking about how much he'd hate it if she got fat made her want to head into the kitchen and see what *else* there was to eat.

Luckily, she was feeling too roly-poly to move right now. She put her hands over her stomach, groaned once and then keeled over—head down, feet up—onto the cushy leather. Maybe she'd just sleep on the couch tonight.

She shut her eyes, ready to drop off, when suddenly, outside the window behind her, something went *plink*.

She sat up, her heart beating fast, either from the sugar or from the sound. What was that? She tried to re-create the noise in her head, tried to tag it to something familiar. But she couldn't. It wasn't a *plop*, like water, or a *clink*, like glass.

It was a *plink*, like...

Like nothing she recognized.

She listened carefully, but the apartment was so quiet she began to wonder whether she'd imagined the sound. No live animals were housed in the adjoining barn, and she was too far from the stables to hear any horse noises.

And none of the workers lived on the property. Dusty Barley had been the last to leave. He'd stopped by about nine, asked her if she needed anything, and when she said no he took off for home, wherever that was.

With Grant, Crimson and Molly all gone, Becky was the only human inhabitant of Campbell Ranch tonight.

Her skin shivered oddly. Now, why had she gone and thought something dumb like that? *The only human inhabitant.* She knew how impressionable she was—and she was usually so careful not to plant unsettling ideas in her own head.

When she was a little girl, she'd been masochistically drawn to scary books, even though after reading one she wouldn't be able to sleep all night. Her mother had always been patient, and never made her feel silly. She'd leave the light on, open the closet door, check under the bed…whatever it took to make Becky feel safe enough to sleep.

But her mother moved out when Becky was eight, and her father had put an end to that foolishness. He'd removed all night-lights and forbidden her to get out of bed and bother him, even if she had bad dreams.

So she'd been very careful never to open a scary book, or watch a scary movie or even tell spooky campfire tales with her Girl Scout troop again. She couldn't risk it, not when there would be no hope of help later.

The only human inhabitant. She tried to laugh herself out of it. Really? She was afraid there was a *ghost* outside, pointlessly going *plink*? She forced herself off the sofa, even though her ankles tingled the way they used to do when she had to step near the bed, which might have witches under it...

"Get a grip," she scolded herself. She'd done the math, just in case, and if she had been pregnant, the baby would have been due sometime early next year. So that meant she would have had approximately seven months to grow up enough to be more like a mother than a child.

And that thought alone made her stiffen her spine. She might as well start growing up now.

Because, by God, when she did decide to have a baby she intended to be the best mother who'd ever lived. She would make any child she had feel so safe and secure that he never got scared in the first place, but if he did, he would never hear her say anything so cruelly dismissive.

"Don't be so pathetic, Rebecca. Stop that whimpering and go to sleep."

Plink...

And suddenly, as loud as an alarm in the dead silence, her cell phone began to ring. It was Rory...she had a special ringtone for him. The

Police, "Every Breath You Take." It had seemed romantic, once, but she must not have been paying attention to the lyrics. Now she could see what a creepy, stalker song it really was.

She didn't answer it. It rang about ten times. She listened to each one, with her heart knocking at her throat. She swallowed hard, to keep it where it belonged.

When the ringing stopped, she felt a wash of cool relief.

And then it started again.

He called three times before she turned off the ringer.

Even then, it still vibrated and lit up as Rory called yet again.

And that's when she realized ghosts were the least of her problems. There were actual living human beings who were far scarier.

There was a new alarm system on the whole house, including the barn where she was staying. Probably especially the barn, because of course she knew why Grant Campbell had suddenly spent all that money to protect his house.

He knew she might bring trouble his way.

She should have been smart enough to take Marianne up on her offer to spend the night there. But it wasn't too late. Better to wise up belatedly than to be dumb forever.

She picked up only two things. Her car keys and her purse. When the phone began to buzz again, she decided not to even take the time to change out of her bunny slippers, or throw on a sweater. Being a little cold and a lot embarrassed sounded way better than sitting here alone, waiting for Rory to appear, angry at being ignored.

She didn't want to take the phone, but she might need it if anything went wrong with the car. She slipped it into the pocket of her pajamas and then walked slowly out of the apartment. She didn't think he was at the ranch, but just in case he was, she didn't intend to give him the satisfaction of seeing her go dashing out into the night, squealing like some TSTL heroine in a horror movie.

The car started up right away, and her headlights cut long white cones out of the darkness. She'd been holding her breath, and it felt good to exhale.

No one—not ghosts, not monstrous ex-boyfriends, not even a startled deer—showed up in those cones of light. Only white fences and the outline of trees.

It was raining lightly, so she forced herself to drive carefully, even though downtown Silverdell was only about fifteen minutes away, and hers was the only car on the road. She would not become a statistic tonight. She refused to give Rory that satisfaction, either.

When she turned onto Elk Avenue, and could actually see the Kelly-green awnings of Donovan's Dream, she reached into her pocket and pulled out the still-buzzing phone. She held down the button that would power it off.

Let him call all night if he wanted. She wasn't going to listen.

Donovan's Dream was the best-lit storefront on the avenue. She parallel parked methodically in front—her dad would be so proud—and then climbed silently up the cold metal outdoor staircase to Marianne's apartment above the café.

The windows were dark, and she had to knock twice before she heard noise from inside. Her bunny slippers weren't made for a rainy June night in Colorado, and her toes had begun to ache when Marianne finally opened the door.

"Oh, my gosh, Becky!" Bleary-eyed with sleep, Marianne still managed to smile as she clutched Becky's arm and dragged her inside. "Are you okay? Why didn't you call and tell me you were coming?"

Becky laughed, relief pouring over her like warm bathwater, and for the first time she allowed herself to recognize just how terrified she had been. In fact, she wondered whether she might be in shock, a little bit, as the adrenaline receded.

"I'm sorry," she said. "I should have, but...I turned my phone off." She laughed, and the sound must have been odd, because Marianne frowned and put one arm around her shoulder. "The darn thing just wouldn't stop ringing."

CHAPTER FOURTEEN

THE DREAM WAS the same. It was *always* the same.

As Crimson propelled herself deeper and deeper into the river, she couldn't see anything, so she tried to turn her hands into eyes. She grasped frantically at every shadow that moved past her. Waving river plants. Crisp, frightened, darting fish. A hundred lumpy, jagged things that had no names up there, up in the light and air.

When she reached the silt floor, she spread her arms and swept them back and forth, back and forth, as if they were sonar antennae, scanning the river bottom for dead women. Sometimes something silky would slide between her fingers, and she'd make a desperate fist, praying it was Clover's long brown hair.

But it never was. Her screams came out only as gurgling bubbles. She dug like a dog in the silt, and though she'd thought her eyes were already blind, suddenly it was darker still.

She had to fight her own spongy body's instinct to rise like a buoy toward the surface. She grabbed a razor-sharp, oozy plant and held on. She couldn't breathe, her lungs were on fire, but she didn't care. If she couldn't bring Clover up with her, she would rather die down here.

And then, as if her fingers were no longer her own, her grip on the plant released. She began to float upward. And she knew... With a sudden, sickening clarity, she knew that wasn't true.

She *didn't* want to die.

Whether or not she had the right, she wanted to live.

"I'm sorry," she said. And in the dream world it seemed to make sense that her words could be heard underwater, clear and edged with anguish and shame. "I'm so, so sorry."

She woke, then, on a choking gasp. She was shivering. Her heart was a sharp, jabbing pressure in her chest, as if she were being stabbed. Her face streamed with tears.

She felt still half-tangled in the remnants of her dream, and heavy with a penetrating sorrow.

Just a dream. Just a dream. And yet...this one had been so much worse than the others.

Failing to find Clover in time...that was a nightly torture. But choosing to move on without her...

That was impossible to bear.

She hung her head, trying to breathe. Every inch of her skin ached—she had never felt so alone in her life. It was as if she'd lost Clover's memory now, too. Not even Clover's ghost would walk with her in this new, terrifying world.

She kicked her legs free of the covers and started to stand. But for a minute, only half-awake and disoriented by the dark, unfamiliar room, she couldn't remember where she was. Not her apartment…not the ranch…certainly not her grandmother's Victorian farmhouse.

She almost panicked. Out in the hall, the muted metallic ping of the elevator could be heard…and she remembered. Nevada. Molly's mother. Grant. *Grant.*

As if she'd been lost in a dark mine and suddenly saw a pinprick of light, she moved toward it, weakly grateful. Grant's name was that light.

She unlocked her side of their double door. She started to knock on the second door, but first, instinctively, she tried the handle. It was open.

"Grant?" She didn't wait for him to answer. She couldn't wait. She needed his warmth, his arms, his breath on her skin, or she would freeze. She moved into the room. "Grant?"

The bedcovers rustled as he swung his feet over the side of the bed. "Crimson?"

He was up in a heartbeat. He was moving, and she was moving, and they collided somewhere in the middle, in the darkness. She felt his body heat and she melted into it, riding a wave of relief, and something that felt like joy.

"Are you all right?" He held her tightly with both arms, one rippling, warm muscle, and one

be bewildered, after all she'd said before, after the thorny walls and icy ramparts she'd hidden behind…

Even she was confused. She didn't know why yesterday she had needed him to say no, and tonight she was begging him to say yes.

"I can't explain it," she said, as if he'd asked. "All I know is I need you tonight."

"But—"

"It isn't… There's no need to worry," she said. "I'm not taking back anything I said before. I'm not asking you to save me, or to heal what's broken, or to take me on as your wounded bird. I'm not asking for forever, or even for tomorrow. I don't want anything but tonight."

He didn't speak. Under her breasts, his heart was a sledgehammer. Under her hands, his back was vibrating iron.

"You can say no," she said. She lifted her head and looked up at him. "If it's too much to ask…"

"No." But his arms tightened as he spoke, crushing her up against the wonderful, rigid heat of him, and she knew he wasn't turning her away. "No, it's not too much to ask. It's too little. But whatever you want from me, it's yours."

He kissed her, his lips hard against hers…and so hot.

She was almost undone by the passion that flooded her; she almost couldn't stand. As if he knew, he swept her into his arms, even the broken one, as if she were no heavier than Molly, and carried her to the bed.

When they fell together, she was ready. She rolled him quickly onto his back and straddled him. She lifted his right arm, with its heavy cast, and brought his fingers to her lips. She kissed each one separately, slowly. And then she gently laid his arm on the mattress, high above his head.

Moonlight filtered in through the curtains and drew a silver line along his graceful, muscled length, from arm to hip. It stopped the breath in her lungs. He was magnificent...

And, just for tonight, he was hers.

He watched, with half-parted lips and gleaming, gold-flecked eyes, as she fumbled with the drawstring of his pants. When he was free, she tilted her hips and let their bodies find each other.

She cried out as he filled her.

"Grant," she said on a breathless spasm of pleasure. "I think...I think..."

But when he began to move inside her, all thought stopped. She was made of light, and he was made of fire, and nothing, *nothing* she'd ever known in her life had been more beautiful—or more impossible to put into words.

He woke to the sound of the phone ringing. Ringing, ringing, so insistent, so indifferent to how much he longed to stay asleep. He sensed the change in light, even from behind his closed eyelids. He felt the sun sneaking in, uninvited, to warm the room.

Even his subconscious knew what that warmth meant. It meant the end of the night.

The miraculous, mind-blowing night he'd just spent in Crimson Slayton's arms.

He opened his eyes. And that's when he realized…she was no longer there. Her side of the bed—the side she'd used when she wasn't melded into him—was rumpled and empty.

Gone. Without a goodbye, without a kiss, without a morning-after talk that had been his last hope for turning this amazing night into more than a few hours of stolen pleasure.

So she'd meant what she said. Why had he tried to tell himself anything different?

She was gone. He no longer had a lover. And he couldn't help but wonder…did he still have a friend? Everyone knew what a mistake this was, what a fatal blow one reckless night could deal to two people who once had been good friends.

A hollowness opened up inside him. But the phone was still ringing.

He grabbed his cell from the end table and almost barked a frustrated *"what?"* But then he saw the caller ID—*Unknown*. Just in time, he remembered. They were waiting to hear from Anne, and an angry stranger's voice was hardly going to make her feel safe.

He adjusted his tone. "Hello?"

"Mr. Campbell?"

It was a man's voice. Vaguely familiar, but he couldn't place it.

"Yes," he said. "This is Campbell."

"Mr. Campbell, this is Chad Bartlett, deputy sheriff here in Silverdell."

Grant didn't like the sound of that. He knew Bartlett, in passing. Nice man who took his work very seriously. And he sounded grim.

"Hello, Deputy. How can I help you?"

"Well." The officer took a minute too long to continue, and in that minute Grant recognized that something really bad had happened. "I understand you're out of town?"

"I'm in Nevada. But I'm coming home in a few hours. What's happened?"

"Well, I'm afraid I've got bad news. There seems to have been a fire on your ranch. We're not sure how it started, but the barn's burned pretty bad. And some paddocks. It got a little of the stable, but the fire department had arrived by then, so it didn't do much damage there before they put it out."

"My God." Grant's entire body felt frozen. "The horses?"

"They're fine. Your man—" Grant heard the sound of paper rustling. "Oh, yeah, you work with Dusty? Well, one of our men spoke to him, and he said all the horses are fine."

Okay. If Dusty said it was all right, then Grant could breathe again. But then he finally put the pieces together. *The barn.*

"Jesus. Bartlett, a friend of mine was staying in the manager's quarters, just off the barn. Was she…is she…?" He couldn't think of a way to express it that wouldn't make the imagined horrors real.

"Becky? Becky's fine." Bartlett still sounded grim, though, and Grant didn't like it. He got out of bed, his bare feet registering the sun-warmed plush of good carpet. He paced to the window and looked down at the parking lot. The weather was clear, and, even though it was Monday morning, the traffic seemed light. They could probably make good time.

"Becky wasn't in the barn at the time?"

"No, sir. Apparently, she'd gone to stay with a friend for the night. The barn was empty, thank God."

Yes, thank God for that.

Then what was Bartlett's somber tone all about? He'd broken all the really tough news, surely. Was he merely feeling sorry for Grant, because the damage was so severe? Well, Grant felt rotten about that, too. If the damage was too bad, it was going to set him back, even with the insurance, which carried a high deductible.

After rejecting Stefan Hopler's offer, and absorbing all the expenses that had come with the accident, he didn't have much of a nest egg left over.

But so what? If every living creature had escaped unscathed...then Grant could survive. In the end, the barn, the whole darn ranch was just another *thing*, and he didn't give a damn about things.

"I'll be home in a few hours, Deputy. I should get on the road now." He reached for his sweatpants and managed to pull them on, tucking the phone between his jaw and his shoulder. This would be a lot easier if he could just hang up and focus on not falling over.

"Is there anything else I should know, Bartlett?"

"Well..."

That uncomfortable pause again.

"Deputy? What is it?"

"It may be nothing," Bartlett said slowly. "It's just that...well, the fire department says they don't really like the look of the fire. They said it looks as if it might be arson."

Great. He needed that like he needed a hole in the head. He could only imagine how much a question of arson would slow down any insurance payout.

Grant finally got Bartlett to hang up. Sighing, he moved toward the folding luggage rack where he'd set his case last night. He'd brought very little and hadn't bothered to unpack any of it.

As he turned, he glanced toward the doorway

between their rooms. Crimson was standing there, fully dressed and obviously ready to go home.

Damn it. He had just received potentially life-changing news, and that should have made him immune to her, at least for a few minutes. Besides, she wasn't showing off or coming on to him, just wearing old jeans and a light blue shirt, no makeup, no fancy hair, no flirtatious smile, no heat in those tired eyes.

And yet, she still somehow managed to make his temperature rise.

She was holding her own cell phone in one hand, but she was frowning, as if she might have heard a little of Grant's conversation. He smiled, trying to set her mind at ease.

"That was the sheriff's office. Apparently, there was a fire at the ranch last night, but everyone is fine. Becky, the men, the horses—no one was hurt."

"A *fire*?" The hand that held the cell dropped limply to her side. "Oh, no. Grant. How?"

"They're not sure yet. It seems to have started in the barn." He glanced meaningfully at her cell. "Did Anne call?"

She shook her head. He noticed she was having trouble meeting his gaze.

"No. I mean, I got a call, but not from Anne. It was the hospital."

"*Dear God.* Not more bad news." He looked carefully, to see whether her eyes were simply tired, as he'd first thought, or whether they were filled with tears, fear or grief.

"No." She waved the phone, dismissing that thought. "No, their news was good. I guess they probably tried you first, but you must not have heard the phone."

He had heard a call come through, he remembered now. But he'd been so poleaxed by the news of the fire, he'd completely forgotten to check it out.

"Excellent," he said. "I could use some good news. Kevin's better?" He hoped it wasn't another false alarm. They'd had their hopes raised so often already...

"He's awake," she said. "And not like before. Really, truly awake this time. He's been conscious and talking all morning."

Really, truly awake. What kind of monster did it make Grant that there was a tiny part of him that was selfish enough to remember what she'd said the other night...

When Kevin wakes up...

She'd be leaving soon. If Kevin was awake and getting better, that meant he might be able to come home and care for Molly shortly. Whether they heard from Anne or not, that poor little girl would have a parent.

And that set Crimson free.

Stop being such a selfish bastard, Campbell. Concentrate on being happy for Kevin and Molly.

And even for Crimson. If she wanted to leave, he wanted her to go. A woman who stayed only because she felt trapped wasn't a friend *or* a lover. She was a prisoner.

He smiled. "Well, you know Kevin. If he's really awake, of course he's talking. The coma was undoubtedly the last moment of silence we'll ever get from that man. What's he talking about?"

She fiddled with her phone. "He's talking about Anne," she said. "Apparently, when we stopped by the hospital on our way here and I talked to him, he heard me. He wants to know if we've found her."

EVER SINCE SHE'D slipped back to her own room around dawn, Crimson had been apprehensive about their drive back to Silverdell.

Hours and hours alone in the car with Grant. How would he act? What would they talk about? What would it be like, trying to make small talk after the sublime madness of last night?

It seemed impossible. How could she return to chitchatting about the weather with a man who had, just hours ago, buried his lips between her legs and done things that made her clutch the headboard and try not to scream?

Would either of them dare to speak about it directly? Would they…*could* they…pretend it hadn't happened? She'd assumed those four hours locked together in the car would tell her the grim truth.

Was the trip from friends to lovers a one-way ticket, or was there any way to go back to being friends?

But she needn't have worried. As it turned out, there was no time for chitchat. She drove, so that he could talk. And the hours disappeared in an endless series of phone calls, as Grant tried to sort out what had happened with Kevin, what had happened to the ranch and where they went from here.

Dr. Schilling was first—Grant still called her Elaine—with an update on Kevin, all amazingly good. He wasn't just awake, he was practically normal. Tired, a little weak, of course, but they'd been running tests all morning, and she could state with reasonable certainty that he would suffer no long-term effects.

Dallas Garwood, the sheriff, had called with information about how the arson investigation would be handled. Crimson had been shocked to hear that arson was suspected, and of course her mind shot immediately to Rory and Becky. Poor girl…she must be feeling so guilty, and probably downright terrified.

Then Dusty Barley, with updates on the horses.

After that, so many short calls that Crimson almost lost track. His insurance agent, his financial planner, buyers, former buyers, potential buyers, friends, even his ex-girlfriend Ginny. Everyone wanted to talk to him, to give or get information, offer condolences, make plans.

And when Grant wasn't on the phone, Crimson was. Marianne called to assure her Becky was all right. Becky called, too, safe, but weepy and, incredibly, feeling the need to apologize for leaving the barn unguarded. She felt sure it was Rory who set the fire, and was overwhelmed with guilt…and fear, too, because obviously she had been the target.

After she calmed Becky as much as she could, Crimson talked to Belle, and they made plans for getting Molly over to see her daddy, which Dr. Schilling had tentatively agreed to allow, assuming Kevin's strength held up.

Grant had to go straight to Silverdell to meet with the sheriff and to determine exactly what had been damaged, and whether anything had been stolen. But they knew Kevin was eager to hear news about Molly, to be filled in on everything that had happened since the accident, and, of course, to find out about Anne.

So Grant suggested a compromise. He could drop Crimson off at the hospital in Montrose, which they'd pass on the way back to Silverdell. She could see Kevin and decide whether she thought he was up to seeing Molly. If she thought he was, Marianne would drive over with the baby and take them both back to Silverdell after the visit.

If she decided he wasn't up to it, Marianne

or Belle, or even Becky—somebody would still come to get Crimson and bring her home.

Meanwhile, Grant would be able to start sorting out the mess at the ranch.

Crimson maneuvered the roads while Grant talked to his nearest neighbor, who thought he'd seen a strange truck idling in the Campbell Ranch drive just before dawn.

Of course he had to go home right away. And it was equally obvious that Kevin couldn't just be ignored.

So Grant's plan was such a neat, efficient way of handling things. The only problem was that Crimson wanted to be with Grant when he saw the ranch for the first time. She didn't want him to be alone.

Alone? The word made her smile—judging from the volume of calls, he was less alone than anyone she'd ever met. Even so...

"Maybe I should just go all the way home with you," she said, the instant he hung up. She felt as if she had to speak quickly, before the phone rang again. They were nearly in Montrose already.

"I could borrow a car from someone, maybe Belle, and drive back to see Kevin on my own. It would only delay me an hour or two."

Grant flicked a quick look at her. "Make him wait two more hours? Why would you do that?"

"Because...the ranch... I'll be worrying..."

"Don't be silly. The fire is out. If you just want

to eyeball the damage, that'll still be there when you get back. I suspect it'll be there for quite a while, if I understood Garwood correctly. I can't even begin the cleanup until the investigation's complete."

His phone rang again, of course.

"Campbell," he said briskly. She could just hear a murmuring hint of Dusty's raspy voice on the other end. "Okay, look, have you got an inventory of what was in there? Good…read it to me. I'll tell you which ones we have to replace now, and which ones can wait for the insurance settlement."

The call seemed to go on forever. Dusty apparently read off items on a list, and Grant kept up a running response. "Buy. Buy. Wait. Wait. No, we have to have more of the vitamins. I don't care how much expedited shipping costs—we have to have them on site in the morning. Okay. Yeah, go ahead. Buy. Buy. Wait."

He and Dusty were still at it when she exited the highway at Montrose, and still hadn't finished when she pulled into the hospital parking lot. After she parked the truck in front of the main visitor entrance, Crimson gathered her purse and phone and prepared to jump out.

"Hang on a second, Barley." He stopped. "I'm going to take over the driving, so I'll have to put you on speaker."

He put his palm over the phone and turned to Crimson. "Explain to Kevin for me? Tell him I'll be over as soon as I can. Maybe tonight, but probably tomorrow."

"Of course." She put her hand on the door. They'd talked this over, too. They'd decided to give Anne another day to get in touch before telling Kevin what had happened. They'd just say she hadn't been home when they got there, and leave it at that for now.

She smiled at him, trying to find the old easy camaraderie. "Drive carefully, Grant. Remember, you do still have only one hand, so don't let that phone…"

"Yes, ma'am." He laughed. "I'll be careful."

"And keep me…keep me posted, okay? When you find out the extent of the damage? Maybe… Maybe it's not as bad as we're imagining."

"I'm sure it's not," he said politely. "And…look, Red…"

She paused, one leg out the door, and swiveled toward him.

He didn't speak for a minute. He just sat there, looking at her oddly, with his hand over his cell phone's speaker, and the smell of the truck's exhaust beginning to scent the air.

"Nothing," he said finally. "Just…no regrets, okay? We can find our way back from this. I promise, it's all going to be fine. *We* are going to be fine." He summoned up a smile. "Deal?"

She knew what he was saying. This awkwardness was inevitable, but it wouldn't last. He would make sure their friendship didn't suffer. She managed to return the smile.

"Deal," she said.

She got out, and he got out, too, climbed into the driver's seat and pulled away from the curb. When she looked back from the hospital's double doors, she couldn't see the truck at all.

No regrets. And yet, all the way up to Kevin's room, her heart was so heavy in her chest it was as if she'd been strapped to an anvil and forced to carry it around.

She might not call this *regret*, but it wasn't happiness, either.

She was relieved when, as she approached Kevin's room, she heard the sound of laughter. A man's laughter…followed by a woman's softer echo.

One of the younger nurse's aides was in there congratulating him, no doubt. Crimson had seen the way some of them had looked at the handsome young man over the past couple of weeks, as he lay helpless on the bed.

The nurses were all business, determined to do their best to bring him back to health—friendly, cheerful, supportive, but always focused on medicine first. But here and there a nurse's aide, or a volunteer, had stared at Kevin dreamily, as if he struck them as romantically tragic.

Whoever it was in there with him now, Crimson was grateful for the help. She needed someone else to provide the easy laughter. She wasn't sure she had a celebration in her this morning, and Kevin deserved a party.

She took a deep breath before she opened the door. She arranged a lively smile on her lips. She pushed the door and entered the room, singing out in her silliest, teasing voice, "Well, hello, there, stranger! You certainly gave us a sc—"

"Crimson!" Kevin was sitting up, looking thin and pale, but stronger than she had imagined possible. And he looked oddly peaceful, as if the past couple of weeks had been nothing but the most refreshing nap. "I'm so glad you're here!"

A slim young woman was perched on the edge of his bed, holding his hand. Not a nurse's aide, or a Candy Striper, but someone in street clothes. The woman's whole body tilted toward him, as if he exerted a magnetic pull.

Her shiny, dark brown hair hid her features, but something inside Crimson lit up like a pinball machine registering a connection. She knew this woman…didn't she?

"Crimson, come here! The most wonderful thing…" He grinned at the young woman. "I want you to meet Molly's mother."

CHAPTER FIFTEEN

SILVERDELL TOOK CARE of its own, Crimson had to admit that. She hadn't ever heard of a barn-*burning* party, but so many Dellians brought food to Grant that evening, and stayed to share in the feast while they commiserated—what else could you call it?

Only a few of them had already heard about Kevin's recovery. And none of them had heard about Anne, who had come home with Molly and Crimson, and promptly been invited by Grant to stay here for a couple of days, until she got comfortable with Molly's routine.

Once the other guests learned about the miraculously reunited little family, and met the pretty mommy, who kept Molly in her arms every single minute, as if she were afraid to set her down, the evening turned into a true celebration.

Half the town was there. Well, at least a couple of dozen people. Lord only knew who was taking care of Bell River Ranch, because the whole family had come to the ranch, alerted by Marianne, probably. The half-renovated house rang with laughter and conversation. Someone turned on music. Someone else opened a bottle of wine.

Everyone ignored the lingering hint of smoke and burned wood in the air and concentrated on having fun.

Around eleven, though, Molly began to fuss. She had accepted Anne surprisingly well, Crimson thought, and she realized that the baby's sweet nature would help to bridge this terrible gap—the five months when her mother had been absent from her life.

Because she had been, entirely. Crimson had learned that when she stumbled into the reunion scene at the hospital. Anne had believed the easiest way to survive giving up her infant was to have no contact at all.

At first, watching Anne with Kevin, Crimson had been wary...almost suspicious. Why come back now? And, given that long absence, how serious could Anne be about committing to either Kevin or Molly?

But Crimson had forced herself to set her own anxieties aside. She saw that, for Kevin, there were no doubts.

In fact, though he was still very weak, his new glow had made it clear he had strong feelings for this woman. Obviously their short relationship had been more than just a one-night stand with consequences. He was clearly ready—even eager— for Anne to take over her job as Molly's mother.

The doctors wouldn't let them stay with him long—Kevin didn't have the stamina, though even they could see how much good Anne's presence had done him.

So by early afternoon, Anne and Crimson drove back to Silverdell, in Anne's car. On the drive home, Anne had been quiet and obviously nervous. Crimson didn't push her. She could imagine how large the upcoming meeting with her baby must loom.

Marianne met them at the ranch. And in the minutes that followed, much of Crimson's suspicion and doubt drained away.

As Anne took Molly in her arms, fear, guilt, grief and incredible joy radiated out from the young mother in waves so strong they could have knocked down anyone standing too close.

Crimson and Marianne looked at each other, and they both were obviously fighting tears. This was love, in all its vulnerable, terrifying beauty. No one could fake that raw emotion.

It had been a good day, and Anne's confidence had grown with every passing hour.

But now, Molly had grown tired, and every time Crimson walked by, the baby would cry and reach out her fat little arms. Eleven o'clock was already way past her bedtime, and she'd grown accustomed to seeing Crimson's face as she fell asleep.

"Tell you what. Why don't we both go up?" Crimson let Molly grab hold of her finger. "I'll show you where all her things are, and we can put her down together."

Anne's face looked relieved. "That would be great," she said.

Crimson understood. The young woman must be wrestling with all kinds of guilt already. If her daughter rejected her, or if she seemed to be failing at caring for her, the guilt would be so much harder to bear.

They didn't explain themselves to anyone. They just slipped up the stairs and made their way to the guest room. Grant had already hauled Anne's suitcase up here earlier, when they'd first returned from Montrose.

Anne stood in the doorway awkwardly, as if she were afraid to enter. As if the threshold were some magic portal, and if she crossed it, she could never return to her old life, her old world, her old freedom.

And maybe, Crimson thought, that was true. But she held out her hand and smiled, hoping Anne could see that she didn't judge, and didn't begrudge passing the torch of motherhood. It was going to hurt when she was out of Molly's life forever. But she'd always known mothering the lost little girl was a temporary assignment, and she'd always prayed for this outcome.

"Come on in, Anne," she said, stretching her hand out farther. "Being Molly's mommy is a pretty amazing gig. I think you're going to like it."

Anne nodded slowly. She took a deep breath, bit her lips together and stepped into the room.

Crimson was careful to let Anne do all the hands-on stuff. She was merely the tour guide, explaining how to work the little countertop bottle warmer, and where to find the new box of baby wipes.

It didn't go well. Molly was hungry and upset by the strange hands. And Anne took forever. Her motions were stiff and self-conscious, and she was awful at fitting the diaper. The first one fell right off the minute she lifted the baby.

Crimson almost laughed. Hadn't the girl ever done any babysitting in high school? But she knew Anne would relax soon, and instinct would take over. By tomorrow, she'd be an expert.

She got busy changing the sheets while Anne settled herself in the big wooden rocker. Anne fit Molly into the crook of her arm and put the bottle next to her mouth. Molly began to gobble hungrily, her hands tight fists at her chin.

"See the way she's holding her hands? That means her fuel gauge is on empty." Crimson smiled over her shoulder, remembering the night Grant had pointed it out. "When she's full, they'll relax and fall to her sides."

Anne looked down, as intent on learning the signals as if Crimson had been teaching her to decode the Rosetta stone. Poor thing…she had so much to prove, didn't she?

"I know you must have been wondering where I was," Anne said suddenly, without looking up. Her dark hair fell over her face, but Crimson didn't have to see her cheeks to know the young woman was blushing.

"Yes, we were," Crimson admitted. What was the point of lying? No human being could refrain from wondering. "But that's between Kevin and you. You don't have to explain anything to us. We're just glad you're here now."

"I'd like to explain, though." Anne lifted her face. "It's not very... It doesn't put me in a very good light. But for all I know you're imagining stuff that's even worse."

Crimson nodded. "Well, we once speculated you might be insane, in prison or..." What had Grant's exact joke been? "Or the madam of a bordello."

She billowed out the top sheet and folded the corners together to center it. "So, whatever your story is, it's got to be more flattering than that, right?"

Anne finally smiled, as if Crimson's light-hearted honesty had broken down the barrier between them. Crimson had made it clear they didn't have to pretend this was a picture-book romance, which apparently made Anne feel safe enough to tell the truth.

"We met in Vegas," she said. "I was at one of

the big resorts on the strip, with friends, celebrating. We'd just graduated from high school."

She ducked her head again when she said that. She knew how it sounded.

"Kevin was there at a conference. We met, and we hit it off. I kind of let him think I was a little older, I guess. But it was just a fling. All we had was that one weekend. Then, after I got home, I found out I was pregnant. It was…it was really a shock."

"I can imagine." With the blanket in one hand, Crimson reached over and tilted the bottle a little higher with the other. Molly had drunk most of the formula and was slurping in a lot of air. Burping time would be exciting tonight.

"Anyhow, I wasn't going to tell my parents. You see, they…" Anne swallowed hard and looked out the window at the trees in the distance. "My mother… She's…"

Crimson chuckled. "We met her. Enough said."

The other woman sighed and nodded. "Yeah. Well, anyhow, I didn't know quite what I was going to do. I thought maybe I could get a job out of town, have the baby and give her up for adoption."

With a small, anxious, "Oh!" she glanced down and pressed her lips together again, as if she shouldn't have uttered those words out loud in front of Molly.

"I don't think Molly knows what *adoption* means yet," Crimson said. "I'm counting on very limited word recognition, frankly, because I've been a bit unguarded around her, myself."

"Well, yeah. That was silly, wasn't it? I guess I just feel guilty now, remembering."

Crimson grunted as she lifted the bottom of the mattress to tuck in the hem of the blanket. "Good thing people can't be arrested for what they're thinking. The jails couldn't hold us all."

Anne smiled gratefully. "Anyhow, I couldn't bring myself to contact Kevin. But one day he found me. He had looked me up. He said he'd just wanted to be sure…sure there weren't any consequences from the weekend." She shook her head. "I never heard of anyone so conscientious, have you? I mean, none of the boys my age…"

"My sister was conscientious like that," Crimson volunteered. "But mostly, no. You're right. I don't know many people that careful."

She suspected what Kevin's seeking Anne out really meant. The Kevin she knew wasn't reckless, but neither was he abnormally meticulous. She had a feeling his reason for looking Anne up was much simpler—he'd missed her.

"When he heard I was pregnant and planning to give the baby up for adoption, he was mad that I hadn't told him. He said he wanted the baby. He offered me a lot of money."

Crimson cocked her head, unable to hide her surprise.

Anne colored brightly. "I didn't take it. It wasn't

about money. I just thought…the baby would be better off with her real father, especially since he wanted her so badly. That makes sense, don't you think?"

"Of course."

"So, anyway, he drew up documents—he's a lawyer, you know. I had to promise I wouldn't…"

She shook her head, a subtle movement that seemed to be directed more at herself than at Crimson. "I agreed not to seek custody of Molly. In exchange, he paid a lot of my expenses while I was pregnant. He found a place for me to live in Price, and he even found me a job in a dentist's office, just like I'd had at home."

"What did you tell your parents?"

"Just that I wanted to get out on my own, get a job in another town. My mother was so mad, and that made it easier, really, to hide everything. There was no question of her coming to visit. And it was only about four months, anyhow…"

She let the thought dwindle off.

"Did you see Kevin at all during those months?"

Anne nodded. "Oh, yes. He came to see me a lot, to be sure I was all right, and everything. He went with me to the doctor, sometimes. He even offered to try to make it work, if I changed my mind and decided I wanted to be in Molly's life. Sometimes I even wondered…"

She swallowed hard. "But I was just too scared. I didn't think I could be a good mother. I didn't see how I could tell my parents, and change my whole life. All my plans…"

She looked at Crimson, her eyes moist and bewildered. "When she was born, I didn't even want to see her. I made them give her to Kevin right away. We'd already done all the paperwork, of course. I was so naive. I thought I could go back to my regular life, and everything would be… everything would be like before."

"Except it wasn't."

Anne shook her head slowly, staring down at her baby, now almost asleep. Anyone who had ever seen a painting of a Madonna and child would recognize that gracefully curved neck, that soft, bemused smile, instantly.

"No, it wasn't. It was torture. I tried so hard to be normal. But I couldn't stop thinking about her. I even found myself thinking about Kevin…"

Molly whimpered, and, clearly driven by pure instinct, Anne said, "Shh. Honey, hush." She lifted Molly gently to her shoulder, where she began to make soft circles on her back.

"I got your messages, you know. And your note. I'm sorry I didn't call you back. I…"

Crimson shook her head. "It's all right. I know it must have been a shock."

"It was. But it was a shock I needed, I guess. I realized I couldn't go on like that. If he was sick, I had to see him. I had to see Molly. But I wanted to do it on my own, you know? So that he'd know

I did it because I wanted to, not because someone called me and made me do it."

Crimson nodded.

"So the first thing I did was tell my parents." Anne's voice broke. "That didn't go well."

"I can imagine."

"Then I drove to Montrose. I was going to call you after I saw Kevin." She looked up. "Really, I was."

At that moment, Crimson's lingering doubt evaporated, and she decided Anne Smith would probably make a darn good mother. Facing down that dragon of a mother had taken determination. It had also taken courage to decide to correct her mistake, even if it meant asking her older, legally sophisticated baby daddy to void their contract and give her another chance.

And ironically, she admired Kevin Ellison right now, too. She'd melted inside when she'd seen that look on his face in the hospital today. Crazy. She didn't really know whether their attempt to be parents together would work, but it was brave and loving to try.

She plumped the pillows in their new cases and lined them up at the head of the bed. She hoped fate would be kind to this vulnerable trio.

"Everybody settling in okay?"

At the sound, both women looked over toward the doorway. Grant stood just on the other side of the threshold, a beer in his hand and a pleasant smile on his face. "Molly ready for bed?"

Anne stood so fast she made the rocker sway, like Goldilocks caught in the act by one of the bears. "Yes, we're fine. Thank you so much, Mr. Campbell, for everything you've done for Molly. And I'll be glad to sleep on the sofa, if that would be more convenient."

"Don't be silly!" Crimson shook her head firmly. "You need to be with Molly. And if you think you're getting out of the three o'clock feeding, you're so wrong. This is my night to get eight hours for a change."

She moved toward the chest of drawers. "Let me just grab a nightgown, so I don't have to disturb you later. You look tired, and I know I am. I'm going to get a bath. Grant, can you make Anne's excuses downstairs so she can go ahead and get some sleep?" She smiled at Anne. "Believe me, you'll be glad you did, come three o'clock."

Anne still looked uncertain. "If you're sure… I don't want to put anyone out…"

"You're not," Grant assured her. "I'll say goodbye to everyone for you—I don't think they're staying much longer, anyhow. Red, why don't you take my room? I'll sleep on the sofa downstairs."

Take *his* room? A streak of something hot moved through Crimson's midsection. She couldn't. Everything in there would smell like him. Everything in there belonged to him. She wouldn't get a wink of sleep.

She hoped her thoughts weren't written on her features. Turning away again, she grabbed the first nightgown her hands landed on. It was an old, shapeless thing, two sizes too big—a mannish nightshirt, really, in a mystery gray that could once have been any color at all…way back before it had been washed about a million times.

Clover used to say Crimson looked like a muddy, half-deflated balloon in that nightgown. She'd tried twice to throw it in the trash, though Crimson had always rescued it. It was comfortable, and she didn't care if she looked shapeless and faded, because who was looking, anyhow? Clover had been the one with the fiancé. At that point, Crimson hadn't yet found a man she gave a damn about impressing.

"Sleep in *your* room? No way, Campbell." She raised her eyebrows, smiled rakishly and adopted a playful tone.

She hoped he could tell what that particular smile, and that particular tone, really meant. She intended to communicate that last night had been…well, it had simply been one of those things that sometimes happened between friends, when they were very tired, very emotional or very drunk.

It had been nice—very nice, in fact. The smile was meant to show she wasn't going to carry around any angst about it—or any regrets, because regrets were pointless—but it wouldn't happen again.

The tone meant he could go back to being lady-killer Grant Campbell, and she would go back to being Crimson Slash, his outspoken, no-nonsense buddy with *no* benefits.

"No, seriously, Red, sunrise hits that downstairs picture window like a laser. You'll sleep a lot longer in my room."

"Nice try, Campbell," she said, patting his shoulder as she edged past him, her arms full of nightshirt and underthings, to start the bathwater. "But the room next door to the squawk box is all yours. As soon as you run the entire population of Silverdell out of the living room, that big, comfortable, blissfully quiet sofa down there is *mine*."

GRANT COULDN'T SLEEP, which didn't surprise him much. He had been walking around all day with a hurricane raging inside. The fight to keep it from bursting through to the surface had been exhausting—but the turmoil kept him wide-awake.

He'd spent several hours with the horses, who were still agitated, memories of the fire kept alive by the lingering smell of smoke. Dawn, in particular, seemed restless, and his presence calmed her down. Of them all, only the new, nameless foal seemed unaffected.

Maybe that one was too young to understand their near miss.

After that Grant had wandered around the shell of charred lumber and wet debris that used to be the barn. The water they'd used to put out the fire still pooled in the grass, the liquid shining eerily in the moonlight.

This was the end. He knew, even before he got an estimate from the insurance adjuster, that this might be the straw that was going to break him.

God, fate loved a good laugh, didn't it? Three hard years to build this ranch, always on the cliff edge, but somehow managing to keep from tumbling over. Three nail-biter, all-nighter years. And just when he thought he'd turned the corner, just when he thought he might have found solid ground, *this*.

It was truly ironic that the dream of Campbell Ranch might be ended by one whack job with a crappy temper, a defiant ex-girlfriend and a gas can.

He spotted something, something mud-colored with spots of bright pink, lying just outside the main field of debris, sticking up from a puddle of water. He bent over and retrieved it. He brushed at the filthy surface.

It was Molly's teething ring. The one Crimson had bought her the day of the accident. The day it all began.

He threw it back onto the ground. It was trash

now, like everything around it. No one would ever put a singed, half-melted piece of plastic in a baby's mouth.

And the baby would be leaving soon, anyhow. Maybe as early as tomorrow. Anne had assured them she wouldn't be here long. She'd be getting a hotel in Montrose right away, or maybe a small apartment. She wanted to be able to see Kevin often while he remained in the hospital. Even when he got out, they'd need easy access to any therapy or recovery treatments he might need.

And of course when Molly and Anne left, Crimson wouldn't be far behind them.

Becky was already gone, staying with Marianne Donovan—and she wouldn't be coming back, not now that her quarters were burned to the ground.

For the first time since Kevin showed up at his door, Grant would once again be alone at the ranch.

Unless he, too, decided to sell off and move on.

He was actually surprised he hadn't heard from his father-in-law yet. Ever since Brenda and Jeannie died, Benjamin had been urging him to come to Memphis and run the foundation. Ben tried not to apply too much overt pressure, but the subtext was always there.

Grant was almost tired of fighting it. Maybe the foundation job was the answer. At least helping disadvantaged kids was something he believed in, something that did good in the world.

And, hell, maybe he was ready, anyway. He'd needed these three years to heal in peace. Solitude, with only the horses for company, had been therapeutic. But suddenly, solitude didn't sound so great anymore.

He turned to go back to the house. An hour spent staring at smoldering ashes was all the wallowing he would indulge in tonight.

As he climbed the steps to the kitchen door, he decided he'd pour a glass of milk. He'd like to warm it up, but that took too long and made too much noise, especially with his clumsy, one-handed maneuvers. He didn't want to wake Crimson, who slept in the great room, just a few yards away from the kitchen.

But to his surprise she wasn't sleeping. She was in the kitchen, sitting at the counter in that ridiculously sexy nightshirt, her head bent sleepily over a cup of hot cocoa that smelled like heaven.

"Oh," she said as he opened the door. She stood, her chair legs scraping across the floor. "I…I thought you were upstairs."

He didn't let his eyes linger on the curve of her breast, outlined by moonlight. But it was a fight. Compared to the mud and ruin he'd been dwelling on for the past hour, she looked like an angel.

"Couldn't sleep," he said. He glanced at her

steaming cup, with its dusting of cinnamon on top. "You don't have any more of that, do you?"

"Of course." She went to the stove and stirred a pot sitting there. The spoon seemed to release a waft of chocolate air, so sweet he found himself inhaling, trying to catch as much of it as possible.

She reached for a mug, and his gaze followed the hem of her nightshirt as it slid slowly up, revealing the satiny skin of her thigh, all the way to...

"You want marshmallows, not cinnamon, right?"

He had forgotten she'd know that. Last Christmas, he'd gone to a party at Fanny Bronson's house, and Crimson had been in charge of the food. They'd both hidden in the kitchen for hours, drinking too much hot chocolate and talking about how they hated the holidays.

"Yours looks great," he said. "I'll have whatever you're having."

She sprinkled some cinnamon on it, taking him at his word. Surprisingly, she spilled some on the counter, as if her hand shook.

She handed him the cup. "Enjoy," she said. "I'm...I'm heading back to sleep a little more, I guess. Good night."

But now that she'd spoken several words, he could hear that her voice didn't sound right. Her throat was raspy, as if she'd gone hoarse. It was a frightened-little-girl sound.

"Red." He reached out with his casted arm. "Wait."

She paused. She turned toward him, and for the first time the moonlight fell full on her face. To his shock, her eyes were red, haunted, gleaming. Her face was both pale and oddly blotchy.

What a fool he'd been! What a stereotypical caveman male. He'd been so busy admiring the curves of her body he'd completely missed the misery in her face.

She'd been crying. A lot.

"Are you okay?"

She nodded, angling her face away. "Just half-asleep. And…you know. Pretty tired."

He came closer, set his mug down on the break-fast table and reached out to feather her hair out of her face. It was, as usual, an adorable mess, but it was also damp and stuck to her cheeks.

"You've been crying. You don't cry because you're tired. What's wrong?"

"Nothing." Crimson shook her head. "It's just… I had a dream."

He touched her shoulder, and to his surprise, he realized she was trembling slightly. She needed to sit down.

"Come here," he said. He set her cup down next to his own and then led her into the great room. She didn't resist, though her feet were slow, as if they were made of lead.

He guided her back to the sofa, which was a sea

of tumbled blankets and pillows. Had she gotten any rest at all? Those chaotic, knotted bedclothes suggested she hadn't.

Whatever sleep she'd managed had been more like a war.

As they walked, he rubbed her shoulder and arm with his good hand. The subtle shivering hadn't stopped. He couldn't tell if she was just cold, in that way you could be when you woke in the middle of the night, or if she was in a mild shock.

It didn't really matter. As they reached the sofa, he snagged a blanket with the fingers that extended from his cast, wincing slightly as they tried to close over the soft cotton. He settled her on the cushions, spread the blanket over her and then sat down beside her.

"Do you want to tell me about it?"

She shook her head. "No. I just didn't… I just needed some cocoa to help me get back to sleep."

He let that pass, rubbing his hand across the tops of her thighs, with the blanket in place to prevent the touch from becoming too intimate. She needed to stop shaking. He needed more friction, more coverage…

Damn this broken arm! He hadn't wished for two healthy hands, not in the whole time he'd been wearing this cast, as passionately as he did at this very moment.

Finally, her muscles started to relax, and the

shaking subsided to a subtle tremor. He reached up and tucked her hair behind her ears. It was such a hopeless mess of tousled layers...the minute he got one damp strand off her face, another fell down and tickled her cheek.

"Sometimes," he said, making sure there was no pressure in his tone, "it helps to talk about a dream. It can help put it in perspective, help you figure out what it means."

She leaned back, finally, as if she didn't have the strength to hold herself up anymore. Her eyes fell shut. The dark lashes that brushed her cheeks were damp.

"I *know* what it means."

"Is it about your sister?"

"Yes. I dream about her a lot. About the night she died. She..." Her voice caught. "She drowned."

Grant tried not to show how surprised he was that she had volunteered any information at all. But the thigh muscles under his hand had begun to quiver again, and he realized that she hadn't yet fully recovered from the dream. She was still half caught in its tendrils...whatever they were made of.

She might not even realize she was talking about forbidden things.

"That must have been heartbreaking. To lose a sister...a twin..."

"We weren't just sisters. Twins are different.

We were best friends. We were inseparable. And even that doesn't really capture it. We—"

She seemed, now that she'd begun, to have a difficult time stopping the words from flowing. She'd started out looking at her hands, but suddenly she raised her eyes to him, their expression yearning and fierce, as if she needed to know whether she was saying it right, whether he understood.

"We were *connected*. In some ways, we were complete opposites. I was wild and willful. She was smart and sensible. And yet we were exactly the same, too. That didn't seem strange to us. We understood how that could work."

He nodded. He'd known a few sets of identical twins through the years, and he'd glimpsed their incredible connection. It was almost mystical. He'd envied it, sometimes. A twin seemed never to be alone, not like the rest of the world.

But he'd never thought about the flip side of that coin. If you lost your twin, if you lost that mystical other half, you could never be anything *but* alone again as long as you lived.

He didn't say any of that. He didn't want to interrupt this compulsive flow, now that she'd finally started to talk. This was the heart of her, spilling out into the open for the first time.

"Clover was…" She smiled wanly as he made an instinctive move. "Yeah, *Crimson and Clover*. Silly, huh? Our parents were throwbacks to another time… They were activists, do-gooders, hippies—at least those were the words my grandmother used. They loved that song."

He smiled, too. So that was why she wore that shamrock around her neck. Last night, while they were making love, it had winked back and forth above him, catching the streetlights that knifed in through the crack in the curtains. He'd felt oddly hypnotized by it, hypnotized into believing he was just a long, fiery column of intense physical sensation.

But he had to stop thinking about that. Sex wasn't the kind of intimacy she needed now. She was letting him discover a part of her that was even more precious, even more private.

"I love that song, too," he said. "And I love your names. I probably would have loved your parents."

"Yes," she said absently. "They were very good people, I think. They died when we were only three. They were abroad, helping in the Caribbean, after an earthquake."

This was also tragic, but he'd let her get sidetracked. He held his breath, hoping she'd return to talking about her sister. He wanted to know. And he had a feeling this might be his last chance.

"So…Clover was…?" He nudged the subject gingerly.

"Clover was so talented. We both loved to cook, but we were opposites that way, too. I was the dessert chef—I loved the sweet things, the frills. She was the savory—she made the food that kept you alive. But together we made the perfect team."

She shut her eyes again. "We'd always dreamed of opening a restaurant together, and it was finally going to happen. It was exciting…but it was scary, too. That night, we…"

She stopped for a minute, reaching up to rub her forehead. Finally she nodded, as if giving herself permission to continue.

"We were supposed to sign the loan documents the next day, and the lease the day after that. It was such a huge step…all that money, all that commitment. It was like…" She looked up. "I thought of this tonight, when I was watching Anne with Molly. It was as if we were passing through a door that would close and lock behind us. As if we were leaving our carefree days behind forever."

He had no idea what all this had to do with her sister's death, exactly, but he knew she was going somewhere. Somewhere that hurt.

Very subtly, her voice had tightened, as if this was more than simple narrative. This was making a case. She sounded almost as if she was defending herself from an accusation that he hadn't heard anyone make.

"We were trying to think how to celebrate, and as usual I was coming up with all the crazy ideas. She was always so sensible…so much more mature than I will *ever* be. I said we should go to the railroad truss bridge and jump into the river."

She had opened her eyes again, and she was staring down at his hand where it still lay on her thigh. Suddenly, she put her own hand over it, and began to move his fingers nervously, compulsively, as if it was her own hand, and she was trying to calm herself.

"I used to do it all the time when we were teenagers...with boyfriends, with other girls, even alone, when I was feeling angry or hurt. But Clover had never joined me, not even once. She said I was insane, that it was way too dangerous."

Oh, shit. He could almost see the disaster coming. He could almost run ahead of her in the telling, and see, hear, *feel* the terrible conclusion of this story.

She lifted her eyes toward him, and he saw with horror that they were swimming in tears. *"Why didn't I listen to her?"*

"I don't know," he said simply. "I don't know why we make terrible mistakes. I just know that we do. We all do."

"I jumped first, to show her how easy it was. She was so scared. And I made fun of her, calling her names from the water. So finally she jumped, too. But then...she didn't come up."

"Oh, God," he said, though he'd commanded himself to remain completely silent.

She was crying openly now. "They said later that she'd hit her head on something. A rock or something. But at first..." She wiped her cheeks.

"For a while, they actually thought I might have been the one who hit her. They thought…"

She clutched at his hand so hard he felt his bones bend. "They thought maybe I'd killed her."

His blood froze in his veins, all in an instant. He'd known from the start that he was walking with her through a terrible memory, a place she was cursed to revisit every night in her dreams. But he'd never, even for a split second, realized just how terrible that nightmare was.

"What? *Why?*" He shook his head angrily. "For God's sake, why would *anyone* ever think such a crazy thing?"

She looked at him through dull eyes. "Because of the insurance. We'd just taken out a very large policy. If either of us died…" She couldn't go on. "They thought that I…the money…"

"What?" A furious sound erupted from him, not loud, but thrumming with contempt. "Were they *insane?*"

She smiled at him, those wet, streaked cheeks dimpling in a way that made him want to kiss them until…

Until what? He could kiss her until doomsday, and he couldn't kiss this memory away.

"You're a very sweet man, Grant Campbell," she said. "But you know better than that. They didn't really know me. They didn't even know Clover. They just knew the circumstances looked suspicious. They would have been insane if they *hadn't* suspected me."

He felt part animal right now, and so he made an animal noise. A growl. "I assume they finally came to their senses and saw how absurd that was."

She nodded slowly. "Yes. Finally. But it didn't matter to me. I didn't care about the insurance money, and for a long time I didn't care whether I went to jail, either."

She sounded so tired. Tired of crying, tired of explaining, tired of dreaming. Tired of pain.

"Red." He put his hand on her face and brushed his thumbs over the wet streaks. The words she spoke were painful enough to hear. But the unspoken words…those were the ones that haunted her, torturing her even in her sleep. "Red, you *know* it wasn't your fault."

Her eyes widened briefly, but she just smiled sadly.

"It *wasn't*," he repeated. "You had no idea she'd be hurt. You'd just made the jump yourself. You had every reason to believe she would be fine."

The small, strange smile seemed frozen to her lips. She shook her head back and forth, the movement slight but unmistakable beneath his palm.

"She was so scared." She licked her lips as if they'd gone dry. "I won't ever forget the fear on her face right before she jumped."

He couldn't stand it.

He racked his mind. Surely there was something he could say to make this better, even if he couldn't make the guilt and horror go away entirely. He couldn't look on this much pain and not do something to help.

But what? He remembered, suddenly, all the horrified, pitying faces that had stared at him in just this way, back when Brenda and Jeannie died. All those people searching their minds, scouring their hearts, trying to figure out what to say to him, praying they could ease his pain, if only a little.

They'd offered up a million words. And none of them had mattered. Every one of them had bounced off his shell of grief, and had fallen, impotent, into the emptiness around him.

He wasn't arrogant enough to believe he could do better than all those good, caring people. All those true friends.

He wasn't anything special. He was no philosopher, no orator, no sage. The only thing that made him different was how much he…

His hand stilled on her face. *How much he loved her.*

Yes. Those were the only words that didn't seem ridiculous right now.

I love you.

He could tell her that. And maybe she would see that, even if she had to hurt, she didn't have to hurt alone.

But the universe knew, even if he'd forgotten,

that those were the three words she absolutely did not, under any circumstances, want to hear. She didn't want to love or be loved. She was leaving Silverdell rather than be caught in a sticky, dangerous web of emotion.

The universe knew that, in Crimson's mind, love was just another word for pain.

And so the universe stopped him.

Upstairs, Molly began to scream as if a thousand monsters had just converged above her crib.

Anne's quivering, panicked voice called down the stairwell, *"Crimson?"*

Someone, maybe Dusty, knocked hard at the kitchen door.

In Grant's pocket, his cell began to ring.

And through the picture window, Tuesday morning dawned, streaming in on a blinding beam of light.

CHAPTER SIXTEEN

WHEN CRIMSON GOT home from her errands Wednesday afternoon, she wasn't surprised to find strange cars parked in the drive. Detectives and insurance people had been crawling through the rubble of the barn all day.

Maybe they'd been at the ranch all the day before, too. Her days were beginning to run together, blurred with exhaustion, emotion and nonstop activity. In fact, Crimson would be hard-pressed to explain exactly what had happened to Tuesday. Between taking Anne and Molly to visit Kevin, acquire a rental car and reserve a hotel room in Montrose for when Anne was ready to leave the ranch, Crimson had been gone most of the day.

When she finally made up the sofa and lay down for the night, she'd crashed. She'd slept for ten hours straight, and none of the noises, not Molly, not Grant, not even the endless ringing of phones and knocking on doors, had roused her.

She hadn't even dreamed.

Wednesday morning, while Grant went over to visit Kevin for the first time since he'd woken up, Crimson spent hours giving Anne last-minute instructions about Molly.

So many details to share before Anne took over on her own. The rash Molly had developed from that one ointment. The best remedies for teething pain. Which outfits were getting a little tight around her thighs. The name of the pediatrician Kevin had used that time she had a cough. Her inexplicable dislike of orange things, and her fear of dogs.

Anne was a sponge, soaking up all the information she could get. Most of it she typed into her computer tablet. She had created elaborate branching files to cover every aspect of Molly's life. She had a similar tree of folders and files in which she took down notes Kevin's doctors gave her about his condition and care.

It was cute, watching Anne bite her lower lip and squint hard as she concentrated on recording it all accurately. She was clearly a methodical person. She was bright, too, Crimson had discovered. She absorbed information quickly. She was especially good with medical details, which made sense, given her background in a dental office.

And Molly was getting used to her quickly. So quickly, in fact, that Crimson suspected there must be some magical mother-daughter alchemy at work. By the time Crimson headed out to do a few personal errands around noon Wednesday, Molly didn't even seem to notice she was leaving.

That was good, Crimson told herself. Anne and Molly were falling in love with each other, as parents and children ought to do. It was more than good—it was a miraculous gift to all three of them, Kevin, Anne and Molly.

The fact that Crimson felt a selfish pang…that was nothing. This wasn't about her.

Anne and her daughter would leave in the morning, and Crimson would find a way to be okay with that. She'd say goodbye to Molly tonight, in her own way. Maybe Anne would let her feed Molly dinner, and she'd savor the moment, imprint every detail on her memory.

But when she got upstairs, she was shocked to see that Anne had already packed up all of Molly's things…and all of Kevin's, too.

She must even have loaded them into her car already. The room was practically stripped clean.

All that was left was the furniture, the bed, bare of its linens, and the beautiful wooden rocking chair, where Anne sat with Molly in her arms.

"Oh, I'm so glad you came back early," Anne said, smiling as Crimson came into the room. "We wanted to wait for you. We wanted to say goodbye."

"Goodbye?"

"Yes." Anne's eyes lit up. "Kevin wants us to take the place in Montrose right away. Tonight." She pressed her lips together, smiling shyly. "He says it'll make him feel better if we're close by. And the hotel we picked out has plenty of vacancies, so…"

"Of course," Crimson said automatically. She let her gaze sweep the tidy, almost-empty room. "You need any help with anything?"

"Nope. I'm pretty sure I got it all. Grant helped me load some of it into the car, although I tried not to be a nuisance, what with his arm and all."

Grant had helped her?

"He knows you're leaving?"

"Yes. Of course we wanted to say goodbye to him, too, and thank him. He was very nice about it, said we didn't have to leave so soon, but he has to be relieved to have his house back to himself."

Relieved...

Crimson wondered, suddenly, whether that might be true. Maybe he'd had enough of all their drama. Poor man. He'd been minding his own business, getting his ranch up and running, and making a success of it. And then suddenly an old college friend shows up at his door...

Things pretty much skidded downhill from there. And they'd reached the bottom of the emotional pit Monday night—or was it Tuesday morning?—when Crimson had come apart so melodramatically. She'd been mortified every time she remembered that.

Still, this conversation felt surreal. Anne was acting as if this...this *rushing off* was perfectly normal. As if she might, in fact, have been doing Crimson and Grant a favor. As if it had never occurred to her they might actually have started to care about her poor little girl…the baby who, up until forty-eight hours ago, had been essentially an orphan.

But of course she couldn't guess how intensely Crimson had come to love Molly. Anne was so young—young in years and young in love. She had only just now sampled her first taste of maternal love. She probably found it preposterous that anyone could love a child who was not her own.

And maybe it *was* preposterous.

Maybe it was one of the most foolish things Crimson had ever done.

Second only to the spectacularly self-destructive mistake of having let herself fall in love with Grant Campbell.

Crimson dropped onto the edge of the stripped bed, feeling a little dizzy.

"Oh, and I started a load of laundry, with the used sheets and such," Anne said, pointing to the mattress Crimson had just perched on. "I know you'll be glad to be back in your own bed. You were so good to let me borrow it."

Crimson nodded numbly. She'd only been gone three hours…four at most. And she'd returned to a world turned upside down.

"Thanks," she said, though the condition of the sheets meant nothing to her. She would never sleep in this bed again. "I guess you should get going."

She thought of the empty house she'd just passed through. "Where *is* Grant?"

"I think he's in the stables. Or maybe they drove off. I'm not sure. His father-in-law is here, and they had a meeting somewhere. Grant apologized for not being able to see me off, but I told him not to be silly. Molly and I are fine."

She stood. "But I am so very glad we could stay till you got back. I was starting to worry." She looked at her cell phone, checking the time. "I promised Kevin I'd check into the hotel before dark."

Crimson understood. With her dim-witted inability to process what was happening, she was delaying Anne. She was messing up the schedule.

She stood, too. She looked at Molly, and she felt the first sharp, surgical knife-slice of loss—just a tiny streak of lightning in the distance, warning of the tempest to come.

"Mind if I say goodbye?"

"Oh, of course not!" Anne looked down at her daughter. She lifted one of the baby's hands. "Molly, say bye-bye to Crimson! Say 'thank you, Crimson, for taking such good care of me!'"

She didn't seem to realize Crimson had wanted to hold Molly. And Molly didn't seem to have the slightest desire to leave her mother's arms. She was focused on trying to get hold of Anne's pretty earrings, small, gleaming hoops of gold.

And Crimson couldn't bring herself to ask.

Leaning down, she settled for kissing the top of Molly's round head. As she inhaled the powdery sweetness of her, a second, stronger bolt of lightning moved through her chest.

"Bye-bye, Molly," she whispered.

Before she could make a fool of herself by tearing up, she straightened and smiled at Anne. "I forgot to mention that it's probably better not to wear too much jewelry. At this age, they'll put anything in their mouths that'll fit."

Anne touched her ears self-consciously. "Oh, gosh, I should have thought of that! Thank you, Crimson!"

She impulsively leaned in and used her free arm to squeeze Crimson in an emotional hug. "You are so wonderful, and Molly was so lucky to have you. I'll see you the next time you come to visit Kevin, okay? Maybe tomorrow?"

"I…I'm not exactly sure what tomorrow holds," Crimson equivocated. "With the fire, and everything so up in the air…"

"Of course. I know it's crazy. I was just being selfish. But…Kevin's law firm, the one that hired him just before the accident, has held his spot, so as soon as he's well, we'll be coming back!"

"Yes," Crimson said, wondering where she, herself, would be when that moment came. Would she have found the cause she hoped would give her life purpose? Or would she still be trying to live like a bird on a wire, never touching the ground, never getting involved with anyone or anything?

As Anne gazed down at her baby, her smile

deeply content, Crimson was surprised to realize the young woman seemed to have matured five years in the past forty-eight hours.

"And when we do come back," Anne said, reaching out to take Crimson's hand, "I really hope the two of us can be friends."

FIFTEEN MINUTES LATER, as Crimson stood on the front porch of the ranch house and watched Anne's car bump down the drive, alternately waving and smiling, she decided she had two choices.

One, she could go upstairs, lie down on that bare mattress and cry until her heart was empty. That might take a while.

Her internal organs began to ache, as if someone had punched her repeatedly. She put her hand against her stomach. This was why she'd vowed not to care like this anymore. When she cared, she was vulnerable. When she cared, fate knew exactly where to hurt her.

Okay... Choice One sounded awful.

So, Choice Two: she could pack the few things she'd brought when she came to stay at the ranch, and she could get the heck out of here.

She picked Choice Two.

As usual, it took her only about ten minutes to gather everything that belonged to her. A couple of nightshirts, toothbrush and toothpaste, paperback books, underclothes, jeans and T-shirts. Oops...the bottle of multivitamins was hers, too.

This time, though, the dearth of material belongings surprised her. She had imagined there was more, and she stood in the kitchen, a little confused until she remembered that so many of the utensils, pans, mugs and plates she'd been using and feeling so bonded with…they all belonged to Grant.

The pottery vase she'd put fresh wildflowers in every morning? His. The pillow that fit so perfectly at her back when she sat on the sofa? His. The fern she watered every afternoon? Yeah, his, too.

Even the soft blue blanket she'd almost folded into her suitcase, just because she'd tucked it around her cold feet so often…that belonged to Grant, too.

She filed that mistake away in the "never do again" box in her brain. When she'd tossed her two small suitcases into the trunk of her rental car, she sat down at the kitchen table and did the most important thing of all.

The hardest thing of all.

She left a note for Grant, saying goodbye.

GRANT CAME INTO the house around ten, glad to be home after a long, unpleasant dinner with Ben. He was surprised, at first, to see that all the lights were off. Where was everybody?

But then he remembered, Anne had headed over to a hotel in Montrose, and she'd taken the baby with her. Kevin had been such a dork about it. When Grant finally saw him early this morning…

Wait. Wow, was that only this morning? He stretched his tired back. It felt like about five years ago.

But in reality it had been only this morning. Grant had sat in Kevin's room for more than an hour, listening to a monologue about Anne, about how hard he'd tried to convince her to give marriage and motherhood a chance, right from the start.

He'd been defeated by her youth, her fear. And now, ironically, because he'd almost died, he was going to get a second chance to make everything right.

Grant hoped it would be that easy. He could have cautioned that six months of acquaintance wasn't really enough to know whether they could make a life together, but he didn't.

What did he know about love? He hadn't been able to make it work in his own life, so he was in no position to give advice now.

So he just listened. All the information Kevin had refused to divulge earlier came pouring out now. A rockslide of details, an avalanche of emotion.

Grant had practically been buried by it. But the bottom line was, Kevin really felt something for

Molly's mother, and he was going to give everything he had to make it work.

He might be trapped in his hospital bed, waiting for his bones to heal, waiting for the doctors to clear him to go home, but he couldn't bear one more night of being fifty miles away from Anne and his little girl.

As Grant grabbed the mail from the foyer table, he took a couple of seconds to "read" the house. He couldn't hear anyone…no TV or talking, no running water to indicate dishes. He didn't smell anything cooking, but he did just barely recognize the hint of fabric softener and electric heat that told him the clothes dryer had been running sometime recently.

"Red?" Resting the mail against his cast, and flipping through it with his good hand, Grant went to the bottom of the stairs and looked up. He wondered why she hadn't appeared to greet him. He was getting spoiled, he supposed. He was used to having her dance down the stairs and ask about his day. "Red, you home?"

No response. He climbed a few stairs, almost to the landing, in case she was in the tub. She did love long, hot baths filled with scented oils.

But he didn't detect any lavender-sweet steam. The mirror in the upstairs hallway wasn't misted over with condensation, and, besides, the bathroom door stood open. She wasn't in there.

He went up the rest of the way. He rapped his

knuckles lightly on her door. But once again he got no response.

"Red?" His voice took on an edge. He poked his head into the bedroom.

Immediately, he frowned. The room was all wrong. It felt empty. No, more than empty. *Lifeless.* And not just because Molly's things were gone. Granted, there was something especially poignant about not seeing the baby's crib, but this room was missing something more than that.

His skin prickling, he entered, heading straight for the dresser. He pulled open the top two drawers, one after the other. Those were the two he'd cleared out for Crimson when she'd first arrived.

They were empty.

She was gone.

He scanned the room, hoping to see a note. She wouldn't go without leaving some message. He had no trouble believing she'd bolted, rather than stay another night without Molly and Anne to stand as buffer between them.

And he could easily accept that she'd choreographed her departure to coincide with his absence, so that she wouldn't have to say goodbye in person.

But he could *not* believe she hadn't left a note.

When he was sure the note wasn't in this room, he descended to the first floor, his feet taking the stairs two at a time. Without hesitation, he chose the kitchen first. That was *her* room.

And sure enough, there it was, on the breakfast table. A white envelope, with "Grant" scrawled in dramatic black ink on the front. He picked it up, unsealed it and began to read.

Grant, you've opened your home to everyone who needed you. It doesn't seem right that you should have to pay such a high price for that generosity. I know you won't want to accept this, but I'm praying that you will. I've had this money a long time, and I haven't known what to do with it. It was the insurance settlement I told you about. It would make me happier than I can say if you'd use it to rebuild, and maybe even expand, the ranch.

I think it would make Clover happy, too. She would have admired you very much.

As I do.

Thank you for being my friend…and so much more.

Love,

Red

PS…Come on, Grant. Stop scowling and take it! Deal?

Halfway through reading it, he had lowered himself into the chair. As he let the note fall, he smiled at that PS, in spite of his growing frustration.

Deal? He could almost hear her saying it.

She would be using her sassiest voice to rob the moment of melodrama.

Behind the note was a check. Not an insurance check, but a personal one, drawn on the account of Crimson Rochelle Slayton. He had to read the amount written there once…twice…and even a third time, before he could believe what he was seeing.

He dropped that, too, as if it had scalded his fingers. He leaned back in the chair and tried to steady his brain. Before he could stop himself, his mind was reeling with thoughts of what that money could do. He could rebuild…even, as she suggested, expand. He could breed and show and open international markets…

At the same time, his heart was reeling from knowing what this check really meant. It meant she wasn't just gone from his house. She was gone from this town. She was gone from his life.

And there wasn't enough money in the world to make up for that.

He shook his head slowly.

"No, Red," he said to the dimly lit room. "We do *not* have a deal."

"HI," CRIMSON SAID politely to the middle-aged woman behind the front counter at Needles 'N Pins. "I'd like to get a tattoo."

The woman, whose nametag read Needles 'N

Pins/Tanya, pushed a hank of blond hair off her heavily rouged face.

"Sure," she said, sizing Crimson up with a quick, professional eye. "Do you know what you're looking for?"

Crimson shook her head. "Not exactly," she said.

Tanya slid a black portfolio folder across the glass-top counter.

"Take a gander," she said. "I can do custom, but this might give you some ideas."

"Thanks." Still not quite able to believe she was doing this, Crimson settled herself on the bar stool and began to study the images.

As she turned the pages, she scanned the parlor out of the corner of her eye. Someone had redecorated the waiting room since she'd last been here. Where the space used to have faux zebra-striped armchairs and shiny black vases filled with terrible fake sunflowers, it now had light, streamlined Nordic-looking furniture, one sofa and one chair.

A vast improvement, which meant somebody had been able to rein in Pete's dreadful taste in decor. Crimson stole a glance up at the blonde behind the counter. Tanya, maybe?

Pete was at the far back, in his regular station, and he was bent over a muscular back, inking something very big and very red that Crimson couldn't make out from here. He hadn't noticed her yet.

"These are beautiful," she said to Tanya as she moved through pages of the standard flowers, hearts, stars, flags, fairies and skulls. She meant it. These might be the "standard" offerings, but they were far from ordinary. Tanya was an artist.

Suddenly, she was very glad she'd decided to stop in here on her way out of town.

At first, she'd just wanted to say goodbye to Pete, who had been good to her—in spite of the whole firing thing. But the minute she walked through the door, she knew what she really wanted. She wanted to get a tattoo.

And then, as if it were meant to be, she turned one last plastic-covered page, and there was the picture she wanted. It was so perfect it could have been drawn straight from her imagination.

A simple shamrock, green and graceful, looking as if it had just been plucked from a windy field on the Irish coast.

She loved it. "How about this one?" She held the book up for Tanya to see.

"Sure. That'll be quick and easy. And cheap. Where do you want it?"

"I…" This really was impulsive, wasn't it? She really had no idea. "Maybe on the inside of my wrist?"

Tanya tilted her head, squinting. She raked that narrow gaze from the top of Crimson's head to her shoes. "You sure about that, honey? How about your shoulder, instead? You don't look like the type who really wants to flaunt her tats. It's pretty hard to cover up one on a wrist."

Crimson smiled. If only Tanya could have seen her a few months ago, with her spiky red hair and black leather everything. "I don't plan to cover it up," she said. "You see, I'm getting it in memory of my twin sister, who died last year."

For a split second, her shoulders tightened, and she wanted to take the words back. She didn't talk about this. Not to anyone. *Ever*.

But slowly her muscles relaxed. Maybe…maybe she *did* talk about it…now. Clover had been the most important person in her life for twenty-five years. Clover was the other half of her. How crazy had it been to try to pretend she hadn't existed?

"Her name was Clover." Crimson touched the little four-leaf clover. "That's why I chose this."

"*Aww.* I think that's lovely." Tanya's eyes softened. "I had a brother who died. He was in Afghanistan. It's awful, isn't it? I taught him to ride his bike, and now he's gone."

Crimson nodded slowly. "It's beyond awful," she agreed. "But at least we have the memories. I used to wish I could forget, but now…"

"Ah, honey. You can't forget."

Even as she spoke, Tanya was writing out a ticket for the fee. Crimson knew they always got payment in advance, of course, so she had her credit card and driver's license ready. Tanya took them, turned to the copier to make a duplicate and raised her voice so she could be heard over the machine.

"No, we might as well accept there's no forgetting," she said loudly. "And anyhow, we'd be heartbroken if we did, wouldn't we? If we woke up one day and couldn't remember them, then they really would be gone."

Crimson's throat closed up, hot and steely. But she nodded. Tanya wasn't only an artist. She was also a very wise woman.

As Tanya walked her back to the station, Crimson kept a smile on her face, ready for the moment when Pete looked up.

She was already situating herself in the chair when he finally straightened, wiping the back of his forearm against his damp brow. Pete took his work so seriously he lost a couple of pounds on every tattoo.

"Red?" When he recognized her, he did an adorable double take. Crimson laughed as she rolled up her sleeve. There was something ridiculously endearing about a six-foot-four man sitting with his eyes popping and his mouth open, looking as shocked as a kid who'd just seen Santa Claus.

"Red? *Damn it*, Red. What are you doing?" He scowled hard. "Didn't I tell you if you ever decided to get a tattoo *I* wanted to do it?"

He pointed an angry finger at Tanya, who was carefully washing her hands. "Her tat's free, whatever it is. I don't care if she wants the Gettysburg Address running down her leg. It's on the house."

Tanya shrugged. "She already paid."

"I don't give a damn. I'll tear it up." He winked at Crimson. "I knew you'd come over to the dark side eventually, Red. It was just a matter of time." He threw a smile at Tanya, and that smile said he was sorry for barking at her.

Crimson wondered what the relationship was here. Had Pete finally found a woman who would put up with him?

"She was a holdout for a long time, this one," Pete went on, playfully. "What's she getting, anyhow?"

"A shamrock."

"Yeah? You Irish, Red? Slayton doesn't sound Irish to me."

She shook her head and held out her arm as Tanya tapped her, signaling that they were ready to start. Tanya didn't work from a stencil...so they went straight to the nitty-gritty.

"No, not Irish. It's in memory of my twin sister, Clover."

She smiled to herself. Saying her name got easier every time. And somehow it made everything feel lighter. Brighter. It was as if talking about her allowed some part of Clover to remain real and relevant. Not alive, but significant. And true.

"For real?" Pete's eyes widened. "I didn't even know you had a sister."

"No one did. She died last year, and for a long time it was hard to talk about her. I guess I thought if I didn't talk about it, it wouldn't hurt so much."

And speaking of hurt…the machine was on, and the needles were doing their thing. She concentrated on breathing deeply.

"What's wrong with hurting?" Pete waved his hand dismissively. "Hurting isn't the scary thing. Feeling nothing, that's what you gotta watch out for."

"Hey!" The man with the bare, muscular back rose onto his elbows. His bearded face looked decidedly pissed off. "Am I getting inked here, or what?"

"Yeah, yeah, you're getting inked." Pete rolled his eyes at Crimson, to show what he thought of the man's impatience, and then turned back to his work with a chuckle. "But I guess this is your lucky day, Jerry, 'cause today you get a little free philosophy on the side."

CHAPTER SEVENTEEN

WHEN CRIMSON OPENED the door to Donovan's Dream, and the doorbell notes rang out, the crowded lunchtime restaurant sang their part with such enthusiasm her ears rang lightly from the sound.

In one way, she was happy to see the place so full. Good traffic meant a good investment. But selfishly, she had hoped maybe she'd catch Marianne at a slow moment, and it would be easier to talk.

She looked around, but Marianne was nowhere in sight. Was she even at the café today? Crimson's excitement faded slightly. She'd come marching straight down here from the tattoo parlor with such a full head of steam, so eager to follow through on her crazy, wonderful, bold new plan. If she couldn't act on it, she felt as if she might pop—as if someone were filling her up with helium and the shut-off valve was broken.

She spotted Becky over by the window, talking to an older man. She had her order pad out, and the man was looking at the menu. Crimson knew she shouldn't interrupt, but...

"Hey," she said breathlessly, after maneuvering across the room, between tables, over purses, under trays of food carried by irritated waiters. "I'm sorry to interrupt, but I was wondering if Marianne's here today."

Becky smiled. "She's in the kitchen. Want me to go get her?"

"Would you mind?" Crimson could have just burst into the kitchen herself, of course. But with this kind of crowd, it was probably like waging a war back there. She knew just enough about running a restaurant to know how unwelcome an extra body would be. "If you'd just tell her I'd really like to talk to her when she gets a free minute?"

"Sure." Becky glanced at the man whose order she'd been taking. "I'll be right back," she said. She gave Crimson a quick smile. "Have you met my father?"

As Becky dropped that bombshell, she hurried off to find Marianne and pass along the message.

Crimson looked at the dignified, middle-aged man, with his aristocratic nose and his cool blue eyes. She was proud of how composed she was, even though this was a man she'd wondered about often.

Several times, she'd even considered calling him up and offering him a piece of her mind. What was he thinking, ignoring his daughter like that? Didn't he know Becky could really use a champion?

"Hi," she said, putting out her hand politely. "Great to meet you, Mr. Hampton. I'm Crimson Slayton."

"So I gathered." The man made an old-fashioned half rise, which he undoubtedly meant to be respectful. "I've heard a lot about you."

She grinned. "All good, I hope?"

He grunted, but he nodded. "Apparently, I owe you a lot. I hear you took my daughter in when she desperately needed a place to stay."

"No," she said. "I didn't take her in. Grant Campbell did. I just happened to be staying there at the time myself." She smiled. "Grant was running quite a wounded-bird sanctuary there for a while."

"And it was his barn this Rory…this lowlife who got hold of my daughter…set on fire?"

"Yes."

"I hear they've arrested him."

"Have they?"

She hadn't heard that, but how would she? She hadn't been in touch with Grant, or Becky or anyone else who would tell her, since she'd left the ranch yesterday. They undoubtedly all assumed she'd left town…which she almost had. She'd settled up with her landlord, cleared out the rest of her things and loaded them in her rental car.

An hour ago, she'd been on Elk Avenue, driving west, and hadn't intended to stop until she reached California, which seemed like a big enough state, surely, to offer Crimson the chance to find her purpose, big enough for her to be helpful to *someone*. But then she'd seen the neon sign for Needles 'N Pins.

Becky had returned. "She says she'll probably be able to take a break in about five minutes, but she will only have about three minutes to spare. She told me to get you something to eat while you wait."

"I'm fine," Crimson said. Her stomach was so full of butterflies, she wouldn't dare eat. If the next ten or fifteen minutes went as she hoped they would, everything in her life was about to change. And that was both thrilling and terrifying.

She smiled at Becky, who looked remarkably serene, given what she'd been through the past few days. "So…the barn. Scary stuff, huh? Have you seen what's left of it? Thank God you got out of there when you did."

"Yeah." Becky shivered slightly. "But it wasn't exactly ESP or anything. Rory had been calling and calling…and I wasn't answering the phone. I knew that would make him crazy. I mean, I didn't know he'd get *that* crazy. I had no idea he'd burn anything down, but I knew he'd do something. I know him too well."

"Too bad you didn't know him that well *before* you moved in with him." Becky's father's voice was caustic.

Crimson saw Becky's hands tighten on her order pad. "Dad. *Don't.*"

"Are you still staying with Marianne?" Crimson was eager to change the subject. Something in Becky's face said she wasn't going to let another domineering man belittle her today.

"For now. I'm looking for my own apartment, though. I could probably swing a studio if—"

"That's absurd," her father interjected. "You'll come home, where you belong."

Becky stared at him coldly for a minute. "No," she said. "I won't."

Her father's eyebrows rose, and behind that expression of mild surprise Crimson thought she glimpsed true anger.

"I'm not living there again, ever. I have two jobs, and I can support myself." Becky drew herself up so straight Crimson felt like cheering. "And you can stop giving me that look, Dad, because it's not going to work. In fact, until you stop trying to bully me, I'm not going to interact with you at all."

She began walking away. "I'll get Nora to take your order," she said, and with another two steps she was too far for him to bother replying.

He watched her go, his hands immobile on the table, his lips thinned and pale.

Well done, girlfriend, Crimson thought. But to the older man, she just offered a cordial smile. "She sounded like she meant it, don't you think?"

Luckily, Marianne arrived at that moment, holding out her hands to hug Crimson. Mr. Hampton took advantage of the distraction to toss his menu aside, stand up and leave the restaurant. If he'd thought he could exit without drawing attention, he must have forgotten about "Danny Boy." As they sang, the entire restaurant seemed to be cheering his departure.

"What on earth are you doing here?" Marianne released Crimson and surveyed her with a curiosity she didn't—or couldn't—hide. "I heard you'd left town. And talk fast, because I meant it when I said I only had three minutes."

"Okay." Crimson might not need that much. She took a breath so deep she practically felt her lungs tickle her hips. "You remember when you said you'd like to sell the restaurant? Well, I'd like to buy it. I don't have much of a nest egg, but I have decent credit, I think. I can apply for a loan tomorrow and—"

But to her dismay, Marianne began shaking her head. She put her hand on Crimson's forearm to stop her before she went too far.

"I can't do that," she said.

"I'm not asking for any special deal," Crimson assured her. "I'll see if I can get the financing to pay your full asking price. It might take a little while, but—"

"No. Crimson, listen to me." Marianne's bright green eyes were somber. "I'm not saying I won't.

I'm saying I *can't*. It's not the money. I can't sell you the restaurant because I've already accepted another offer."

For a minute, as if she'd been drunk on the adrenaline high of her dreams, Crimson simply couldn't process the words. She stared at Marianne stupidly, and she felt disappointment trickle into her veins, like water dripping through a bad pipe, slowly eroding the foundation of a house.

She put her hand out and touched the table. She needed to steady herself. Her house of cards, built so impulsively back there at the tattoo parlor, was listing badly and threatening to fall apart.

"Someone else has already bought the café?"

Marianne nodded. "It's not final, but they've offered, and I've accepted. I can't go back on that now."

"No. Of course not." Crimson forced herself to smile. "I'm sorry for myself, but I'm glad for you. Congratulations."

"Thanks." Marianne squeezed her arm. "You know…there are other restaurants in Silverdell. If you're really ready to commit…"

"Yes." Crimson still had that awkward, uncomfortable smile on her lips, and she didn't know how to get rid of it. She didn't want to diminish Marianne's joy.

And she wasn't going to let go of her own dream that quickly. Right now, substituting some other restaurant for this one felt like substituting rhinestones for diamonds. But that was disappointment talking. If she was going to create a new life, she'd have to learn to roll with the punches. She'd have to learn to fight for her victories.

"Yes," she said firmly. "I'm ready to commit, and if you have ideas, I'd love to hear all about them."

"Great! But not right now, I'm afraid." Marianne looked at her watch and groaned. "I'm so far behind I'd have to run to qualify as late. There's no chance you could come back to the kitchen and help me with a cake, is there? I've got to decorate it, write on it, package it up and deliver it, all in the next ten minutes. And you know me…I just don't have the touch."

For a minute, Crimson almost said no. But *no* was a word she'd used far too often over the past year. The new Crimson—who was really the old Crimson trying to reemerge—much preferred saying yes.

"Sure," she said. "I'd be glad to."

"Hurray!" Threading her arm through Crimson's elbow, Marianne hurried her back to the swinging doors that led to the kitchen. She elbowed them open expertly, and guided Crimson through just in time to avoid getting slapped in the rear when they closed.

"Hey, where's that cake? I've brought in the marines to save us! Crimson can get that baby iced with one hand tied behind her back, and it'll still look better than it would if we did it."

Two men stood in the room, working. One was the young chef Marianne had been training for quite a while now. Andy...Andy something.

Crimson gave him a smile, which he returned fleetingly, because he was elbow deep in dough, kneading it like someone wrestling an alligator.

The other man was facing the back counter, and he was bent over what must be the cake in question.

Then he turned around, an icing dispenser in his hand, and smiled.

It was Grant.

Crimson couldn't speak. Literally. She opened her mouth, but her voice had simply quit working.

What was he doing here?

Marianne grabbed a pair of oven mitts and scurried to the stove. "Grant, can you show Crimson what to write on the cake?"

"Sure." He held out the tube, which was full of white icing. He backed away from the cake. It was small, but exquisite. White, with roses and swags and fondant icing. A wedding cake.

"I have to admit it's a relief to see you." His eyes twinkled. "I'm right-handed, you see, and my left hand was about to make a horrible hash of this."

"But..." Crimson couldn't bring herself to take the icing, or to join him at the counter, until she understood. "But what are you *doing* here?"

Grant smiled, but he didn't get a chance to answer. Marianne came over, her green eyes dancing. "You know that offer I told you about? It was from Grant. He's buying the café."

Crimson shook her head. "Is this some kind of joke?"

"Of course not," Marianne said. "He made me a wonderful offer. Full price. *Cash.*"

Crimson's gaze shot to Grant. But he was merely standing there, looking as innocent as a child.

"What?" He shrugged. "I unexpectedly came into a great deal of money."

She was still shaking her head. "No. No. You don't want to run a restaurant. You need that money to rebuild Campbell Ranch."

"How do you know I don't want to run a restaurant?" He tilted his head quizzically. "Maybe it's a secret dream of mine, owning a restaurant. Or maybe it's a dream of mine to give a restaurant to someone special. You know…as a gift."

No. This was madness. She couldn't stop that ridiculous shaking of her head. Anyone would think she was some kind of clockwork person, with a metronome for a brain.

But how was she supposed to make sense of any of this? It was as if she'd stepped into an alternate universe. It was simultaneously the most wonderful and the most confusing experience she'd ever had.

"Grant, I don't understand."

His smile was so beautiful… half teasing, half tender. "Sure you do."

"No. I honestly don't. I mean, if you're talking about me, about giving the restaurant to me…"

"The thought had crossed my mind."

"But that wasn't what I wanted. I wanted you to use the money for the ranch. For Dawn. I know you saw your father-in-law the other day, and I know what that must have meant. He heard about the fire, and he thought maybe it was a good time to talk you into coming back to Memphis to work for the foundation."

He smiled. "Right. Benjamin is definitely not the type to miss an opportunity like that."

"But you can't say yes, Grant. Don't let anyone take your dream away from you. Especially not Rory. It would be…it would just be…" She couldn't find a word bad enough. "It would be an *abomination*."

At the dough-kneading station, Andy guffawed rudely.

Crimson ignored him. "Please. Please, Grant. Use the money for the ranch."

"What does it matter to you how I use the money? I thought you were leaving Silverdell for good."

"It matters because I know you. And…I love you."

There. She'd said it.

She tested herself to see if the admission had

damaged something, if it had left her weak, or weepy or embarrassed. But it hadn't. In fact, she felt great. Saying those words out loud had somehow felt quite natural.

Maybe it was like talking about Clover. It was only hard if you didn't do it.

"I love you," she said again. "And it doesn't matter whether you love me, too. I love you so much I can't be happy if you aren't. And I know you wouldn't be happy in Memphis, sitting at a desk. Without Dawn, without Campbell Ranch, without the whole stressful thrill of it all."

He didn't respond to the declaration. Instead, he responded, quite calmly, to the part about the job. "But I'm not going to Memphis. I'm going to stay here, and I'm going to dig Campbell Ranch out of the ashes and raise it up again, if it takes the rest of my life."

"But it doesn't have to take that long, not if you use the money."

"I'm sorry." He smiled serenely. "Can't. I've already spent the money."

Again her automatic head-shaking started.

"Grant, be serious. You *couldn't* have been buying it for me. You thought I was leaving town. I *was* leaving town. What if I hadn't come back?"

He lifted one shoulder, as if none of that mattered. "I would have come after you. You see, I love you, Crimson Rochelle Slayton. I told myself I had to let you go, that it was wrong of me to try to talk you into staying. But that's baloney."

The blood rushed to Crimson's face. "You… you…"

"I love you." He repeated it placidly. "And so if you'd left I would have found you, and I would have done whatever it took to make you love me, too."

Finally, Marianne laughed, and put the tips of her fingers into the small of Crimson's back. She shoved gently, nudging her toward Grant.

"This is all very touching," she said, "but I've got an order to fill. Could you guys please get the writing on that cake, and finish this circular conversation afterward?"

"Yes, ma'am." Grant grinned, and extended the icing dispenser toward Crimson one more time. "Come on. If you'll write, I'll dictate."

With numb fingers, Crimson accepted the tube. She kneaded the icing with the tips of her fingers, relishing the familiar feel of the tools of her trade in spite of herself. She moved up to the counter, spun the cake a couple of times to study its landscape and then nodded.

"Okay. How many words are we going to have to accommodate?"

"Just four." Grant was very close behind her, watching over her shoulder as she readied the icing and held it poised over the cake.

He was so close she could feel his heat against

her back. It wasn't fair…her fingers were shaking, and she'd end up making a mess of it, just as much as he would have.

"Come on," she said, jiggling the dispenser impatiently. "Four words…"

"Okay." He put his hands on her shoulders and spoke against her ear. "Will…"

She looped the letters into place. Thank goodness this was her one real talent. Even at a moment like this, with the echo of his words reverberating inside her, spinning and giving off sparks, her fingers knew what to do.

"You…" He nipped lightly at her earlobe. "Marry…"

She turned, crying out a single syllable of inarticulate joy. But she forgot to stop squeezing the icing, and a lovely ridged piping of white cream spurted all over his shirt.

He ignored it. "Me…"

Will you marry me…

She looked up at him, her eyes burning and her throat so narrow she didn't see how words could possibly fit through it.

But she didn't need words. She only needed one.

"Yes," she said.

His answering smile was a beam of heat, and it moved directly into her core. "Good," he said. He tilted his head. "You did hear the rest of the question, right? You didn't think I said, will you marry Kevin, or will you marry Andy over there…"

Andy growled. "I'm going to be sick," he declared.

But Crimson laughed. She did so love this man. Her friend, who could always make her laugh. Her lover, who set her soul on fire.

"I heard," she said. "And the answer is still, and always, yes. I'll marry you…if you'll forgive me for being such a fool, for not seeing how right you were about…about everything. I've been such an idiot, Grant. I've wasted so much time. I've been so trapped in the past, in feeling guilty about Clover…"

"Our pasts are part of who we are," he said softly. "I don't want you to forget her. I just want you to share her with me."

She nodded. The movement dislodged two warm tears she hadn't realized were gathering in her eyes. He brushed them away with his thumb, so gently she barely felt the touch.

"Yes," she said, though she wasn't sure exactly what she meant. She just knew her spirit was singing and soaring and everything was *yes*.

"I want to be a part of whatever happens in your life, Red." He leaned in and put two slow kisses where the tears had been. "Not just the happy things. Not just the sex and the fun, but the sadness and the pain."

She nodded. "But the sex, too, right?" She grinned. "Because I really, really loved the sex."

Marianne sputtered, and had to cover her laughter with her apron.

"You have got to be kidding!" Andy wheeled toward Marianne, his voice deeply aggrieved. "I thought you said their problem was that they didn't talk to each other enough! Now you can't get them to shut up!"

"He's right," Marianne said, her voice thick with amusement. "Considering you're going to own this restaurant, you don't seem very concerned about helping us please our guests. If you can't be useful, at least take that sappy stuff outside. And leave through the back door. I don't want the customers to see you. You look like you've been playing sex games with that icing."

"Yes, ma'am," Grant said, leaning in to give Crimson the first of what she hoped would be at least a million kisses. When he lifted his head, she was dizzy in the most beautiful way.

She started to set down the icing dispenser, but he blocked the move with his cast.

"Bring it," he said. He swiped a dollop from his shirt and carried it to her lips. "It's delicious… and, frankly, Marianne has given me some excellent ideas."

And as the back door swung shut behind them, they heard Andy groan one last time.

"I'm going to be sick," he said.

* * * * *

COMING NEXT MONTH FROM

HARLEQUIN

super romance

Available June 2, 2015

**YOU CAN FIND MORE INFORMATION ON UPCOMING
HARLEQUIN® TITLES, FREE EXCERPTS AND MORE AT
WWW.HARLEQUIN.COM.**

HSRLPCNM0515